Aloha, Lady Blue

Aloha, Lady Blue

Charley Memminger

MINOTAUR BOOKS

A Thomas Dunne Book
NEW YORK

This is a work of fiction. All of the characters, organizations, and events portrayed in this novel are either products of the author's imagination or are used fictitiously.

A THOMAS DUNNE BOOK FOR MINOTAUR BOOKS.
An imprint of St. Martin's Publishing Group.

ALOHA, LADY BLUE. Copyright © 2013 by Charley Memminger. Printed in the United States of America. For information, address St. Martin's Press, 175 Fifth Avenue, New York, N.Y. 10010.

www.thomasdunnebooks.com
www.minotaurbooks.com

Library of Congress Cataloging-in-Publication Data

Memminger, Charles.
    Aloha, lady blue : a mystery / Charles Memminger.—First U.S. edition.
       p. cm.
    "A Thomas Dunne book."
    ISBN 978-1-250-00778-0 (hardcover)
    ISBN 978-1-250-02099-4 (e-book)
    1. Private investigators—Fiction. 2. Older people—Crimes against—Fiction. 3. Hawaii—Fiction. I. Title.
    PS3613.E476A46 2013
    813'.6—dc23

                                                                2012038368

First Edition: January 2013

10 9 8 7 6 5 4 3 2 1

For Martha

Acknowledgments

There are many, many people who helped and encouraged me complete this, my first novel. First, of course, is my wife, Margie, who I love dearly and who stuck with me on what, at times, was a very rough road. My daughter, Sarah, the light of my life, was a great inspiration for me. Over the years working on the book, I often felt the presence and support of my Mom and Dad, both buried in the stunning and incredibly moving National Memorial Cemetery of the Pacific at Punchbowl (which I made sure had a cameo in the book). My brothers, Lucien and Steven, who pestered me about getting the damn thing done. And a legion of friends and extended family—my "ohana"—as we say in the Islands.

I hesitate to list all of my supporters by name, knowing I'll likely hurt some feelings because they were either left off the list or included on it. But, in no particular order, are some people I want to thank for their help, guidance, and encouragement: Richard Pine, Elisa Petrini, Marcia Markland, Kat Brzozowski, Andre and Maria Jacquemetton, A. J. Jacobs, Kinky Friedman, Carl Hiaasen, W. Bruce

Cameron, James W. Hall, Andy Bumatai, Joe Moore, Frank South, Starling Lawrence, Tom Mayer, Paul Theroux, Wally Amos, Calvin Branche, David Houle, Patricia Wood, Murray Eden-Lee, Kitty Lagareta, Michael W. Perry, Howard Daniel, Jim Borg, John Radcliffe, and John Perkin.

Aloha, Lady Blue

Prologue

November 12, 2001, 5:14 A.M. Waikiki Beach. Chester McArthur, eighty-three, is walking along the water's edge off the Moana Hotel, moving the search coil of his Cobra Beach Magnet metal detector evenly back and forth through the gentle lapping waves. He's hoping to hear the magical ping through his headset indicating the presence of a thumping big gold ring or bracelet that some hapless tourist lost playing in the surf the previous afternoon. He is untroubled by his role as one of society's scavengers, comfortable with the concept that someone else's mischance is his good fortune. If people are too fucking stupid to take off their jewelry before jumping into the ocean, that's their own damn fault.

The sun is just rising above the horizon on the windward side of Oahu, but the Koolau Mountain Range blocks the lowest rays, casting a shadow over Honolulu and the South Shore. In the hazy half-light Diamond Head crater looms like a crouching lion looking out to sea. The beach is lit up by spotlights on the Moana's seawall and pool deck, but the ocean is dark, and the muffled sound of waves can be heard in the distance.

Staring down at the metal detector, Chester suddenly notices some movement to his left in the water. At first he thinks it must be a surfer on dawn patrol getting ready to paddle out, but then the form materializes into the shape of a man inexplicably walking from the ocean with something heavy in his arms. Chester pulls off his headset and gapes at the approaching specter.

The man walks unsteadily toward the beach. Once out of the water, he falls to his knees and gently lays the limp body of a woman on the sand. He looks up with what Chester would later describe as a tired, mournful expression and says, "This is police officer Jeannie Kai. Jake Stane killed her."

The man then collapses unconscious onto the sand.

Chapter One

It was one of those typically blustery mornings in late August when rain squalls march across Kaneohe Bay from the eastern ocean, one after the other like soggy invading battalions. I was in the day cabin of the *Travis McGee*, my fifty-foot-long Vagabond houseboat, nursing along my first meal of the day, which I had come to refer to as Honey Bunches of Budweiser because it sounded healthier than "swigging beer for breakfast." The gods were restless, pacing outside the screen door on the covered aft deck, waiting to be fed. The two German shepherds, Kane and Lono, had been on duty all night, patrolling the grounds of the Bayview Yacht Club, a small suburban club on the windward side of Oahu where I kept my boat. As the nominal night watchman, I was the only club member allowed to live on his boat. Keeping an eye on two piers berthing about seventy-five boats, a swimming pool, two tennis courts, and the club's longhouse and bar wasn't as difficult as guarding Fort Knox or even Taco Bell, especially with the gods doing most of the heavy lifting.

I took the gods two large metal bowls with dry dog food

mixed with leftover spaghetti and meat sauce from the night before, which they tucked into with the restraint of hyenas bringing down a Serengeti wildebeest. They were still wet from their last patrol, so I couldn't let them inside. I'm not the greatest housekeeper in the world, but you don't spend a couple of hundred thousand bucks on a houseboat just to have it smell of Eau de Damp Dogs.

I had already taken my morning exercise, diving off the end of A Pier and swimming the half mile along the edge of the channel to the last reef marker and then back. I was still in pretty good shape for a gentleman of a certain age. Nothing like when I was a nationally ranked butterfly specialist, but I wasn't ready for a walker and ear trumpet just yet.

I finished my breakfast with a last swig and walked back inside. The houseboat came with twin Merc 230-horsepower engines, two seventy-five-gallon fuel tanks, two bedrooms with baths, two wet bars, galley, covered lanais fore and aft, and a day cabin big enough to stage the finale of *Oklahoma!* The day cabin was ringed by picture windows that let in light no matter what time of day when the blinds were open. It was bordered on one side with a leather sofa facing the big Sony. A wet bar was in the corner, and elsewhere in the room were coffee tables, another couch, and a couple of chairs for hypothetical guests. The galley was separated from the main room by a counter and contained all the usual appliances you'd find in a regular kitchen except for a garbage disposal. There was no sewer hookup.

Upstairs, or up the ladder, as the grumpier old salts at the club liked to remind me, was a second deck with a state-of-the-art flying bridge, the other wet bar, a hot tub, a couple of kayaks, surfboards, and a Kawasaki Ninja ZX-14 Jet Ski. A guy has got to have his toys.

I'm told there are also a couple of anchors somewhere on the boat, but I hadn't had to use them because I had yet to put the *Travis McGee* in the water. The thing about a smallish yacht club is that there are only so many wet slips, especially slips that can handle a fifty-foot-long houseboat, and Bayview Yacht Club boat owners tend to hang on to their slips until they die.

You'd think that since the average age of a club member seemed to be about 114, boat slips would become available rather frequently. But it's the members of the tennis fleet, the ones who get daily exercise and restrict their alcohol intake, who die off regularly. The geezers who own boats, who drink all day in the Longhouse Bar reliving the glorious days of sail when Admiral Nelson ruled the sea, these guys apparently live forever. It must be all those vitamins in the rum.

So the *Travis McGee* had been sitting on blocks at the water's edge for the past year and a half, sort of like my life.

I looked at the cluttered desk near the hallway that passed as my office. The red light on the telephone blinked on and off indicating there was a voice message, one I had already listened to three times. It was from Amber Kalanianaole Kam, a girl I had had a huge crush on in high school but hadn't laid eyes on for probably twenty years. I pushed the button to hear the message a fourth time. Her voice sounded fragile, like a piece of fine porcelain about to shatter.

"Stryker," she said. "You might not remember me, but we went to Punahou together. My grandfather Wai Lo Fat died in a terrible accident a week ago. Stryker, I think I need your help."

Chapter Two

An hour after sunrise, steady trade winds blew the rain squalls over the Koolau Mountain Range toward Honolulu and eventually out into the southern sea. The late-summer sun quickly dried everything in sight: boats, piers, cars, tennis courts, and the gods themselves. Kane and Lono, sated from their Italian breakfast, had plopped down under the awning on the stern lanai and gone to sleep. I headed across the lawn toward the longhouse to see if I could find a *Honolulu Advertiser* with news of Wai Lo Fat's death. Before I called Amber back, I wanted to know what I was dealing with. Old reporter's instincts die hard.

Passing the swimming pool, I glanced out of habit at the fifty-five-foot-tall sailboat mast set in a concrete base that served as the club's flagpole. The Stars and Stripes and the Hawaii state flag were at the top of the mast, but the smaller ocean blue club flag was flying halfway down. One of our members apparently had gone to that big yacht club in the sky.

At the club office, I saw Commodore Fleetwood Richardson on the other side of the sliding glass counter windows shuffling some papers. I slid the glass partition open, feeling a rush of cool air from the air-conditioned room.

"Morning, Commodore," I said.

He looked up from the papers.

"Stryker, I swear you are positively turning into a ghoul," he said. "We just lowered that burgee an hour ago, and you are already running in here to find out who died. It was Old Lady Baldwin. She had a heart attack, God bless her. And she didn't have a damn wet slip."

"I just wanted to say good morning," I said, smiling.

"A ghoul!" he growled, the way only a seventy-two-year-old former marine jet pilot who had done two tours in Vietnam could growl. "Why'd you get such a damn big boat in the first place? My God, it's like the *Queen Mary*. You're lucky we let you live on the damn thing."

"We haven't had a major theft since I volunteered to keep an eye on the place at night," I countered.

"That's because of those two monsters patrolling the grounds," he said. "Hell, if we kept those dogs and got rid of you and the USS *Enterprise* out there, we'd have room for another tennis court."

I knew he was just firing the afterburners for the hell of it. He owned a thirty-five-foot-long power boat and had no love for the tennis fleet. If he could get rid of one of the two existing tennis courts to create more dry slips for boats on trailers, he would do it. For a small club, it was amazingly segregated. The fishing fleet boat owners didn't socialize with the pleasure boat owners. The sailboat owners hated all the power boaters. And all the boat owners turned their noses up at the non-boat-owning tennis players. The only place where peace and harmony seemed to reign was the drinking fleet, which met every afternoon at four at the large round table in the Longhouse Bar and of which I was a member in good standing.

After his verbal broadside, the commodore went back to his work. So I closed the glass partition and wandered over to a corner of the open Longhouse where members left paperbacks, magazines, and newspapers to share. I flipped through a few *Honolulu Advertisers* and some copies of the *Honolulu Journal*, the newspaper I had worked for before becoming nominal night watchman for the yacht club. Wai Lo Fat was a fairly prominent businessman and an elder in the Chinese community, so there were large feature obituaries in both papers. His decades of business success and public service were well documented, but there weren't many details about his death, other than he had apparently drowned in a taro field. As a former investigative reporter, my surprise meter is set pretty high. So I wasn't surprised that an old man drowned in a taro field. I wasn't even surprised to learn that the taro field was smack in the middle of Kahala, a posh residential colony east of the less photogenic side of Diamond Head and one of the most expensive chunks of real estate on the planet. Strange things happen all the time, even to elderly Chinese guys with weird names and the net financial worth of a small country.

That isn't to say I can't be surprised. In the summer of 1998, about a year after I started working for the *Honolulu Journal*, a local character known as the Rev. Franky Five Fins had somehow contrived to commit suicide by locking himself in a fifty-five-gallon drum, shooting himself fourteen times from outside the drum, and then tossing the drum off of a cliff near the Makapuu Point lighthouse. Now that was fucking surprising.

In a way, I considered the Rev. Franky Five Fins a friend. He was a former professional surfer, an ordained minister, and an underworld hit man. He must have been about fifty years old, part Hawaiian, part Portuguese, and part who-knows-what-else; what island locals called a poi dog. I used to run into him at Bowls, a surf spot off Ala Moana Park on Oahu's South Shore, between Honolulu and Waikiki. He was called Franky Five Fins because his nine-foot-ten Turbo Thruster surfboard had five fins instead of the standard three, the leading edge of each filed as sharp as a chef's knife. On the board's deck was airbrushed Guido Reni's *Archangel Michael Defeating Satan*, the seventeenth-century painting showing the Archangel Michael with his foot upon the head of Satan and sword poised for a fatal thrust. The expression on the face of the Archangel Michael was the same look the Rev. Franky Five Fins assumed when any other surfer was stupid enough to drop in on a wave Franky figured belonged to him. The penalty for a first offense was a stern lecture on good and evil and God's will. Should the offender prove unrepentant and try to steal a wave from Franky a second time, he would feel the wrath of the Archangel Michael when the good reverend launched the holy board into his back or legs. I had seen it happen more than once and can report that being struck by five sharpened fins in the back can really ebb a surfer's zest for wave riding.

For some reason, Franky liked me. Maybe because at one time I had been a nationally ranked competitive swimmer, like his idol Duke Kahanamoku. Or maybe because I never tried to steal any of his waves. We always sat together, outside the pack, waiting for the biggest swells. I was usually the only haole out at Bowls but never got hassled by the locals. Yes, I was a white guy, but I was the white guy sitting with Franky Five Fins.

One day, sitting in the water waiting for waves, I asked Franky Five Fins how, as a man of the cloth, he could justify firing a surfboard armed with hellishly sharpened skegs into the backs of clueless high school kids, practically decapitating them and causing them to wipe out onto the shallow reef.

"Stryker," he said, "Our Lord Jesus Christ didn't like pussies. Sometimes you just gotta knock the Word of God into these little cocksuckers."

He also saw no conflict between his religious calling and his professional career as a hired killer.

"You see, Stryker," he said, pointing to the Archangel Michael on his board, "that buggah right there is whacking Satan, but in real life Satan is people like that degenerate Mongoose Pacheco or Samoan Johnny. Sometimes it's God's will that certain cocksuckers get whacked."

At the time, I was an investigative reporter focusing on white collar crime—crime in the suites, not the streets—but I knew about the death of Samoan Johnny. He was a notorious leader of an organized crime group that controlled cockfights, drugs, and protection along the West Shore of Oahu. His partially eaten body had been found a few weeks earlier at a Waianae pig farm said to be favored by certain criminal enterprises wishing to make trouble disappear. But Mongoose Pacheco was still alive.

"I just saw Mongoose in Chinatown the other day," I said to Franky. "He's not dead."

"Not yet," Franky Five Fins said, giving me the official underworld hit man death stare.

Then he smiled.

"I'm just fucking with you, Stryker," he said. "Mongoose is okay."

A beautiful six-foot swell moved toward us, explosions of sunlight bouncing off of its blue face.

"Take it, Stryker," Franky said.

"You sure?" I asked, turning my board tentatively toward shore.

"All yours, haole boy." He laughed. I paddled for the wave, and as it took me I heard Franky Five Fins yell, "Go in peace, brother Stryker."

The next day the body of Mongoose Pacheco, a lowlife gambler, meth mouth, and sometimes bagman for Chinatown crime interests, was found slumped at the foot of a large iron cross in Our Lady of Redemption Roman Catholic cemetery on King Street with a trinity of .22 caliber bullet holes in the back of his head. And a week after that, some fishermen pulled a fifty-five-gallon drum with more bullet holes than Bonnie and Clyde's Ford sedan onto their boat off of Makapuu Point. Franky Five Fins had gone to meet his maker.

So while the unusual death of Wai Lo Fat in the taro patch didn't surprise me, the phone call from Amber Kalanianaole Kam did. We had attended high school together at Punahou, the most exclusive private school in Hawaii. But Amber was way out of my league. While she perched on the higher branches with the school's elite, kids from some of the richest and most politically powerful families in the state, I was in the "Downward Bound Program," a struggling C-student from the wrong side of the island on a swimming scholarship. I held the state record for the 50-meter and 100-meter butterfly, but Amber was senior class president, honor roll, and Blue Lotus Blossom Queen.

She was an absolute knockout, a gorgeous Chinese-Hawaiian with long black hair and green almond eyes. Our relationship basically was that I ached for her with the intensity that only a seventeen-year-old boy with raging hormones could and she ignored me from afar. Close up, too. So why would she be calling me twenty-two years later in connection with the death of her grandfather?

After going through the newspapers I walked back to the *Travis McGee* and finally called the number Amber had left. As the phone rang, I realized I actually was nervous about calling her. Maybe you never grow out of that rigid psychological caste system that exists in high school. On the fourth ring, she answered. This time her voice wasn't soft and fragile, it was all business.

"You've reached the Kam residence. Leave a message."

I did. I take direction well.

"Amber, it's Stryker McBride returning your call," I said. "Sorry to hear about your grandfather. I'd be happy to help you out however I can. Call me and let's talk about it. Aloha."

I was pretty happy with my message: professional, yet tinged with concern. And I didn't sound overly excited that she had bothered to honor me with a phone call. The "aloha" at the end was kind of cliché, but better than "Tag, you're it."

I pulled a beer from the refrigerator and climbed the stairs-slash-ladder to the top deck with the telephone handset. The Jet Ski was sitting near the port rail, covered in a custom-designed elastic waterproof cover. Last thing you want is your Jet Ski getting wet. I couldn't remember the last time I took it out. The six-person hot tub also was covered. It hadn't been used for a while, either. I guess I was being optimistic getting a six-person hot tub. I'd never had more than four in it, myself and three friendly premed students who had come to Hawaii from Oregon on a sail-boat skippered by one of the girls' father. It was a hell of a night. How long ago had it been? A year?

I stood at the flying bridge, turning the stainless steel steering wheel back and forth. An elderly club member known as Football Mike because he had played in the NFL as a linebacker a million years ago walked by on his way to his boat.

"Hi, Captain!" he shouted. "How's the bay today? Little rough? Hahahahahaha!" The *Travis McGee* being on blocks was a source of constant amusement for passersby.

"Lono! Kane!" I shouted down to the two gods, who now were loafing on the lawn. "Kill!"

They lumbered over to Football Mike and began licking him to death. He rubbed their heads and patted their sides as their tails whipped back and forth. Then they followed him along A Pier toward his boat, knowing he was a soft touch for a couple of potato chips or a piece of beef jerky. Traitors.

Just then the phone rang and I almost jumped out of the seat. Jesus. I took a breath and let it ring a few more times. Then I answered.

"McBride."

"Stryker!" Amber said, sounding genuinely enthused. "It's been so long! How are you?"

"I'm great, Amber!" I said, with more excitement than intended. Then I shifted into a more serious tone. "I was sorry to hear about your grandfather," I said.

"Yeah, it was really horrible," she said. "But the police aren't telling me anything about what happened. I remembered reading about you a while back. You're like this famous reporter guy now. I thought maybe you could help me, as a former classmate and everything."

"I haven't been a reporter for a while, Amber," I said. "I can probably find a reporter for you to talk to."

"No," she said quickly. "I mean, look, can you just come to the house?"

"Sure," I said. "When?"

"This afternoon?"

I almost jumped at that. Then I thought, *Hey, man, have a little pride. Act like you have a life.*

"How about tomorrow morning? I'm in the middle of something this afternoon."

"That would be great," she said.

She gave me directions to her house, which I didn't need. I had already looked it up in a street map book I keep on my desk. I assumed we'd engage in a bit of pointless chit-chat, sharing stories of the great times we didn't have together in high school, but she said someone was ringing her doorbell and she had to go. For some reason, I suspected the doorbell was just as hypothetical as the something I had to do that afternoon. I took a sip of beer and decided to look at my Jet Ski some more.

Chapter Three

The next morning I pointed my Ford F-150 pickup toward the Pali and headed for the leeward side of the island. The Koolau Mountain Range divides Oahu in half from the North Shore to Makapuu Point on the southeast side of the island. The range stands like a giant green barrier of heart-stopping beauty, nothing but jagged peaks, sheer cliffs, and waterfalls. In the old days you had to travel along the eastern shoreline to get from one side of the island to the other; the mountains were considered impassible. It was a long trip. Then a treacherous footpath was carved over a section of the range called the Pali, best known as the place where King Kamehameha chased a few hundred fellow Hawaiians off a cliff when he consolidated all the islands under his control. The footpath eventually became a horse path and finally expanded to a road, which eventually was made less terrifying thanks to a tunnel built through the most vertical part of the mountain range. The road became a highway with a turnoff to the Pali Lookout, the spot where so many Hawaiians met their death. With its thousand-foot cliffs and dramatic views of practically the entire windward side of the island, the Pali Lookout became both a favorite scenic attraction for tourists and a point of departure for suicide cases.

Eventually, three highways were poked through the Koolaus, cutting a trip from the windward side of the island to the leeward to just about ten minutes. As I came through the Pali Tunnel, Honolulu and the South Shore of Oahu opened below me.

As it turned out, I hadn't spent the previous afternoon staring at my Jet Ski. I decided to hop on my laptop computer and see what I could find out on the Internet about Wai Lo Fat, Amber Kam's family, and Chinese migration to Hawaii in general. Unfortunately, even in the waning months of the Year of Our Lords (Bill Gates and Steve Jobs) 2003, there was no wireless Net access on the windward side of Oahu except at important locations like police stations, hospitals, and overpriced coffee shops. So I went to the Longhouse Bar, sat on a tall stool, and plugged my computer into an ancient cable jack in the wall. When I started out as a reporter, collecting information involved pawing through piles of newspaper clips kept in the paper's morgue. You literally had to get your hands dirty to find the information you were looking for. Thanks to the Internet, the information I was looking for poured off the computer screen, and all I had to do was not spill beer on my $5,000 Apple PowerBook.

I think it took three hundred pages of James Michener's novel *Hawaii* before the first coconut finally washed up on Hawaii's shores. I wasn't going to go quite that far back. I knew that Polynesians got to Hawaii first in sailing canoes but eventually found out that calling dibs on an unpopulated chain of islands doesn't mean you get to keep them.

When the first white sails appeared on the horizon, the Hawaiians initially welcomed the exotic, pasty-faced visitors. But once they realized that Captain Cook wasn't the physical manifestation of the god Lono, the Hawaiians—as Franky Five Fins might have said—whacked him. Things got rather bleak after that for Hawaiians, as things always seem to do for cultures just a few technological steps behind strangers who show up on the doorstep. Imagine how the residents of the British Isles and the coast of France felt when Vikings showed up like heavily armed Jehovah's Witnesses. It was sort of like that for the Hawaiians when American whalers, missionaries, and plantation owners—supported by U.S. Navy gunships—decided to make the Islands home.

Once the haoles were settled in Hawaii, they began to look for cheap labor to work in the sugarcane fields. One boatload of Norwegians was coaxed to the Islands, but they found the weather too hot, the fish too mild, and their bosses too bossy. So the plantation owners looked west, where they ironically found the Far East. The Chinese first came to Hawaii in the 1850s. I tried to imagine how bad life in your own country would have to suck before sailing ten thousand miles to work in a sugarcane field in a strange foreign land under a hot tropical sun seemed like a good idea. It sucked bad enough for the Chinese that they came and stayed. They seemed have a natural affinity for the Hawaiians, especially the way they revered their ancestors and honored their elders. They also admired the way Hawaiians had woven the values of tolerance and hospitality into their lives, making it a fundamental part of their culture, a thing the Chinese would learn was called "aloha."

According to Wai Lo Fat's obituary, his father came to
Hawaii in 1895. Wai Lo Fat was born in 1914, fourteen
years after the great Chinatown fire. He apparently was
one of those Chinese who admired the Hawaiians, or at
least saw the value of a strategic union with a well-placed
Hawaiian family. He married Hoku Kalanianaole, a cousin
of Prince Jonah Kuhio Kalanianaole, an heir to the Hawaiian throne. Prince Jonah Kuhio Kalanianaole was impris-
oned after the overthrow of the Hawaiian kingdom but
later embraced the idea of Hawaii being a legal possession
of the United States and was elected to the U.S. Congress.
As a Republican, of all things.

Wai Lo Fat and Hoku Kalanianaole had several children,
including a boy named Clarence. Clarence, who grew up
to become vice president of a major Honolulu financial
institution that served Chinese residents, married a beautiful Chinese model and sometimes actress named Julie
Young, who appeared in three episodes of the TV show
Hawaiian Eye.

Julie gave birth to the future Blue Lotus Blossom Queen,
Amber, but her marriage to Clarence wasn't a long one. I
came across a 1969 news item about the death of Clarence
Lo Fat headlined CHINESE BUSINESSMAN KILLED IN FREAK
ACCIDENT. I thought, *Please don't let this be about a taro patch
and six inches of water.* It turned out to be a bit more surprising than that.

Clarence, apparently bored with his life as a captain of
business, took up hang gliding. The sport was just becoming popular in Hawaii at the time, particularly above the
fifteen-hundred-foot-high Koolau cliffs overlooking Sea
World Hawaii, a big tourist ocean theme park and aquarium on the eastern tip of Oahu. Sea World Hawaii featured

the usual waterlogged zoo attractions: a bizarre assortment of disgruntled fish who would never associate with each other in the ocean, thrown together in the same aquarium. It also had the mandatory porpoises jumping through flaming hoops and hunky guys in Speedos racing around in huge tanks of saltwater on the backs of false killer whales.

Behind and high above the ocean park, men attached to flimsy triangular kites would throw themselves off perfectly good cliffs and soar for hours above Waimanalo and Makapuu beaches before eventually landing on a sandy strip of land across Kalanianaole Highway, just a few yards from the ocean. At least that's the way it was supposed to work.

Clarence Lo Fat, who had made many successful flights, liked to equip his kite with pyrotechnic canisters that emitted trails of red and yellow smoke as he flew, much to the delight of people watching from the ground. On that day in 1969, he launched himself off the cliff and, according to eyewitnesses, everything looked fine. He started the colored smoke and made lazy turns along the towering cliff face, riding the updrafts. Then one of the canisters apparently exploded, and he suddenly dove like a Red-footed Booby with its ass on fire into the main marine tank at Sea World Hawaii during the noon show, killing himself, a guy in Speedos riding a false killer whale, and a porpoise named Mr. Whippy.

Julie Young Lo Fat, though financially secure after Clarence's death, apparently wasn't ready to just sit back on the oars and eat bonbons. She quickly married another rich Chinese businessman, Michael J. Kam, thankfully allowing the future Blue Lotus Blossom Queen to enter high school with the name Amber Kam instead of Amber Lo Fat. I know what kind of shit I had to take from classmates in high school with the name Stryker. I can imagine how brutal the razzing would have been for a sensitive sixteen-year-old girl with the last name of Lo Fat no matter how common it might be in China.

I took the Kahala off-ramp from the H-1 Freeway and passed by Kahala Mall, a curious outpost on the border between Hawaii's haves and the want-to-haves. The strange thing about Kahala Mall is that the want-to-haves consider it a ritzy shopping plaza while rich Kahala residents think of it as a quaint market frequented by the common folk.

In nineteenth-century Russia, a city named Novgorod was situated halfway between culturally backward Moscow and sophisticated St. Petersburg. It is said that when the unsophisticated travelers from Moscow reached Novgorod they thought they had reached St. Petersburg, and when pampered travelers from St. Petersburg entered Novgorod they thought they had reached Moscow. Kahala Mall is sort of like that. There's even a pierogi kiosk.

When you pass Kahala Mall and enter Kahala proper, you know you are entering some of the priciest real estate in Hawaii, if not the entire world. The first clue is that many of the houses are behind walls with huge iron driveway gates with sculptures of whales on them. Big iron gates in themselves are not a big deal and not all that expensive, but when you start adding custom-designed sculptures of whales and dolphins on the gates, you are hanging out in the high country.

The other way you know you are entering rarefied terra firma is that a lot of the houses have names, and their names are written on large metal, wood, or ceramic plaques attached to the wall or fence surrounding the house. The names of the houses usually end in "hale," which is Hawaiian for "house." I drove past Baldwin Hale, Sunrise Hale, Eagles Nest Hale, and the strangely named Hale Hale. I think this guy was trying to out-Hawaiian his neighbors. Most of the houses should have been named "Haole Hale" since they were owned by white people.

The second thing you notice is that despite their multimillion-dollar price tags, the houses are extremely close together, not surprising when you consider Hawaii real estate is practically sold by the square inch.

But there are worlds within worlds even in Kahala, as I was reminded when I reached a massive guarded gate at the entrance to Kala Lane Estates, where Amber lived. "Kala" means "money" in Hawaiian, and judging from the enormous manors, mansions, and tropical domiciles on the other side of the gate, Kala Lane Estates was where money lived. The security guard was a blond-haired kid in white shorts and a red polo shirt with a Diamond Head Security patch. After he took a photo of my truck and I had produced a valid driver's license and proof of vehicle ownership and insurance, he passed a plastic gate card in front of a sensor imbedded in a chest-high column of lava rock and the gate began to magically open.

"Guess you're waiving the DNA sample and body cavity search," I said, smiling. He apparently was one of those minimum-wage gate Nazis who don't appreciate sarcasm, because he didn't laugh or anything.

As I drove along Kala Lane, I noticed flashes of green between the stately homes, glimpses of the taro field where Wai Lo Fat drowned. Why would someone put a taro field in the middle of such a posh housing development?

As I neared Amber's house, I reminded myself that I had merely gone through a teenaged infatuation with her and that it was more than twenty years in the past. Things change. People change. She most likely had ballooned to the size of a sea mammal you might find on a Kahala driveway gate and was no longer that striking Blue Lotus Blossom Queen of my memory. Then, as I approached her house, I saw her standing near the driveway, and she looked—excuse me while I dip into my huge stock of hackneyed adjectives—breathtaking, gorgeous, stunning, and sexy (see: HOT); in short, nothing like any sea creature I could name except maybe one of those mythical Greek sirens of the sea who lured unsuspecting sailors to their deaths. Time and gravity had been amazingly generous to Amber Kalanianaole Kam.

I parked my truck behind a Mercedes in the driveway, with all the self-confidence of a yard boy come to collect that month's wages, but she greeted me like an old, close friend, giving me a hug and a kiss. And not one of those air kisses on the cheek. She planted one right on the lips. Then she pushed me back arm's length.

"Stryker McBride! You look fabulous! Look at you! God, if I knew you were going to turn out to be such a hunk I would have grabbed you in high school!"

I could not trust what might come out of my mouth, so I just smiled and nodded my head.

"It's good to see you!" she gushed, taking my hand. "Come on, let's go inside! I made some coffee. Unless you'd rather have a beer. Do you want a beer?"

"Coffee sounds great," I mumbled like a barely ambulatory mental patient.

Her house was huge, like something that might grace

the cover of *Luxury Island Living* magazine, which it had a year earlier. And unlike the houses in the outlying provinces of Kahala that are so close together you could jump from roof to roof, this one had a huge yard, a combination of lawn and exotic flowering shrubs that looked like they had been groomed with fingernail clippers and comb. Forty-foot-high coconut trees were strategically placed around the grounds as if it were a Hollywood back lot. We entered through one of two massive double arched koa wood doors, and I was surprised that the inside of the house was in no way as manicured as the outside. In fact, it had that just-ransacked look I came to know from my days on the police beat. We walked into a kitchen whose sheer size would have amazed Emeril Lagasse, except there were dirty dishes piled in the sink, and a long line of small black ants marched along one of the counters to a half-eaten piece of toast. A smallish cockroach darted from behind a Coke can and disappeared under the paper towel dispenser.

She laughed when she saw me looking at the mess.

"I know, I'm the worst housekeeper," she said, taking a couple of coffee mugs out of a cupboard. "I have a Filipino girl who comes on Thursdays. I wish I could get a Vietnamese. They are so much more manageable than the Filipinos these days. Don't you think?"

"I live on a boat," I said. "Not much call for domestic help."

"A boat? How cool!" she said. She poured coffee and then took a small carton of half-and-half out of the refrigerator, shook it, smelled it, and then peered into the opening like Sherlock Holmes.

"Black's fine," I said.

She led me out to a living room in a similar state of disarray, clothes piled on the several couches in the room and boxes of papers and junk piled up against the wall. The floor-to-ceiling windows looked out over a beautiful wooden lanai deck and lushly landscaped lawn and to the green taro field beyond.

She looked around the room at the devastation.

"Let's sit outside," she said. "It's not too hot yet."

We stood at the lanai rail, overlooking the yard and taro field. Two fields, actually. It was an amazing sight: a sea of broad green taro leaves, at least two football fields' worth in two rectangular patches. Through the middle of the fields was a wide, raised dirt pathway that headed in the direction of the ocean. I knew Kahala Bay was just beyond a row of houses in the distance. A small Hawaiian grass shack stood on a wood platform at one end of the dirt pathway, shaded by a couple of coconut trees. The taro patch was a living postcard—but what was it doing here?

"All this land used to be marsh," Amber said, apparently anticipating my question. "Then for a long time before the war it was all rice paddies. Then developers started reclaiming the land for houses."

"Reclaiming?"

"Yeah, I know. More like claiming it," she said. "Back then, nobody thought it was valuable land. The big money development was on the other side of Diamond Head. Waikiki and downtown."

I looked at the nonphotogenic side of Diamond Head, which stood like a giant brown discarded bookend in the distance. From this side, you wouldn't know it is probably one of the most recognizable natural landmarks in the world—a dormant volcano that, from the Waikiki side, has been the backdrop for probably a hundred million snapshots.

"My grandfather was one of the investors who developed all of Kahala," she said. "But he decided to save one part of Kahala from development in memory of his wife, my grandmother, Hoku Kalanianaole, who died giving birth to my father. My grandfather planted taro, a sacred plant that the Hawaiians call kalo, and he vowed this plot of land would never be developed."

"What about his partners? Didn't they have a say in the matter?" I asked. "Looks like you could put a lot more homes in here."

"You don't understand the Chinese," she said. "They don't think in terms of five years or ten years. They think in terms of generations. His partners were all Chinese. My great-grandfather Wen Lo Fat and other contract workers came from the same province in southern China. My grandfather was born in Hawaii, but he shared their views. My grandfather and his Chinese partners were willing to let this taro field remain undeveloped. If anything, it would just get more valuable with time."

"What about the younger partners in whatever corporation controls this property?" I asked. "Maybe they aren't as patient as the Chinese."

"Four Gates Enterprises developed Kahala. They are all Chinese," she said. "Mostly second and third generation. A few, like me, fourth."

"You work for Four Gates?" I said.

"Yes," she said. "I manage that little strip mall out in Hawaii Kai along the water, the Blue Ocean Centre."

"That's a nice place, great shops. Little restaurant out there on the pier, what's it called?"

"Whaler Cove Inn," she said. "Yeah, it's nice out there, but it's not like working downtown. The Four Gates Plaza. That's where the action is."

She looked out across the taro patch wistfully.

"What can I do for you, Amber?" I asked. "You sounded pretty upset on the phone about your grandfather's death, but you don't seem to think anyone might have wanted him dead."

She slipped her arm through mine, a clear violation of my personal space that I didn't mind a bit. She looked at me with those almond eyes that had only become more beautiful with age.

"I'm not sure why I called you, Stryker," she said. "My grandfather was eighty-nine years old. He lived in a house about three down from this one. He was one of the original founders of Four Gates, but he wasn't involved in the day-to-day corporate business. He was like a figurehead. He had live-in caregivers. He was a sweet old man. He spent his time taking care of his taro. He used to spend his days puttering around the taro patch and napping in that grass shack. His death was probably an accident, but I just want to be sure. So I thought of you."

"Why me?"

"Because I need someone I can trust. I read some stories about you. They made it sound like you are some untouchable Eliot Ness kind of newspaper reporter. You even got shot by the bad guys, right? I just thought I needed someone who wasn't afraid to take on the powerful."

"You're laying it on a bit thick now, sister," I said, laughing. "Besides, I'm not a reporter anymore. Just a citizen trying to get by in a troubled world."

"But didn't you get shot?"

"You know the press, always blowing things out of proportion," I said, avoiding what had become my least favorite subject.

"Stryker, the police don't care that my grandfather's dead. Just another old guy who died. He was loved in the Chinese community. Tomorrow they will have a great memorial service for him up at the temple and burn incense and all that. But then it will be business as usual. I just want to know that everything is kosher. That's all."

"Kosher?"

She smiled.

"I spent a few years in Hollywood. L.A. lingo."

"I'd be happy to make a few calls, Amber," I said. "It was probably just an accident. But you're right, the police don't go out of their way to make family members think they care one way or the other. Can you show me where he, uh, where he was found?"

She looped her arm in mine again. She gave me a peck on the cheek. I might have blushed, but my tan is dark enough so it would be hard to tell.

We walked down a worn track to the taro field until we reached the raised dirt pathway cutting through the middle of the two patches. Amber's foot slipped off the path at one point and into some mud. She grabbed me as if she had stepped in hot lava.

"Ahhhhhh! I *hate* it down here," she said, shaking the mud from her slipper. She looked up at me, suddenly smiling sweetly. "It's just so, you know, wet, and there are lots of mosquitoes and things," she said.

"Still the Blue Lotus Blossom Queen," I said, smiling, feeling manly. I'm not afraid of mud.

We walked the length of the fields, and just before the

grass shack on the ocean side of one field, she pointed out an area about twenty feet away where Wai Lo Fat's body was found. The newspaper report said Wai Lo Fat had drowned in six inches of water. From where I stood, it didn't even look that deep. Aside from the mud along the banks, the water was crystal clear and moved slowly in the direction of the ocean. A frail old man falling facedown into even that amount of water wouldn't have to work hard to drown. The closest I came to drowning was bodysurfing over a shallow reef to get my board after a wipeout when some whitewater splashed into my face and went down my throat, causing it to seize shut. If I had been in water over my head, I probably would have drowned. But I was able to stand on the reef in just a few feet of water until I could breathe again. Here in the taro field, Wai Lo Fat just might not have had enough strength to push himself up.

"He worked in these fields all the time and never had any problems," she said.

"He worked these fields by himself?" I asked.

"No, there are some university students who volunteer to work out here," she said. "They get college credits or something. It was one of them who found him. Or maybe the security guard."

"There are security guards?"

"Yeah, usually just one old guy in a gray uniform," she said. "I don't see him. He's probably sleeping someplace."

We walked on toward the grass shack.

"That's my grandfather's house," she said, pointing across the field. "The house I'm in belonged to my mother. She died about ten years ago. Cancer. "

"You live with your dad?"

"No, he and Mom divorced and she got the house. He wasn't my real dad. My real dad died when I was seven."

The image of Clarence Lo Fat in flames plunging into a Sea World Hawaii porpoise pool from fifteen hundred feet ran through my mind, but all I said was "Sorry to hear that, Amber."

"I'm okay," she said. "I'm Chinese-Hawaiian, I've got millions of relatives."

That struck me as a tad cold, but I let it pass.

"Were there any problems between your grandfather and your stepdad?" I asked.

"No," she said. "My stepfather really didn't get into the whole Hawaii thing. He was from New York. After my mom died he went back to the East Coast."

"I know this will sound stupid . . . kind of *Murder, She Wrote*, but did your grandfather have any enemies? Was he involved in any legal disputes? Did he cut down his neighbor's banana tree or anything?"

She laughed and then stopped herself.

"I'm sorry," she said. "It's just that he was this sweet old man. I can't imagine anyone wanting to hurt him. But I really didn't know anything about the business side of his life. Four Gates is a big company, and I'm sure there are a lot of secrets."

This sounded a bit odd to me, too. She couldn't imagine anyone out to hurt Wai Lo Fat but in the next breath opens a door to shadowy business dealings at Four Gates? This was a smart girl. As she looked innocently up into my eyes, I was getting an uncomfortable feeling that she was sure she was a lot smarter than a former high school swimming star and ex–newspaper reporter. My surprise meter may be set pretty high, but my bullshit meter is finely tuned, and it was beginning to hum a bit.

"Look, Amber," I said. "I can't do much. I can check with the cops and the medical examiner and make a few other calls for you. It might make you feel better."

"Thank you, Stryker," she said, giving me a slight hug. She put her arm through mine again, and we began walking back to her house.

"So how'd you end up in Hollywood?" I asked.

"My mom was an actress," she said. "An unsuccessful actress. So she put her ambitions on me and became a stage mother, pushing me into trying out for all kinds of plays and things in high school and college. She's the one who made me enter that Blue Lotus Blossom pageant. I hated it. When I graduated from UH, she persuaded me to go to Los Angeles. She said she still had some Hollywood connections."

We got back to her house, and this time she broke out some beers. We sat on the teak deck chairs on the lanai. I noticed she sat close enough so that she could reach out and touch me when she wanted to make a point or kick me playfully with a bare foot when she thought I was being funny.

"So how was it?" I asked. "L.A."

"Insane. Unless you are ready to blow every director and producer in town—I'm sorry," she said, reaching out and grabbing my arm. "I mean unless you are ready to quote, read lines, end quote for every director and producer in town, you aren't going to get any work. I tell you, I'm surprised someone doesn't rent knee pads in Hollywood. They could make a fortune."

I laughed and took a sip of beer.

"That wasn't for me," she said. She looked at me sideways, and I just smiled. "It wasn't! And don't you smile like that, Stryker McBride. I'll have you know former Blue Lotus Blossom Queens do not . . . you know what . . . to get jobs."

We both laughed at that, and I realized I really kind of liked her. Yes, my BS meter was humming, but she was incredibly gorgeous and there was a certain charm there. It also was clear she had a way of getting just about anything she wanted without the use of knee pads.

"I was an extra on a couple of *Baywatch* episodes," she said. Then, looking at my reaction, she kicked me and added, "I got that job fair and square! I actually had a line of dialogue with David Hasselhoff in one episode."

"What was the line?"

She laughed. "Don't even start!" she said.

"Come on, you must remember it."

"Of course I remember it," she said. "It was my first TV line."

"Well?"

"I come running up the beach to the lifeguard tower, boobs bopping up and down in the classic *Baywatch* fashion, I grab Hasselhoff's arm, point to the water, and say, 'Mister, I think someone's drowning!'"

"And the rest is film history," I said.

"It might have been," she said. "Except they cut the line and all you see in that episode was me pointing to the water. After a year in L.A. I came back home, went back to UH and got my master's in business, and went to work at Four Gates."

She took a sip of beer and gazed across the taro patch,

maybe wondering what could have been had her *Baywatch* line not been cut and she went on to become a star. She sort of shook her head, as if to break the spell.

"What about you?" she asked. "How did you go from being a great swimmer at Punahou to some hotshot reporter?"

I've learned that when most people ask you to tell them your life story, the last thing they want to hear is your life story. I put Amber in that category. The fact was that I had actually swum my way to Punahou School. I had been a swimmer since I was two years old, according to McBride family lore. I learned to swim in Morocco, Africa, where I was born. My dad was in the air force, a B-52 pilot, and there was a pool at the Officers Club on Nouasseur Air Base. There is absolutely nothing for a child to do in Morocco, except avoid the 120-degree heat, scorpions, and camel rides. The base pool was our oasis. My brothers and I stayed in the water until our little fingers and toes were wrinkled and blanched white like cadaver flesh. My mom practically had to force us out of the pool at gunpoint.

We left Morocco when I turned three and moved to Tampa, Florida. Then Bellevue, Nebraska. Then Montgomery, Alabama. Then Agana, Guam. Then Osan, South Korea. It's a horrible thing to do to a kid, drag him all over the world, especially to places like Morocco, Guam, and Alabama. But the one thing all these places had in common, what every air force base had wherever we went in the world, was an Officers Club. And every Officers Club had a swimming pool. And the swimming pools were always the same. So I swam. From Morocco across the United States and then to Guam and South Korea. By the time we came to Hawaii in 1977, I was fourteen years old and one of the fastest swimmers in the state. At age fifteen I went to Radford High School, just off base from Hickam AFB, where I set a state record in the 50-meter butterfly. When I turned sixteen I was offered a scholarship at Punahou School.

"It's a short story," I said to Amber. "After Punahou I swam for the University of Hawaii for a few years. Then I transferred to the University of Oregon. Eventually, I got a degree in journalism and started working at newspapers."

That was true, as far as it went. Sort of the *Reader's Digest* version of the story. The whole story was something I didn't like to dwell on. My dad had retired from the air force and moved with Mom to Oregon, where they bought a ranch. My mom came down with cancer, and so I looked into moving to Oregon to be closer to them. The timing worked out because the University of Oregon swim team was looking for a butterfly specialist. The Oregon swimming coaches put visions of a possible trip to the Olympics in my head. That and a nice scholarship sealed the deal. I became a University of Oregon Duck.

My mom died a year later, and I was sort of happy that she wasn't around to see what a knuckleheaded son she had raised. One day, I drove with a friend of mine from Eugene to Newport on the coast to try some cold water surfing at a place called Agate Beach. We had to wear full wet suits to ward off hypothermia, but I refused to wear the wet-suit booties because they felt too weird after surfing barefoot in Guam and Hawaii. As a result, my feet froze into numb stumps and I took a heavy wipeout on my first wave, dislocating my right shoulder. The injury was so serious that the little medical clinic in Newport didn't want to touch it. I was raced by ambulance all the way back to

Eugene where specialists put in a titanium shoulder socket. The surgeon did a great job, and I eventually regained complete use of my arm. But competitive swimming on the level where I had been is a game of microseconds. My competitive swimming days were over.

I always knew there was no professional future in swimming—I mean, back then there was no such thing as *Monday Night Swimming* with Al Michaels and John Madden doing the commentary—but I thought being a nationally ranked swimmer might propel me into sports journalism, maybe a staff position on *Sports Illustrated* after college. After the injury I lost interest in the whole sports journalism thing. I got to keep my scholarship and after graduating I was unable to stop the momentum from moving every two or three years of my life. I ended up just joining the Peace Corps and going to Sierra Leone, an African country so miserable and backward it made Morocco look like Monaco. After that I backpacked around Europe for a while before returning to Oregon to work on my dad's ranch. I finally put my journalism degree to work at the *Oregonian* newspaper in Portland and after a few years got a job at the *Honolulu Journal*.

That was way too much backstory to throw at Amber. And I was right about her not really wanting to hear my life story anyway. After I mentioned the University of Oregon and getting a degree in journalism, she said, "Oh, God!" and looked at her watch. "I've got to get out to Hawaii Kai before noon. Burger King wants to open a store in the Blue Ocean Centre. Can you believe that? I mean, it is an upscale commercial space. We just got Trisha's EuroAsia Boutique as an anchor client. But I have to go let down the Burger King people nicely. See if I can steer them to another Four Gates property in a less desirable area."

I just smiled at her. She was amazing. She really didn't care about what I had been doing, my work, the swimming, or even being shot. She couldn't even keep up the ruse of interest long enough for me to try to weasel out of telling the tale. This interview was over.

She walked me to my truck and surprised me by giving me a hug and a kiss good-bye. This one wasn't an air kiss, either. It was right on the smacker, and just a tad too long. Then she looked straight into my eyes and said, "Thank you for your help, Stryker. I'm really glad we are finally friends."

And, you know, I almost believed her.

Chapter Four

I was up before dawn the next morning. Way before dawn. Because Kane and Lono had heard some kind of commotion on the end of B Pier and raced out to investigate in a loud and annoying way. During Admiral Nelson's day, crews from British frigates would slip into harbors in small boats under cover of darkness and cut out enemy ships. I doubt anyone was trying to cut out one of the yacht club boats, but some knuckleheads might have thought they could sneak in and steal stuff off a boat or two, like an outboard motor or marine radio. It had happened before, but not since Kane and Lono were around.

I made the long walk out to the end of B Pier, where the gods were still barking into the darkness. I finally got them to shut up and could hear the rumble of a small engine on the other side of the coral patch. Whatever craft it was, it was moving away from the club. The gods had done their job once again.

I sat down and dangled my legs over the end of the pier. A green light a few yards away marked one side of the channel through the reef. Across the basin, just off the other pier, a red light marked the other side of the channel. There were a couple more red and green lights farther out where the channel between the reef patches widened. The green light reminded me of the green light in *The Great Gatsby*, the light Gatsby could see across the bay at the end of Daisy's dock. The green light was supposed to represent Gatsby's hopes for the future, his desire for Daisy. F. Scott Fitzgerald apparently wasn't a boat owner or he might have had a more pragmatic, less romantic view of green lights in bays. When you're looking from land to the water, green lights or green signs mark the right side of a channel entrance, while red lights and red signs mark the left edge. The first thing new boat owners learn is "Red, Right, Return." That means on your return to port entering a channel, make sure the red lights are on your right or else you'll end up on the reef or rocks. When I think of the green light shining on Daisy's dock, I wonder, Where the hell is the red light? How irresponsible is it to have a green light and no red light to tell you where the channel is? I mean, if Gatsby had tried to sneak up to Daisy's dock at night and whisk her away, he probably would have run aground. The famous last line of the novel was "So we beat on, boats against the current, borne back ceaselessly into the past." It should have been "So we sit stuck on the reef forever, our boats beat to pieces by the ceaseless currents, because there was no red channel light. Man, Daisy, what a fucking bitch."

Kane and Lono were still fired up, hoping to find more action. They tore down the pier, and a few minutes later I saw them across the boat basin at the end of A Pier, gazing out into the bay, hoping the mystery boat would return.

The sky was starting to lighten. On the east horizon,

the edges of a cloud bank were shining gold with the sun behind it. Overhead was clear with just a few stars. The moon hung over the bay, just a blue-white sliver, like God's eyelash. I thought, *That's pretty good. God's eyelash. I should be a writer. I bet F. Scott Fitzgerald never thought of calling a sliver of moon God's eyelash.*

Since I was already up, dressed in just some old surf trunks and a T-shirt, and it was a long walk back to my boat, I decided to get my swimming in. I dove off the dock and swam across to A Pier, where the gods were happy to see me. I tossed the wet T-shirt on the end of the pier, where I knew they would ignore it with their lives. They were excited to see me swimming away. They probably thought I was going to drag their mystery intruder boat back for them in my teeth.

I stroked freestyle along the left reef edge toward the channel buoy a half mile away. I was thinking about the gods, how they had turned out to be a perfect fit for the yacht club. I had adopted them about a year and a half before from a Hawaiian kahuna, or priest, out in Kaaawa, a little seaside town on the windward side, settled in ancient times by islanders who enjoyed hunting, fishing, and, judging by the name Kaaawa, vowels.

When word got around that I was looking for a couple of dogs for guard duty, everyone told me to call Puka in Kaaawa. They always added, "And let the phone ring." They weren't kidding about that. The first time I called, I let the phone ring about ten times before I hung up. The second time about twenty. Finally, the third time I let it ring about thirty times and someone picked up. Whoever answered sounded out of breath.

"Is this Puka?" I asked.

"Yes, confoun' it!" he said hoarsely. "You da buggah who been calling me all day and hanging up every time I just get to da phone?"

"Well, I called earlier but no one answered."

"I was trying for answer, confoun' it!" he wheezed in pidgin English, the patois common to many local Hawaii residents. "Ho! I'm one old man you know! Da phone rings, I come running for da house from feeding those damn chickens and you wen' hang up on me!"

I had been told that, aside from being a Hawaiian priest, Puka ran a sanctuary for abandoned dogs and fighting cocks. I could hear a lot of crowing and barking in the background. I was going to tell him that they have phones these days with built-in answering machines, but I decided it would be better just to cut to the chase.

"I'm looking for a couple of dogs," I said.

"What they look like?"

"No," I said. "I didn't lose any. I want to buy a couple of dogs. Guard dogs."

"I get plenty those kine," he said. "You like rooster, too?"

I told him I didn't need any roosters, just dogs. I asked him for directions to his place. He laughed hoarsely into the phone.

"Bruddah," he said, "you drive out Kaaawa. You find 'em, no worry."

So I drove out to Kaaawa along Kamehameha Highway, which, though called a highway, really was just a two-lane country road that ambled along so close to the shore that at times the spray from the waves hitting the rocks was so bad you had to turn on your windshield wipers. It's a lovely drive, past rows of coconut trees bordering small, clean sand beaches on the ocean side and ramshackle wooden houses with large, well-kept lawns on the other. I understood what Puka meant when he said I'd have no trouble finding his house when the speed limit dropped from forty-five miles per hour to twenty-five at the outskirts of town. The windows on my Ford F-150 pickup truck were down, so I had no trouble hearing the ungodly racket of crowing roosters and barking dogs coming from a nearby valley. I turned off the highway and headed in the general direction of the noise.

I finally came to a slightly askew main house and some tumbledown outbuildings that looked like something out of *The Grapes of Wrath*. Or maybe *Bananas and Papayas of Wrath*. Now I understood why Puka didn't have an answering machine. I was surprised he had electricity.

When I turned off the truck, dogs starting pouring out of everywhere. They surrounded the truck, wagging their tails and looking happy to see a visitor. But since I was vastly outnumbered, I thought it would be better to wait for Puka to show up. A little brown man with white hair shuffled out of one of the outbuildings.

"Move, confoun' it!" he yelled, wading through the dogs. They parted, allowing him through.

"You da haole who wen' call looking for dogs, eh?" he asked. "Come on out, these buggahs won't bite you."

When I got out of the truck, the dogs seemed to lose interest and started wandering away in small packs. I then noticed the feral chickens and roosters hanging out on the rooftops and in the branches of a large avocado tree in the front yard. Considering the number of dogs on the premises, that seemed like a prudent place to be.

Puka pointed out several dogs he thought would make

good guard dogs. It looked like you could get just about any kind of dog you wanted as long as he was part pit bull. The pit bull/Chihuahua was particularly disturbing to look at, a mostly hairless sixty-pound shivering animal with a bad attitude. I watched a fairly sinister-looking pit bull/rottweiler mix eyeballing a Rhode Island Red on a tree branch, apparently calculating the vertical jump distance. The mental image of Bayview Yacht Club members sprinting from their cars to their boats with Cujo in hot pursuit popped into my mind. I explained the kind of dogs I was looking for had to be able to get along with people, lots of different people, as well as guarding property.

"No worry, bruddah," Puka said, walking toward a small wooden building. "I got some special dogs. Try come."

Inside the shack was a gorgeous female German shepherd, jet black with tan paws, and four similarly colored puppies scampering around her and wrestling with each other. There was no pit bull in these pups.

"Try sit down," Puka said, plopping down on the wooden floor. I joined him, and the puppies, not more than six months old, came racing over and dove into our laps.

"That one there, he Lono," said Puka. "That one Ku. The little buggah, he Kanaloa. And that big bruddah in your lap, he Kane. They named fo' Hawaiian gods. Now, I promised Kanaloa to my sista's boy. And I going keep Ku 'cause I need at least one damn dog around this place that's not mental. But if Lono and Kane like go with you, then I let you buy 'em."

Lono came over and began fighting Kane in my lap. Then they both turned on me, jumping up at my face, licking it. It seemed like Lono and Kane were game to boldly go with me where no Hawaiian dog gods had gone before, a suburban yacht club, but not until Puka and I had agreed on a price. Setting the price involved Puka and me consuming many Budweisers throughout the afternoon and then being joined in the evening by his family and friends, who mysteriously multiplied until the lawns between the main house and the outbuildings were filled with people laughing, drinking, talking, and eating (mostly barbecued chicken, much to the horror of the various fowl watching the proceedings from the rooftops and avocado tree). A group of local men armed with ukuleles, guitars, and hollow gourds materialized, and soon Hawaiian music floated through the valley instead of rooster-crowing. Eventually they were joined by young Hawaiian women dancing the hula, and I felt like I had wandered into an Elvis Presley movie (*"Blue Hawaii? Paradise Hawaiian Style? Viva Kaaawa?*). Except this was the real Hawaiian deal.

I don't remember falling asleep, but thankfully it wasn't in my truck driving home on that long dangerous two-lane highway after helping raise the price of Anheuser-Busch stock to an alarming degree. I slept deeply despite the off-and-on rooster crowing throughout the night, but when I finally woke up the next morning, I learned the answer to the age-old question of what happens when you lie down with dogs. The answer: You wake up with dogs. And if you are sleeping on the lawn at Puka's place, lots of dogs. I was amazed to find that Lono and Kane had spent the night curled up against me. The pit bull/rottweiler and the pit bull/Chihuahua weren't among the other dogs crashed out on the lawn around me, so that was good. Someone had thoughtfully provided a grass mat for me to sleep on and a pillow. When I sat up, the two puppies stood, stretched, and looked up at my face. Then they nuzzled their way under my legs, cuddled together and shut their eyes. If I didn't know better, I would say they liked me. Or maybe they were just trying to get warm.

Puka came out of the house with a cup of coffee for me.

"How come you neva tell me you was da kine, the newspaper writer who got shot by that police officer?" he asked, handing me the coffee.

"Not a big deal," I said, taking a sip. It was strong, but just what I needed after a beer-logged night of dog negotiation. Somewhere deep in my hazy memory, I remembered some haole guy making a fool of himself trying to do the hula. The disturbing thing was that I didn't remember any other haoles being at the impromptu luau but me.

"That cop, Jake Stane, the bugga who wen' shoot you, he was one bad bruddah," Puka said. "We knew from small kid time he one bad one. He wen' live just ova there, Laie, wit' all da Mormons. He was good football player but mean, da buggah."

"I don't write for the newspaper anymore," I said. "Life goes on."

"Not for Jake Stane," he said, breaking into a hoarse laugh.

"He's in prison, not dead," I said.

"Same ting in my book," he said. "Da buggah neva getting outta there."

"I'm a bit hazy . . . what price did we finally agree on for Lono and Kane?" I said.

"You said I get your truck and one thousand dollar for each dog," he said. I choked on a sip of coffee. He laughed so loud the pit bull/rottweiler poked his head around a corner of the house to see what was happening.

"Hey, bruddah, I kid you," he said, catching his breath.

"We said you going bring me two hundred dollars and one of those telephones that go answer themselves so I no hafta go running to da house all day, confoun' it. I'm an old man, you know!"

"A hundred dollars for a pure German shepherd is not enough," I said.

"Don't start again," he said, waving a brown hand at me. "I told you, more important da dogs go where they belong, not da money."

And the dogs did seem to belong at Bayview. Puka told me Lono was the Hawaiian god of fertility and peace. He also was identified with rain, which Puka assured me would make this pup a good dog to have on the wet windward side of the island. Kane was the Hawaiian god of light and life. Ancient Hawaiians believed he created the earth, sky, and upper heaven. But, more importantly to Puka, the god Kane also possessed a small seashell that turned into a huge sailboat when placed in the ocean. Anyone using the boat only had to say where they wanted to go and the boat would take them there.

"So this dog, Kane, he going like it at a place where plenty boats stay," Puka said. "He going like living on your boat."

I reached the reef buoy and treaded water, putting two fingers to my neck to take my pulse. I had one. So that was good. I wasn't winded. For a thirty-nine-year-old male with a titanium shoulder and a scar from a bullet wound who considered beer one of the four major food groups, I was in pretty good shape.

I began swimming back to the boat basin, thinking about Amber and our conversation in the taro patch the day before. She displayed an almost clinical detachment talking about the divorce of her mother and stepfather, and the death of her mother by cancer. I found her off-the-cuff statement about having millions of other relatives particularly chilling. That little inadvertent laugh when I asked her about her grandfather's potential enemies was off-putting as well. And while I'm not a bad-looking guy, all the huggy-kissy stuff was over the top. The last time I had been mauled that badly was by three out-of-town aunts at a family Christmas party when I was seven years old.

I wish I was one of those guys who could believe in the basic humanity of man, that people's motives are generally good. But I don't possess that gene. Experience has taught me—sometimes painfully—that human conduct is motivated primarily by self-interest. I didn't know what Amber wanted, but I knew without a doubt the reason she asked me to poke around in the death of Wai Lo Fat wasn't because she was interested in how he had died.

Actually, did it even matter what she wanted? I mean, I wasn't exactly a paragon of good motives. I basically didn't really care how Wai Lo Fat died. It's not that I'm insensitive; it's just that I didn't know the gentleman. I've been to the scene of way too many murders, suicides, and fatal accidents to expend whatever little reservoir of empathy I still possess on people I don't know. What was my self-interest in this equation? I'd like to think that investigating Wai Lo Fat's death at least would get me out of the house, keep me occupied with a task that conceivably could result in some benefit to society. But I suspected it had more to do with the possibility it could lead to me spending an afternoon with Amber in what I assumed was a big Blue Lotus Blossom Queen bed in that messy upstairs bedroom of hers.

As I approached A Pier I decided I had nothing to lose. I'd make a few calls, maybe look up my old buddy Dr. Lew Eden, the city medical examiner, and accidentally run into a few old cop sources.

With just fifty yards to go to the dock, I broke into the butterfly stroke. I still had the perfect dolphin movement for the 'fly, but the little clicking in my right shoulder reminded me to take it easy. I had already put quite a few miles on the titanium shoulder socket and didn't know exactly how many miles it was good for. The next time I took my truck into Jiffy Lube, I'd have to ask an expert about it.

I reached the dock doing an easy breaststroke, and the gods actually got up to greet me. My wet T-shirt was still there. Good boys. I looked across the boat basin. The green light at the end of B Pier blinked steadily. It seemed to be mocking me.

Chapter Five

Morgues are kind of a cross between hospitals and roach hotels. They feel like hospitals, all sterile and medical looking, but, like a roach hotel, they're the kind of places that you check into but you don't check out of. Or, more precisely, you check in when you check out. I'm not a big fan of morgues. It's not that I'm queasy; it's just that I don't enjoy seeing human beings when they are at their worst. And it doesn't get much worse than dead.

That said, the best way to find out exactly how Wai Lo Fat died was to go to Dr. Lew Eden, the CEO of Death, the Honolulu City and County chief medical examiner. I had known Eden for years, a professional necessity. But we had also been known to share a beer or two, and I even played golf with him once.

As I pulled into the small parking lot of the ME's office in a rather run-down, industrial-looking section of Honolulu, a young police officer in a blue uniform was escorting an elderly man and woman to their car. Obviously the couple had been there for a "viewing." I wondered who they had the misfortune of having to visit. A son or daughter? A grandchild? A neighbor? What a great job that cop had.

I entered the double glass doors to the one-story brick building, as I had done more times than I could remember. There was no one sitting in the front office, so I pushed through the little swinging wooden gates by the counter and headed for the part of the facility popularized on all those TV shows as the place with the metal drawers full of dead people and the whirr of circular saws hanging in the air. An attractive woman of about forty wearing blue surgical pajamas stepped out of a doorway with a clipboard and into my path.

"Where you going there, big fella?" she asked. She had dark, shoulder-length hair pulled back in a ponytail, and I know this would seem weird considering the surroundings, but she was very sexy. I just love a woman in uniform.

"I'm looking for Lew," I said. "I mean, Dr. Eden."

"Well, he's up at Punchbowl," she said, sizing me up. She had that confident, relaxed demeanor that I suppose you have to have if you're a sexy woman in blue pajamas walking around a morgue.

"When will he be back?" I asked.

"No," she said, kind of smiling. "I guess I should have said he's *in* Punchbowl. You haven't been around here for a while, huh, big fella?"

She had me there. It had probably been a few years since I had been to the medical examiner's office. Punchbowl Crater, just above Honolulu, is the site of the National Memorial Cemetery of the Pacific, where military veterans and their families are buried. Dr. Eden had been in his late sixties when I knew him, so I guess it wasn't too much of a surprise that he had died. I knew he had been in the army, had even gone to Vietnam as a MASH doctor. It made sense that he'd be buried in Punchbowl.

She saw me doing the math in my head and processing the news that a man I thought was alive was dead and gave me a second to finish.

"Dr. Eden died about a year ago," she said. "I'm in charge of the chop shop these days."

She definitely wasn't one of those warm and fuzzy, overly sentimental medical examiners. In fact, I had never met anyone in the business of cutting up dead bodies who didn't have both a sense of humor and a scientific detachment from the whole life and death thing. Dr. Eden had some really funny dead-people stories if you were into that.

"I'm sorry," she said, going through the motions of being sensitive. "Was he a close friend of yours?"

"No," I said. "Just a friend. An acquaintance. I used to be a reporter with the afternoon paper. Spent quite a bit of time here in the old days. Played golf with Lew. I'm Stryker McBride."

Her eyes widened. "You're Stryker McBride?" she asked. "Lew left something for you."

"Left something for me?"

"Yeah, come on to my office," she said. As we walked she turned, held out her hand, and said, "Sorry. I'm Melba McCall, the medical examiner here."

"McCall," I said. "Of the County Mayo McCalls?"

"The County Passaic, New Jersey, McCalls," she said. "I don't go for all that old country stuff."

I was going to tell her we might be cousins since the McCalls and McBrides hailed from the same part of Ireland, but I had the feeling genealogy wasn't one of her hobbies.

Dr. Melba McCall had a big office, the same big office that Lew Eden had used with the same large desk backed by a wall of books. There were the several jars of medical curiosities that medical examiners seem to like to keep around for that book on medical curiosities they'll never get around to writing. But the thing I noticed about the office under Dr. McCall's tenure, was that it was clean and well organized. It reeked of professionalism. Lew Eden was a professional, but he wasn't what you'd call neat. He had books stacked all over the office, his golf clubs standing in a corner, and empty Big Gulp cups and Taco Bell burrito wrappers decorating the large conference table in front of the desk. This ME cleaned up after herself.

"So you're Stryker McBride!" she said, going over to a rather impressive restaurant-style coffee/cappuccino machine. This lady was a connoisseur of caffeine, or at least a serious adherent.

"Coffee?" she asked.

Before I could answer she had drawn me a cup in a real coffee mug. No Styrofoam for this girl. She didn't ask if I wanted sugar or cream. I didn't. But I noticed she didn't ask, and there wasn't any anyway.

"It's Blue Mountain," she said. "Jamaican. Best coffee on the planet."

"Better than Kona?"

"Kona's okay," she said, settling behind her desk, "but Kona is a breakfast coffee. This is coffee for grown-ups. Grown at fifty-five hundred feet between Kingston and Port Maria. I get it straight from the bean pickers. Jamaican coffee makes Jamaican dope look like shit."

Then she said, "Oh yeah!" and hopped up and went to the bookshelves. She rummaged around, moving some boxes and files, and pulled out what looked like a prescription medicine bottle and tossed it to me across the desk.

I managed to snag it out of the air with one hand, Barry Bonds style, and not spill the coffee, which I thought was both pretty cool and lucky. Unimpressed, she had already flipped open a file and was reading it while I examined the pill bottle with my name on it. Or, rather, a message in Lew Eden's handwriting saying *Hold for Stryker McBride*.

She wrote some notes in the file, apparently connected to the body in the room she had just left when she ran into me. She put the file down on the desk.

"Lew didn't really leave a suicide note," she said, taking up her coffee cup, "but he had sort of organized things."

"A suicide note? He killed himself?"

"I take it you don't read the papers much anymore," she said, sipping her coffee. "What kind of newsman are you?"

"Former," I said. But she had a point. I had pretty much stopped reading the papers. At least for news. I mainly read them for the sports, tides, and weather reports.

"Yeah, he killed himself," she said. "Right back there on Table Number Four. Injected himself with a hundred-milligram concoction of thiopental sodium, alcuronium chloride, and pancuronium bromide. He warned me he was going to do it but didn't tell me when. I had been working here for about a year. He was diagnosed with a rare debilitating brain disease, progressive supranuclear palsy. It's like a slow stroke. Incapacitates you over a year or so until you can't move and can't swallow. He said, 'I'm not going to go through that.' I don't blame him. I'd have done the same thing."

Even after all my years covering crime and death I still

find the rank pragmatism of medical examiners, emergency room workers, and crime scene first responders jolting.

"So you're Stryker McBride," she said.

"Why do you keep saying that?"

"Because Lew talked about you. Said you were some hotshot investigative reporter who had gotten shot in the line of duty or something. It was before my time. He was called to the hospital the night you got hit. Guess you were in pretty bad shape. They gave him the bullet they dug out of you, thinking this would be your next stop. Then you didn't die, and so he ended up just keeping the bullet. I think he was going to give it to you for a birthday present, but I guess he got distracted with his own problems. So when I was cleaning up the office I came across that pill container and kept it over there with some of his other junk. You're lucky I didn't throw it out."

I popped the top off the pill bottle. Inside was a mangled piece of lead.

"Yeah. Lucky. Now I can make an ear stud out of it."

She laughed. I liked her laugh. It was completely natural. It was one of those laughs people laugh when something funny strikes them, no matter where they are—symphony, funeral, city morgue.

"So let's see your scar," she said.

"I'd rather not," I said.

"Come on, I'm a doctor," she said. "I see worse every day."

"It's in kind of a private spot," I said, unconsciously flexing my butt.

"Ah!" she said, "they shot you in the keister! Well, they say discretion is the better part of valor and fleeing is the better part of discretion."

"I wasn't fleeing," I said. "I was making a tactical withdrawal."

She smiled at me, and I confess I was having very non-cousinlike feelings toward her. I have to say I was having the best time I had ever had in the city medical examiner's office. All Lew wanted to talk about was oversized gallstones and golf. And this doctor's coffee was great. I don't know if it was better than Kona, but it's good to know Jamaica has something going for it other than jerk chicken, dreadlocks, and joints the size of baguettes.

"You're a fairly young man to be retired, Stryker McBride," she said. "Getting shot in the fanny rob you of your zest for life, did it?"

I didn't say anything. I had never really thought of it that way, but there's no denying I had become something of a recluse since quitting the paper.

"I see," she said. "Another private spot. Well, then tell me what brought you looking for Lew today. Just in the neighborhood? On a walking tour of city facilities?"

"Actually, a friend of mine wanted me to look into the death of her grandfather," I said. "Elderly Chinese man, Wai Lo Fat."

"So now you're a private eye? Good, it'll get you out of the house," she said. "Although Wai Lo Fat was a run-of-the-mill drowning."

"Run of the mill? He was in six inches of water."

"Not actually drowning. More like asphyxiation," she said. "Results are the same. It takes surprisingly little water to drown. You can drown in six inches of water. Especially if you aren't very mobile or ambulatory."

"What kind of water was it?"

"Ah! So you're going after a *Hawaii Five-0* scenario here,

huh, Stryker? Or Charlie Chan? If the victim drowned in the ocean, why were his lungs filled with Evian!"

The question seemed a lot dumber now than when I asked it.

She pressed on.

"But it's amazing you asked that, because the weird thing is that Mr. Lo Fat didn't have taro patch water in his lungs, he had chlorinated swimming pool water," she said.

I sat up a bit and almost . . . almost . . . said, "Really?" But I caught the gleam in her eye in time.

"Mr. Lo Fat had plain old fresh, yet a tad muddy, water in his lungs. And not much of it," she said. "There are some toxicology tests still to come back, but from everything I saw, he appeared to be a very old man who had a very unlucky accident in a taro pond. The only notable thing, or I should say ironic thing, is that for someone named Lo Fat, he had a fairly serious case of atherosclerosis. Clogged arteries. Must have been all that mu shu pork and Peking duck. If he hadn't drowned, he likely would have been dead of a myocardial infarction within a year. Heart attack in layman's lingo."

I fought off the urge to ask another dumb question, like "Any signs of foul play?" knowing that if there had been, she would have let that drop up front. Instead I said, "When you're eighty-nine years old you should be able to eat all the mu shu pork you want."

"Good point, Stryker," she said. "However . . . I don't want to burst any bubbles here, but I doubt you and I are going to reach eighty-nine."

"Why's that?"

"How long did your parents live?" she asked.

"My mom died of cancer when she was sixty-three. My dad is still alive. He's in his seventies."

"Well, maybe you'll hit eighty. My parents both died in their late sixties, and so did their parents," she said. "So I come from a genetic line that doesn't favor longevity. How long you live generally comes down to genetics. Unless you go around getting yourself shot. Of course, everyone dies eventually, so there's no point in worrying about it. It's the quality of life that counts."

I had no real response to that so I said, "Good coffee!"

"Yeah, isn't it?" she said, laughing. "Well, I've got a date, big fella. Pedestrian fatality waiting for me on Table Three. Hit by a Handi-Van. Can you believe that?"

"So much for quality of life," I said.

She stood up and finished her coffee. I stood up and shook her hand.

"Thanks for the information," I said.

"Nice to meet you, Stryker," she said. "You ought to go up to Punchbowl sometime. Say good-bye to Lew. And don't get shot anymore."

I laughed. "I'm trying not to."

I walked back to my truck and sat there a while, looking at the pill bottle containing "my" bullet. I couldn't believe Lew Eden had actually saved it. I chuckled to myself. It was a nice sunny afternoon. I tossed the pill bottle on the passenger side of the seat and started the truck. Maybe I would take some flowers up to Punchbowl.

Chapter Six

Honolulu Police Department headquarters is a large, tan, neo-Gothic affair on South Beretania Street that was apparently designed to project a sense of strength and security but instead looks more like a pork barrel post office or a cross between a medium security prison and a community college auditorium. It had been a while since I had walked into the cop shop, and I knew I wouldn't be getting a warm welcome. I didn't have many friends left in HPD, and those who were my friends didn't like to brag about it.

I had made an appointment to meet the head of the Communications Division, Captain Gordon Watanabe, who, once upon a time, had been a good source of mine. He was a lieutenant in charge of the Special Crimes Investigative Unit when I first started at the *Honolulu Journal*. Although I wasn't technically the newspaper's police reporter, I had cultivated a few sources inside the police department. I sometimes met with Gordon and his crew in the Club Buy Me Drinkee, a Korean bar on Kapahulu Avenue featuring some of the hottest hostesses in Honolulu but, curiously, run by a black six-foot-eight former professional football player transvestite who called himself Enola Gay.

It was during one of these booze-soaked "background briefings" in 1998 that I tried to get some information from then-Lieutenant Watanabe about the deaths of Franky Five Fins, Samoan Johnny, and Mongoose Pacheco. But he was coy, insisting that all three deaths were suicides and if I reported them any other way my access to him and his unit was history.

"Lieutenant," I said, "I can't believe that three underworld figures committed suicide within a three-week period."

"Okay," said Watanabe, "one suicide, one accidental, and one natural causes."

"Which was the natural causes?" I asked.

"Samoan Johnny," he said.

"He was eaten by pigs," I pointed out.

"Yeah, after the heart attack."

Watanabe, who in those days looked more like an accountant than a cop, with close-cropped black hair and wire-rimmed glasses, laughed and knuckle-knocked two of his men across the table.

About then Enola Gay walked up with a tray of new drinks.

"What is with you homosexuals tonight?" asked Enola Gay in a deep southern baritone voice that belonged to a defensive lineman. "Why aren't you letting any of my girls sit with you? They've got to make money, you know."

Jimmy Neilson, SCIU's newest member, a sandy-haired twenty-four-year-old who looked to be about seventeen, eyed her suspiciously. Watanabe needed someone on his team he could stick in local high schools to infiltrate the

ice trafficking, so he pulled the baby-faced Neilson out of
the last group of police recruits and put him to work. This
was Jimmy's first time out with Watanabe and his crew
for a liquid decompression session and apparently the first
time he had ever seen a six-foot-eight black transvestite in
a blond wig.

"Which are the girls?" Jimmy Neilson asked.

"Well, lookee here!" shrieked Enola Gay, tousling Jimmy's hair. "I don't know whether to ask for your ID or put
you in my purse and take you home, you cute little thing,
you!"

Jimmy grabbed her hand, jumped up, and twisted her
arm behind her back.

"My goodness!" she said. "Now I know I want to take you
home!"

"That's Officer Neilson, Enola," Watanabe said.

"Well, you tell Officer Neilson the rules, Lieutenant. If
he's going to manhandle me in this bar he's gonna have to
buy me drinkee first!"

Jimmy let her go and sat down angrily.

"Jimmy," said Watanabe, "Enola Gay. She owns the
place."

"That's right, Jimmy," Enola said, "and to answer your
question, we're all girls in here."

That caught me in midsip, and I accidentally choked and
spewed beer on the table. Enola glared at me.

"Well, I'm sort of in transition," she said, adjusting her
wig. "Guess you would call me a future gelding." Then,
looking at Jimmy Neilson, she said, "But the rest of the girls
here were born girls, if that's what you're worried about."

"Tell him why you call yourself Enola Gay," said Watanabe.

She leaned close to Jimmy. "Because when I blow you, honey child, you are *blown up!*"

The night went downhill from there. Jimmy Neilson, it turned out, had a bad case of Short Man Complex, combined with You Look Like a Pimply-Faced Teenager Complex and enough other chips on his shoulder to open a Famous Amos cookie store. Within a year, he would get busted by cops from the Sexual Assault Detail for trying to make whoopee-do with one of those high school boys he was investigating for dealing drugs.

I left Club Buy Me Drinkee early that evening after Lieutenant Watanabe made some vague promise that I would be the first to know when the Samoan Johnny, Mongoose Pacheco, and Franky Five Fins investigations bore fruit as long as I didn't turn the whole thing into a big, islandwide mob war in the papers.

As I left the club I saw Enola Gay explaining her name to a table full of drunken Japanese men. Not Japanese Americans from Hawaii. Japanese Japanese. Tourists from Japan. "When I blow you, you are *blown up!*" she cried, and they all howled with laughter. I remember thinking, *I guess the war with Japan really is over.*

It would turn out that the deaths of Samoan Johnny, Mongoose Pacheco, and Franky Five Fins were part of a big crime war, a quick, deadly insurgency over which crime gangs got to supply security to the hundreds of hostess bars and strip joints across the island. The crime war was an embarrassment to the department, and it ultimately led to Watanabe getting promoted to captain instead of fired and shuffled off to the Communications Division. If you fuck up at HPD you are moved up and out of the way, which can hurt more than being fired.

I had nothing to do with Captain Watanabe's problems, but apparently he was still bitter about his fall from grace. He wasn't really happy when I called and asked if I could come by to see him. But he agreed because he knew I had never screwed him over on a story.

The young female officer behind the bulletproof glass at the HPD reception area had no idea who I was. So that was good. She was just another recent graduate of recruit school doing scut work in an office until she could get out on the street and become a real Jane Wayne Police Officer. She gave me a little GUEST badge to snap to the pocket of my aloha shirt and buzzed me into a hall where four elevators stood by ready to render service. The door to the elevator I was standing in front of opened, and two heavyset cops in plainclothes stood looking at me. I sort of recognized one, and he apparently really recognized me, because when he stepped out of the elevator, he shoved his shoulder into mine, sending me flying backward.

"Stryker McBride," he said. "Got ta lot of nerve coming in this building."

I took a few steps toward him, but his buddy held out his hand and said, "Excuse my partner, partner, he's kinda clumsy."

Then they both laughed and walked away.

The elevator door shut, so I waited for the next one. On the wall near the elevators were a number of framed photos of police officers. Above the photos was a sign that said WALL OF HONOR, and I realized that these were all cops who had been killed in the line of duty. One of them caught my eye, an attractive woman in a dark blue uniform who seemed to be looking right at me. At first I didn't recognize her, and then I realized it was Jeannie Kai. She looked confident and proud in her uniform, younger than I remembered her. The photo was probably taken right out of recruit school. I was there when she died, something I had not thought about since it happened. Over the past few years, I had made a job of not thinking about Jeannie Kai, and suddenly here she was staring at me. Why did it seem that the currents of this simple investigation I was doing for Amber Kam were dragging me into the past? First I'm given the bullet that almost killed me, and now cops are knocking into me and Jeannie Kai is staring down at me from the Wall of Honor.

An elevator door opened, and I quickly got in. I was flustered. And embarrassed at being flustered. Did I really think I could just march into police headquarters and memories would stay buried?

On the fifth floor I was buzzed through another set of doors and let into Dispatch, the nerve center of HPD Communications Division, the place where all 911 calls are received.

About fifty operators scanned computer screens and filled the room with a low buzz of conversation, some calming down agitated callers reporting crimes, others directing cops to car crashes, assaults, or other incidents of human folly. It always struck me when I entered Dispatch that if some enterprising team of criminals took over this room, they could send all the cops to the North Shore while their associates ripped off every hotel in Waikiki.

Watanabe's dark hair had gone gray, and he looked old and tired, stuck in a small office with no windows. Or actually all windows, since his office was a raised cubicle of glass from which he could see the entire Dispatch room. Just no windows to the outside world. He looked up from behind his desk and put down a sheaf of papers he had been going through.

"I thought you left the island after you retired from the paper," he said in an almost accusatory tone. It was clear this wasn't going to be a friendly chat. He didn't offer me the empty chair in front of his desk.

"I'm a little young for retirement," I said. "More like resignation."

"Well, you must be living pretty well with all the money you got after suing the police department," he said.

"Lieutenant, I mean, Captain, I didn't sue the police department. I sued the city on the advice of my lawyer, mainly because the newspaper's medical plan was so bad it wouldn't cover my hospital and rehab bills. And it wasn't my fault that HPD had a lunatic like Jake Stane on the payroll."

He obviously didn't want to get into an argument over old times. He just exhaled in a tired way and said, "I don't even know why I said you could come up," he said. "I don't need this kind of shit. You aren't even a reporter anymore."

"Just a private citizen looking for a little public information."

"Yeah, well, I looked at our sheets, and there's not much public information here about the case you asked about," he said. He slid a single page across the desk at me, a computer printout of the dispatch calls.

I scanned the small print quickly, but not as quickly as I could have done in the old days. At my peak as a nosy, aggressive reporter, I could have read it upside down on the desktop from three feet away. Basically it said HPD got a 911 call at 7:56 A.M. for a "possible unattended death" at 576 Waiwai Road, Kahala. Officer sent, got there at 8:05 A.M.

Nine minutes. Not too shabby. He must have just finished his coffee and doughnut at the Kahala Mall Starbucks. Ambulance reached the scene at 8:16 A.M. No resuscitation attempted. Elderly male confirmed dead by emergency medical techs at 8:24 A.M. Homicide Division notified. Deputy medical examiner arrived on scene at 9:10 A.M. No need to rush, apparently. Deputy ME confirms "unattended death" at 9:15 A.M. No apparent foul play. That was the end of the incident report. It didn't say if any homicide detectives actually went to the scene. Probably not. And when Dr. McCall ruled later the death was accidental drowning, homicide would just log the case closed.

"It doesn't say who made the 911 call," I said to Watanabe. He stood up and took the sheet out of my hand, read it, and then held it up to my face.

"Right there," he said, pointing to some initials. "PPA. Paradise Protective Association."

Paradise Protective Association was the largest private security firm in the state. It had government contracts with the Honolulu International Airport, Aloha Stadium, and most of the state harbors.

"What's PPA doing in Kala Estates?" I asked. "When I was there the other day the gate guard was from Diamond Head Security."

"There's the door, Stryker," he said with a nod of his head. He sat down at the desk again and began going through the sheaf of papers.

I folded the dispatch sheet and stuck it in my back jeans pocket. Captain Watanabe looked up at me in a strange, drained way. He looked like a man whose life force had been sucked dry. Or at least taken down a few quarts. I think it was just seeing me that reminded him of how much his life had changed since the time we were at the Club Buy Me Drinkee with Enola Gay laughing and prodding his Japanese Japanese customers to buy the "real" girls drinks. Watanabe was on the inside then, in the exciting heart of the police department running an elite under-cover unit. Now, his glass walls couldn't even contain the incessant annoying chatter of the dispatchers and the beeps and clicks of their computers.

As I reached the glass door, he said without looking up from his papers, "Stryker, don't call me again. We're done."

I took the elevator back down to the lobby and made a point of not looking at the photo of Jeannie Kai again. This little investigation might be trying to drag me into the past but I didn't have to go willingly.

I left the building and walked along Beretania Street toward where I had parked my truck in front of a little saimin diner. About five parking meters back from my truck was a black Cadillac Escalade. I stopped to look at it because several months earlier I had been toying with the idea of getting one myself. It's a cool car, but eventually I decided that driving a huge luxury gas guzzler on an island the size of Oahu was just stupid, even if you could afford it. I felt my old F-150 kept me grounded. When you drive a beat-up pickup truck, it's hard to feel superior to anyone else on the road except idiots on mopeds.

The darkened window on the passenger side went down, and a voice came out of the Escalade.

"Can I help you?"

The tone wasn't neighborly. I looked into the car, and a young man in the driver's seat smoking a cigarette looked back. He was Chinese, maybe about twenty-five or thirty.

"Just admiring your ride, friend," I said.

He blew a puff of smoke in my direction.

"I'm not your friend."

This conversation promised to come to an unpleasant conclusion. In my younger days I might have followed it down the road a bit farther to see where it led, but with age comes something like wisdom. And wisdom told me that if I had left the police station ten minutes sooner or ten minutes later than I had, I wouldn't have even run into this asshole. I really didn't need to make him part of my life through a fluke of timing.

I walked on and climbed into my truck. As I started it, the black SUV drove slowly past. The passenger window was still down, and the driver gave me a hard look as he passed. The Escalade continued on and turned at the first intersection. Out of habit I made a mental note of the license plate as the car went by. It would be easy to remember. It read DRAGON.

Chapter Seven

I was anxious to see Amber again, but I didn't want to seem desperate. So when Football Mike asked me to help him take his forty-three-foot Hatteras around to Haleiwa Harbor on the North Shore for a weekend fishing tournament, I jumped on it. I called Amber and left a message that "something had come up" and I wouldn't be able to get back to her until Friday.

It was a grueling boat trip to Haleiwa, six hours of warm sunshine, cold Budweiser, and wonderful scenery, not to mention catching a big mahi-mahi ourselves on the way to Football Mike's fishing tourney.

Perched on the bow as we cruised past the old sugar mill town of Kahuku and the northernmost point of Oahu, I realized it was the first time I actually had been on a boat outside Kaneohe Bay for at least a year. We pounded over some pretty big swells as we turned the corner to the North Shore. We never were in any real danger, being far out from the reefs of Kawela Bay and Sunset Beach, where surfers were sampling an early gift of waves before the big surf hit in the winter. I was reminded of how exhilarating and rejuvenating just being on the ocean is and how much I missed it. I mean, how stupid is it to live on an actual boat at an actual yacht club and never go out of Kaneohe Bay? A wealthy friend of mine, Jacques Devereux, a Frenchman living in San Diego, had recently asked me to crew with him in the upcoming Pacific Cup sailboat race from San Francisco to Kaneohe Bay. This was the kind of invitation I routinely turned down as part of my self-imposed seclusion from society. But as the Hatteras went up an ocean swell twice as tall as our fly bridge—the boat hanging motionless in the air for a fraction of a second before falling onto the back of the liquid mountain—I decided I'd call my buddy in California and take him up on his offer to race in the Pacific Cup.

With Football Mike's boat freshly filled with diesel and safely tied up at the dock for the next day's fishing tourney, we walked over to Haleiwa Joe's Restaurant next to the famous concrete-arched Haleiwa Bridge. The little bridge is famous for being barely wide enough for two cars to pass each other in opposite directions without exchanging body paint. The narrow bridge has the effect of being a pressure valve that slows everyone down to enjoy the sleepy, country pace of Haleiwa, known for its wood sidewalks, country surf shops, and Matsumoto's Store, where tourists stand in lines a mile long to get Matsumoto's legendary "shave ice," Hawaii's bigger, lighter, and tastier version of a snow cone.

Football Mike's wife had driven over from Kaneohe and met us at the restaurant, where we had the kitchen cook up our mahi-mahi in butter, capers, and white wine. We sat at a table on the lanai overlooking the harbor and watched three local kids aggressively ignore the NO JUMPING FROM

BRIDGE sign, climbing the sand-colored concrete arches of the Haleiwa Bridge and plunging twenty feet into the shallow, muddy water. The jumps looked exceedingly dangerous, but the boys managed to scamper out of the water, climb the bridge, and jump off repeatedly without anyone getting killed. That's just an assumption. There were three of them at the time; I didn't know how many they had started out with.

After lunch we drove back to Kaneohe along the shore on Kamehameha Highway, essentially the reverse of the route we took in the boat. It was the same distance, just a lot drier. We went through the country villages of Laie, Hauula, Punaluu, and Kaaawa, where I swear I could hear Puka's dogs and chickens carrying on. Either everyone in Kaaawa is deaf or there's no noise ordinance.

When we got back to the yacht club I called Jacques and got the message, "Bonjour, I am either flying, surfing, sailing, or making love. Leave a message, s'il vous plait." Ignoring the not-so-subtle implication that his life was superior to mine—and the life of anyone else who called him—I left a message saying I would be happy to sail in the Pacific Cup race with him.

The next morning, I found myself in downtown Honolulu at the city's Building Permits Office. It was the ground floor of a sleek glass high-rise planted not far from city hall, or Honolulu Hale, as it's called. It's also next to the stately Iolani Palace, which had been the only royal palace on U.S. soil but was better known to fans of *Hawaii Five-0* as the location of Steve McGarrett's corner office.

Despite what Amber had said about Chinese thinking in terms of generations, Wai Lo Fat had been the steward of the taro patch, and with him gone, the bulldozers might not be far behind. I wanted to find out if there were any long-term development plans for the taro patch area of Kala Lane Estates before I saw Amber again.

A young haole clerk in the subdivision section of the Building Permits Office dragged out an enormous plat map book that looked like something you find in a wizard's lair. When he plopped it down on the table, dust actually puffed into the air.

"Kala Lane Estates, Kala Lane Estates," he said, turning the giant pages. He had spiked cobalt blue hair and metal studs and rings and other piercings through his lips, eyebrows, nose, and ears. He looked like the victim of a fragmentation grenade explosion.

"There," he said, pointing at the yellowed page with a finger decorated with a silver skull ring.

I looked at the map, running my own finger from where I remembered the front gate of Kala Lane Estates having been and along the roads I had driven to get to Amber's house. I was surprised to see there was no taro patch. Just lines laying out subdivision plans for houses that weren't there.

I showed him where I was looking and said, "There aren't any houses here. I was just there a few days ago."

"This map comes from the original plans submitted for permits when the development was first proposed," he said. "There are a lot of subdivision plans that show houses that don't exist. The plans for Village Green out in Kapolei showed three hundred houses that weren't built until twenty years after the development plans were approved. The housing market crashed, and the developers just hung on to their permits until the market came back."

"So these are houses that could be built in Kala Estates," I said.

"Sure," he said. "Theoretically. I mean, let's see, this was registered in 1953. They'd probably have to come back to the department for new approvals on some things. Building codes have changed. Might even need city council approval, depending on what they wanted to build there."

"Kahala was subdivided as far back as 1953?" I asked the blue-haired clerk as he swept a bit of dust off the table. He laughed at my apparent ignorance.

"Dude, that's just Kala Lane Estates that was created in 1953. Four Gates Enterprises started developing all of Kahala right after World War II. A Chinese investment hui scooped up all that land for next to nothing. It was a brilliant move from a purely mercenary capitalistic perspective. Of course, the Chinese are always thinking about a hundred years further out than the rest of us."

"So I've heard," I said, looking at the map. Then I added maybe just a tad sarcastically, "You really get into your work here, huh?"

"Ah," he said, smiling. "A subtle put-down of a lowly city clerk who doesn't match the stereotypical assumptions about how a minor government bureaucrat should look and act."

"Sorry," I said. "I'm just always pleasantly surprised when I meet someone who is good at his job."

"Dude, I'm a grad student in advanced urban planning at the University of Hawaii and an adjunct professor of urban design theory at Honolulu Pacific College," he said. "Working here, man, is hands-on history. To me, these maps and records are an archaeological gold mine. The entire transformation of Oahu from an idyllic, environmentally sensitive, sustainable agriculture-based society into the fucked-up mishmash of architectural and urban planning bullshit it is today is documented in disgusting detail all around me."

"I take it you aren't fond of the way Honolulu has evolved aesthetically," I said, going to droll instead of sarcastic.

"If I had my way, I'd have the whole island bulldozed and start over," he said. "Bike paths, greenbelts, solar and wind energy farms, integrated seawater-cooled air-conditioning systems, and no buildings over the height of a coconut tree, all laid out according to a lifestyle conducive to health and social equality, not according to where cars and trucks need to go."

I'm always a little jealous of people who exist in a world of complete moral certitude. How comforting it must be to live by a theoretical manifesto that will never be realized. No pressure there, and everything you see around you reinforces your feelings of superiority. Of course, feelings of superiority don't always translate to happiness. Deep down, but not too deep, this was one angry little blue-haired city clerk. I decided to try to cheer him up a little. I pointed to the taro patch area on the map.

"This spot here in Kala Lane Estates where there are supposed to be a bunch of multimillion-dollar houses but they aren't there?"

He nodded, tugging on one of his facial implements.

"There's a big taro patch. Right here in the middle of the subdivision. Beautiful green plants, pure running water, a grass shack, and a raised dirt pathway for strolling through the whole thing."

His metal-fringed mouth actually dropped open for a second. Then he smiled.

"Dude, that is so cool," he said. "I'd like to see it. I'd really like to see it."

I'm not an exceptionally paranoid guy, but when I got back to my truck I noticed a black SUV parked down the street. There must be a few thousand black SUVs on Oahu, so the chance that it was the same guy I had run into at the police station was remote. Still, there's no harm in finding out. I pulled out of my parking spot, jammed the truck into reverse, and burned out backward toward the mystery car. The driver must have had his engine running, because when he saw me coming, he gunned the Caddy SUV out of his parking space, almost smashing into the back of my truck. He raced across the four one-way lanes of King Street, his tires throwing off blue smoke. The last thing I saw was the DRAGON license plate disappearing down South Street toward the waterfront.

Chapter Eight

On Friday afternoon, Amber greeted me at her front door like a long-lost friend with a hug and a kiss. I don't know how to handle such a spontaneous show of joy and affection. I'm not used to people being happy to see me.

"I know!" she erupted after we had entered the house and she saw the surprised look on my face. "Isn't it amazing? I found two incredible Vietnamese sisters who charge hardly anything. I mean, they are practically right off the boat! They clean everything, even do the floor on their hands and knees, the poor little things. Won't use a mop."

The interior of Amber's house had gone from *National Geographic* to *Good Housekeeping* in just three days. There was no apparent wildlife in the kitchen. The Vietnamese sisters knew what they were doing.

Haole plantation owners first brought in the Japanese and Chinese to do the scut work in the fields and be servants in houses. When the Chinese and Japanese moved up the social, political, and financial ladder over the years, the Filipinos, Samoans, and other Pacific Islanders took over the jobs at the bottom. Now those ethnic groups were prominent in the community, their people running for political office and controlling large parts of the state economy. The Vietnamese apparently were now on the bottom. That wouldn't last. I had to wonder who would be cleaning the house of the Vietnamese sisters twenty years from now. Bangladeshis?

Amber looked better than the last time I saw her, even better than the hand-scrubbed floors. She was wearing a tight yellow tank top that put her ample charms on fine display, and short, short cutoff jeans that were so low on her waist they seemed to defy gravity. Her toenails had gone from cherry red to strawberry pink and matched her perfectly applied lipstick. She looked so good I felt I should say something, but I was afraid of what might come out of my mouth. What if I tried to say, "You look very pretty today, Amber," but what came out of my mouth was "You are the sexiest woman I have ever seen in my life. Every minute you spend out of bed is a crime against humanity"?

Luckily, the chance to compliment her on her looks passed when she went to the kitchen to grab a few beers from the refrigerator. We sat on one of the mile-long couches in the living room overlooking the taro field. The couches, I was happy to see, had been cleaned so well that they looked like you could sit on them without first having to get a tetanus shot. Despite the length of the couch, she again positioned herself close enough to me so she could poke me with her bare feet and grab my arm when she wanted to stress a point, like the industriousness of domesticated servants from Southeast Asia. She kept her hand on my arm while I filed my report, seemingly digesting every syllable. I didn't have much to report, so I stretched out the details as far as I could to make it seem like my research into the death of Wai Lo Fat rivaled that of the Warren Commission.

"The medical examiner is finishing up some toxicology tests, but she told me that your grandfather's death was an accident," I said. "He likely just fell over while walking in the taro patch and, because of his advanced age and limited mobility, was unable to push himself up out of the water. A lot of people his age fall all the time, unfortunately, on sidewalks or driveways and break their hips. That usually starts a downward spiral where they become bedridden and eventually lose the will to live."

I almost added, "So, in a way, it's lucky your grandfather fell over in a taro patch instead of, say, at the mall." But I didn't. So that was good.

She looked out through the ceiling-high windows at the taro patch, and I thought I saw the glitter of a tear in her eye. I am ashamed to admit I instantly questioned the legitimacy of that tear. Did I really think so little of Amber's personality that I doubted she could generate a single tear while considering the death of her grandfather? On the other hand, she had lived in Hollywood, and crying on cue was probably one of the first things you learned in acting (Hollywood 101: Turning on the Tears). It nevertheless gave me the opportunity to put my hand on hers and console her.

She turned toward me and in a tiny, fragile voice (Hollywood 202?) said, "Thank you, Stryker." Then she kept moving toward me until her strawberry pink lips touched my sunburned lips and we . . . well, while I might be a cynic, I still consider myself a gentleman, and gentlemen do not provide a play-by-play account of their romantic encounters. Let me just say that the Vietnamese sisters had done a great job in turning Amber's bedroom into a show-place of domestic splendor and emergency room clean-liness and that, while every minute Amber spends out of that massive Victorian four-poster bed might not be a crime against humanity, it certainly is an offense against nature in general.

What surprised me was not the apparent sincere passion Amber brought to the proceedings (Hollywood 303?) but how quickly that passion was replaced, in an odd segue, with a request for me to continue my investigation into Wai Lo Fat's death.

"You said the medical examiner is still waiting for toxi-cology tests, right?" she asked. "Maybe you can poke around a little more. Does anyone profit from his death?"

The question seemed to imply that someone did and it wasn't her.

"Did he leave a will?" I asked. "Or did he have some kind of living trust set up?"

"I don't know. His lawyers are still going over every-thing and haven't told me a thing. Nobody in the family is talking to me."

"What do you mean?" I asked.

"Even at his memorial service at the temple the other day, nobody would tell me anything about the estate, his assets. You know, I don't even own this house, Four Gates does."

I'm not the brightest bulb in the tulip patch, but I was beginning to see where Amber's interests might lie. The image of her bugging relatives and family counselors at Wai Lo Fat's memorial about his financial holdings seemed tawdry. Lawyers don't refer to members of a deceased person's family as "the grubby group" for nothing. And while I was thinking badly of her another small light flickered on.

"Amber," I said, "Did you tell anyone at the memorial service that I was looking into your grandfather's death?"

"I might have mentioned it to a few people in passing," she said, looking at me with a concerned expression. "Was that wrong?"

What could I say? At least it explained why I had Dragon Boy in the black Caddy following me around Honolulu the past few days.

"I wouldn't have mentioned it, especially at a memorial," I said. "But it's okay. Who was at the service, anyway?"

She snuggled closer to me and said dreamily, "I don't know. Lots of people. Chinese elders. The Blue Lotus Society. Members of Four Gates' board of directors."

The question for me was, who from those groups would have been interested enough in what I was doing and who I was meeting to put a tail on me?

"I'm sorry if I messed up, Stryker," she said. "I really appreciate your help. It's just that if I have to look out at the taro patch every day, I want to at least know that I've done what I could to make sure my grandfather is resting in peace."

It was a great line, delivered with moving, dramatic effect (Hollywood 404?), and I certainly couldn't call myself a gentleman if I didn't continue working for her after she had been so generous with her attentions. Apparently just to further inspire me to continue in her cause, she began rubbing her strawberry pink toenails up and down my leg, and her strawberry lips moved in for a docking procedure that I believe is only taught in the higher levels of Hollywood graduate courses.

Chapter Nine

That night I lay on my bed, feeling uncomfortable about having had a, well, an intimate encounter with Amber. Twice. Then I felt uncomfortable about feeling uncomfortable. Hell, we were both consenting, single adults. Aren't we allowed to do certain things that some consenting, single adults do?

Then I realized I wasn't feeling uncomfortable about having sex with Amber. That had actually been a blast. I was feeling uncomfortable because the self-interest equation had clearly shifted in Amber's favor. She had a specific reason for spreading it around at Wai Lo Fat's memorial that I was investigating his death, and I didn't know what the reason was. She was getting more out of our relationship than I was, but it would take a small man to let that get in the way of looking at our *ménage à deux* as just a fun-filled afternoon.

I had to give Amber credit for one thing: If it hadn't been for her phone call from out of the blue, I still would be hunkered down at the yacht club, only making the necessary forays out into the world for errands or to jog. I enjoyed the boat ride to the North Shore with Football Mike. I was looking forward to sailing in the Pacific Cup in a few weeks. I even had some guys at the yacht club help me get my Jet Ski off the *Travis McGee*. Just as the sun was setting the day before, I had been tearing around the bay on the Jet Ski scaring the hell out of the occasional green sea turtle. I'm not saying I deserved the Dr. Phil Semiprofessional Alcoholic and Agoraphobia Recovery Trophy, but I actually had a bowl of Wheaties for breakfast that morning. With milk.

As I lay in bed, I thought about how Amber had inadvertently set into motion incidents that forced me to look at the chain of events that led me to put my life up on blocks like the *Travis McGee*, all the way back to the last time I surfed with the Rev. Franky Five Fins and when I used to hang out at the Club Buy Me Drinkee with Lieutenant Watanabe and the Special Crimes Investigative Unit.

Despite what Watanabe had told me at that time, the deaths of Franky Five Fins, Mongoose Pacheco, and Samoan Johnny were part of a war between Honolulu's underworld crime gangs. The man who actually set the war in motion was a Tongan village chief and rock wall builder by the unlikely name of Three Man Stone.

In 1997, Three Man Stone moved to Hawaii to work in the lucrative lava rock wall-building industry. In Hawaii, just about every house has at least one lava rock wall. The building of a lava rock wall is something of an art, an art perfected by immigrants from Tonga. Unlike most of the other immigrant ethnic groups who came to Hawaii to stay, most Tongans only wanted to come to the Islands to build up a bankroll and then return home. With the money they made in Hawaii building walls, they could live out the rest of their lives in Tonga as the richest dudes in the village. Three Man Stone, though, saw more opportunity in Hawaii than just building walls. He was smart, charismatic, a natural leader, and big as a fale fakataha, a traditional Tongan meetinghouse where kava ceremonies take place. And he was strong. When you build walls of lava rock, some weighing hundreds of pounds, you have to be strong. But Tongan wall builders don't look at a stone as weighing a certain number of pounds. They judge a stone according to how many men it takes to lift it. There are one-man stones, two-man stones, and, the stones just short of needing a backhoe to move them, three-man stones. The Tongan chief known as Three Man Stone got his nickname because he could lift a three-man stone by himself.

Three Man Stone quickly became the CEO of most of the lava rock wall building on Oahu and had plenty of money to spend. He and his favorite headmen would generally hang out on the windward side of the island, up near Laie, home of a large Tongan Mormon community near Brigham Young University. But unlike the devout Mormon Tongans, Three Man Stone drank alcohol. Since there was no booze to be had in Laie, they looked for other places to party.

At that time, there were basically three crime groups on Oahu. There was a mysterious large Hawaiian/Asian group with ties to organized crime going back to just after World War II. This group was allegedly headed by a "Godmother of Organized Crime," a grandmotherly, politically connected Waikiki entertainer known as Auntie Kealoha. Auntie Kealoha, who also owned the largest private security company in the state, liked to keep things low-key and acted as more of a figurehead and mediator, someone used by both the police and crime figures when things looked like they would get out of hand. Her right-hand man and enforcer was said to be a four-hundred-pound Chinese-Hawaiian named Tiny Maunakea. Auntie Kealoha reputedly—because nothing indictable was ever laid at her feet—oversaw organized crime on Oahu through a series of territorial franchises she granted. Tiny Maunakea oversaw Honolulu proper, from Pearl Harbor in the west to Hawaii Kai on the East Shore, with the aid of his right-hand man, the Rev. Franky Five Fins. Samoan Johnny's group controlled most of the west side of the island, and a haole surfing outfit called the Shocka Boys ran the North Shore. Most of the focus of these groups was to provide "security" to the hundreds of hostess bars, strip clubs, and nightclubs across the island, whether they wanted the security or not. In reality, they not only provided security but oversaw the drug, extortion, and prostitution action.

Unable to drink in Laie, Three Man Stone and his entourage first began to take their business to a sports bar on the North Shore called Kooks. Kooks was the haunt of local wave riders and surfers visiting from around the world who came during the winter big-wave contest season. Kooks also attracted filmmakers, surf groupies, rich haole beachfront homeowners from California, and drug dealers. It was the huge waves that drew the "cool" people to the North Shore, but it was the drug dealers who kept them amused when the waves weren't pumping.

Three Man Stone and his crew didn't quite fit into the North Shore scene, mainly because after a few drinks, they liked to fight. And although professional surfers are in pretty good shape physically, they weigh only a few stones and are no match for guys who lift stones all day long for a living. The Tongans won a few lopsided victories in drunken battles with surfers at Kooks, but the end came when Three Man Stone threw Australian surfer Nat Lynch through a plate-glass window, ending his chance to become the only back-to-back winner of the World Surfing Cup's Triple Crown at Sunset Beach. Three Man Stone and his crew were stopped at the door of Kooks two nights later by Freddie "Mad Mouse" Mulligan, head of the Shocka Boys. Mad Mouse, a soft-spoken Irishman transplanted from Hell's Kitchen in New York City and standing all of five-foot-one, "invited" Three Man Stone and his boys not to visit Kooks anymore. Or any other entertainment establishment on the North Shore, for that matter. Two Shocka Boys armed with Uzis standing behind him emphasized the point by cocking their weapons. The sound of an Uzi cocking bar being pulled back is one that makes any linguistic translation unnecessary.

Three Man Stone appreciated the situation immediately. He and his boys then attempted to find their entertainment on the west side of Oahu, where the residents' skin was darker. But the bars there were controlled by Samoan Johnny and his mostly Samoan and Hawaiian gang, who, for some unexplained reason, called themselves the Chicanos. This proved problematic since Tongans and Samoans had been traditional enemies going back hundreds of years to when warriors from Tonga raided what would become Samoa and forced the inhabitants into slavery. The Samoans eventually forced the Tongans out of their islands in A.D. 1600, and Samoan Johnny did the same to Three Man Stone and his boys from Oahu's West Shore bars and clubs at the end of 1997.

Three Man Stone and his oversized retinue faced similar rebuke when they tried to set up shop in a little dive on Hotel Street, finding all the bars and clubs in Honolulu controlled by a local organized crime group with, surprisingly, no official name but a pedigree that encompassed Hawaii's most notorious gangsters going back to the 1950s when a ruthless killer named Tony Kim was considered the island's first godfather.

Realizing there must be money to be made in the bar and nightclub protection rackets, in 1998 Three Man Stone began to move in on smaller, less connected clubs, usually in the hazy, ill-defined demilitarized zones between the three major crime groups' turf. Then using his charm and smarts, he did something everyone thought impossible. Knowing that one thing both Samoans and Tongans had in common was kava, Three Man Stone persuaded Samoan Johnny to attend a secret summit at his fale fakataha in Laie, where during a kava ceremony they agreed to work together to win a share of the strip club and hostess bar protection rackets in urban Honolulu. Once that alliance was sealed with a night of mouth-and-throat-numbing kava toasts, Three Man Stone and Samoan Johnny invited Mad Mouse Mulligan to join their hui. Mad Mouse quietly demurred, saying he was a simple Irish lad happy with the action on the North Shore. He wished them the best in their endeavors and invited them not to consider expanding their adventures into Haleiwa.

Three Man Stone's next step was to enlist the aid of an informant from the Honolulu protection racket's ranks so he could plot his moves. He found the perfect weasel in Mongoose Pacheco, a degenerate drunk, pedophile, and bagman who collected payoffs from the sleazier Hotel

Street gambling holes that even most organized crime figures didn't want to enter. Pacheco fed Three Man Stone
information on which clubs were the most vulnerable for
takeover, which foot soldiers were most amenable to being
bribed, and, most importantly, which people in the Honolulu organization not to fuck with, particularly the eccen-
tric hit man, enforcer, and sometimes preacher, the Rev.
Franky Five Fins.

Unknown to the good citizens of Honolulu, a battle for
control of the protection of the strip clubs and hostess bars
was quietly raging. Police inexplicably found themselves
dealing with an increasing number of assaults, robberies,
and extortion cases connected to the bar scene. The natural order had somehow been upset. The first hint the public had that something was brewing was when police were
alerted to a body dumped at a Waianai pig farm that
turned out to be Samoan Johnny. He hadn't died of a heart
attack as Lieutenant Watanabe had joked to me. His body
had been filled with so much lead that even the pigs were
turned off.

Then Mongoose Pacheco was shot to death and his body
left in a Catholic cemetery. Both murders might have been
passed off as routine underworld housecleaning until the
war went prime time.

First some fishermen discovered a bullet-aerated fifty-
five-gallon drum floating off the Makapuu Point lighthouse. The newspapers and TV stations went nuts when
they learned it contained the body of a reputed underworld
figure and sometimes preacher by the name of Franky Five
Fins. Two days after the city woke up to FRANKY-IN-A-DRUM
headlines, a large local man with a machine gun blew a
huge Polynesian man off of a bar stool in broad daylight at

the Paradise Club on Kapiolani Boulevard, just blocks from the Honolulu Police Department, the state capitol building, and Honolulu Hale. The dead man was identified as Fakaosifolau Tolutau. He was better known in the Tongan community as the lava wall builder Three Man Stone.

The war was over, but it would have the unexpected consequence of leading the Honolulu City Council to do something exceedingly stupid: letting off-duty police officers act as security guards at hostess bars and strip clubs. That would lead to the rise of a corrupt police officer by the name of Jake Stane, the man who shot me.

Chapter Ten

A few days after spending the afternoon with Amber Kam I was jogging along the shoulder of the H-3 Freeway, which is illegal as hell but gives you a great view of the length of Kaneohe Bay, looking all the way north toward Kualoa Point and the oddly shaped island called China-man's Hat. I usually run a five-mile loop a few times a week from the Bayview Yacht Club to the Kaneohe Marine Base and then up onto the freeway and south until I get off at the Saddle Road near Kawainui Marsh. Then I run along the neighborhood streets until I meet up with the yacht club again. It's a nice run, just the right mix of gentle up-hill and rejuvenating downhill, but mostly flat. I had been swimming my entire life, so swimming wasn't exercise any-more. Running felt like exercise, and the older I got the more I felt it. When I was younger, I ran because I could. Now I run so that I can. I knew if I stopped running for a week, I'd never pick it up again.

Running gives me time to think, not in a linear way, but in a disjointed, bouncy way the brain can work that some-times leads to unexpected insights. Albert Einstein said that when he got stuck on a problem, all he had to do was take a long walk and think about other things. Then his brain would mysteriously cough up the answer to the problem he was looking for but couldn't get to by the direct route. I've never thought about the theory of relativity, but once when I was out jogging I suddenly remembered where I had left the TV remote control.

As I ran along the H-3 Freeway my mind bounced to Dragon Boy. Amber let the world know at Wai Lo Fat's memorial that I was looking into his death, which made someone nervous enough to put a tail on me. And Dragon Boy was some tail. I had a friend in the state Department of Motor Vehicles run his DRAGON license plate. The Caddy SUV was registered to a mixed martial arts school in Chinatown called Coiling Dragon Wushu Academy. After checking business incorporation records I found out the school was run by a guy named Danny Chang. And by going on the *Honolulu Advertiser*'s Web site I found out that Danny Chang was a competitive fighter and master of kung fu, karate, aikido, tae kwon do, and some Israeli form of kicking ass called Krav Maga. At the recent Rock the Island Superbrawl III competition Danny, who fights under the ironic handle Tranquility, dispatched a world-ranked California fighter named Mayhem 1.2 seconds into the first round of the championship bout.

Assuming it was Danny driving the SUV, it's a good thing I hadn't tried to drag him out of the vehicle at the police station or in front of the city permits department. When it comes to hand-to-hand combat, I'm pretty sure Champion Kung Fu/Krav Maga Guy beats Former Butterfly Swimmer Guy. I wasn't sure what I was going to do about Danny, but until I found out what he was up to and who he was working for, I'd have to make sure I didn't find myself in lonely spots. I looked up and down the deserted freeway as I ran and realized it was about a three-mile-long lonely spot. Great.

I left the freeway at Saddle Road and headed for home through the neighborhoods, less lonely spots. I thought about the taro patch in Kala Lane Estates. Wai Lo Fat had planted the taro in honor of his Hawaiian wife. That was touching. But was there something more to the taro patch? Taro is taro, right? Or is it? I didn't know shit about taro. Maybe I should find out. I knew just the guy I could ask: a former cop I surfed with sometimes. Hawaiian guy. He ran an agriculture youth project in Waianae. Had to do with growing traditional Hawaiian foods like yams, taro, and breadfruit.

Another half mile to go. I felt pretty good. Had my second or third wind. Someone said middle age is when you are too young for golf but too old to rush the net. I still rush the net when I play the occasional game of tennis at the yacht club. The average age of players in the tennis fleet is about 135, so rushing the net isn't like trying to dodge bullets.

I ran past a house with about fourteen abandoned cars in the front yard. Owner must be popular with his neighbors. There's a sign on the fence. BEWARE OF DOG. WILL BITE. When you run a lot you become an expert on BEWARE OF DOG signs. The dog in the abandoned-car yard means business. No negotiation. He bites. Period. When Kane and Lono joined the yacht club, we didn't put up any signs. Guard dogs should have surprise on their side. Besides, a sign at the yacht club might have confused potential trespassers. BEWARE OF GODS. WILL BITE.

Almost home. I reached a part of the route where there's an acoustical anomaly. It sounds like someone's running behind me. I used to turn and look. Nobody was ever there. Someone said it's probably the ghost of a jogger who got run over or something. I don't think so. I think it's the ghost of a younger me, running because he can, chasing down the old guy in front of him who runs because he must.

As I jogged across Kaneohe Bay Drive toward the yacht club gate, a black SUV came flying out of nowhere. It screeched to a stop, tires smoking, just a few feet from me.

"Watch it, asshole!" a voice yelled from inside the car, and a hand popped up over the top of the vehicle from the driver's side, the universal one-fingered salute. The SUV peeled off with the tires screeching. The license plate was a mishmash of meaningless numbers and letters. On the bumper was a sticker that read SEMPER FI.

It was the first time I actually was relieved to have been cussed out by a jarhead from the Kaneohe Marine Base.

Chapter Eleven

After my run, I showered in the yacht club locker room because I wanted hot water. There's a way to heat up water for the shower on my boat, but it involves propane tanks, special valves, complicated dials, and, well, it's a lot easier just to hoof it over to the locker room.

I donned my usual uniform for venturing off the plantation and mixing with polite company: polo shirt, Dockers, and deck shoes. Sometimes I'd wear an aloha shirt and a nice pair of jeans with leather loafers. It was rumored there was a sports coat and necktie somewhere on the *Travis McGee*, but there had been no sighting of them for ages.

My plan was go out to the Blue Ocean Centre in Hawaii Kai and surprise Amber with an early dinner date. On the way I'd stop by the offices of the Paradise Protective Association, which, I found out, were located in a little commercial office complex in an east Honolulu area known as Aina Haina, right on my way. I wanted to find out why such a hotshot security outfit was guarding a little taro patch in Kahala.

All I knew about Paradise Protective was that it was

owned by Auntie Kealoha, so I would have to be on my good behavior. It's probably not good to be on Auntie Kealoha's radar. Unfortunately, what I didn't know was that Auntie Kealoha hired a lot of retired cops for her security company, sometimes cops who had been forced out of the department for questionable reasons. So, naturally, when I walked into the modern, air-conditioned lobby of Paradise Protective the first person I ran into was a burly former vice squad officer who hated my guts.

"What the fuck are you doing here, McBride?" asked Michael O'Brian, manning the reception desk. I had written about him in the *Honolulu Journal* ten years earlier when he was caught taking marijuana plants confiscated during Operation Green Harvest to his home near Haleiwa. The pakalolo raid had been up by the Dillingham Airfield at Mokuleia Beach on the North Shore. He claimed the operation went long and instead of taking the plants all the way into Honolulu and logging them in to the police department evidence room, he was just storing them at his house overnight. That explained the seventy-five freshly harvested plants in his garage but not the twenty-five other plants hanging upside down from his attic rafters drying. I seemed to remember he got two years in the joint for that. Looked like he landed on his feet, getting a cushy job with Paradise Protective.

"What the fuck am I doing here" I said. "Nice welcome, O'Brian. You learn that at the Walmart Greeters School?"

"The fuck do you want?" he asked again.

Two Irishmen could keep up this kind of banter for days, but I had things to do.

"I want to talk to whoever is in charge of providing your quality security services in the Kahala area," I said.

"Screw you, pal. Nobody around here is gonna talk to any fuckin' reporters," he said. He was certainly adept at decorating his lingo with the better-known copulative idioms.

"I'm not a reporter," I said. "I'm working for one of the homeowners in Kala Lane Estates who is concerned about the security there."

"Kala Lane Estates isn't a client of ours," he said. "That's Diamond Head Security."

"Look, O'Brian, I don't want you to hurt your brain," I said. "PPA provides security for a taro patch out there, and one of the homeowners has some concerns. So call whoever has an office back there with a higher pay grade and more extensive vocabulary than you do and let them know I'm here."

He didn't like it, but he mumbled into the phone to someone and then pushed a clipboard at me like it was infected.

"Sign in," he said.

I did.

"Down the hall, turn right. Operations manager. John Morikami," he said.

Morikami, sitting behind a neat desk, was about fifty and tanned. He looked like a golfing instructor. I decided to play it pretty much straight up with him.

"I've been asked by Kala Lane resident Amber Kam to express some concerns she has about the security situation at the taro patch. You probably know that an elderly man, Mr. Wai Lo Fat, died there recently. That was Miss Kam's grandfather."

"Are you an attorney?" he asked.

"No," I said. "Just a friend. As you can imagine, she's pretty shook up about what happened out there."

"Yes, I understand. We were all sorry to hear about Mr. Lo Fat's accident. But sir—"

"McBride. Stryker McBride."

"Mr. McBride, there are some privacy issues involved here," he said. "If Paradise Protective is providing services within the Kala Lane Estates, the client is not Miss Kam."

"I know, Four Gates Enterprises is."

"I'm afraid I can't even confirm that," he said.

"Miss Kam works for Four Gates Enterprises and has asked me to represent her."

"I'm sure that is true, but there are legal issues here to be—"

So much for playing it pretty much straight.

"Look, Mike," I said, interrupting him. "Let's cut to the chase. It looks like your guy out there screwed up. PPA could be facing a big lawsuit. I'm no lawyer, but it sounds to me like there may be a liability problem here. But Miss Kam isn't interested in pursuing any legal action. She just would like to informally know if the guard saw anything out of the ordinary that morning. Had anything unusual happened in the previous days?"

"Mr. McBride," he said, "thank you for coming by. I'll pass on Miss Kam's concerns to the appropriate parties."

He must have pushed a magic button somewhere that I didn't see, because O'Brian appeared at the open door.

"Mr. McBride is ready to leave now," Morikami said.

O'Brian seemed very happy about this development. He led me down the hall and to the glass doors. He shoved one door open with a beefy paw, and I walked past him.

"Hope I fuckin' see you one day when I'm not on duty," he said, doing a good job of sounding menacing.

"Sorry, man," I said. "I don't date dudes."

As I walked to the little parking lot, I heard him breathing loudly through his mouth like some kind of demented steam engine. Some Irishmen are a tad on the high-strung side.

Back in my truck, I continued south on Kalanianaole Highway, the roadway named after Amber's long-departed relative, the Hawaiian prince who became a Republican delegate to the U.S. Congress. The highway runs along the South Shore, offering amazing views of the ocean on the right and not-so-amazing views of strip malls, McDonald's restaurants, and housing developments on the left. After Hawaii Kai, my destination, Kalanianaole Highway continues past Hanauma Bay, where Elvis Presley frolicked in *Blue Hawaii*; along the rocky eastern side of Oahu past Sandy Beach, the most dangerous bodysurfing beach in the world; past Makapuu Point, known for its scenic lighthouse and as the place where Franky Five Fins met his maker; on through the village of Waimanalo and the beginning of the windward side of the island where Amber's father, Clarence, plunged to his death clinging to a hang glider; and on until it eventually reaches Kaneohe and the Pali Highway. It's a lovely drive when you ignore all the historical death and destruction along its path.

When I reached the Blue Ocean Centre in Hawaii Kai, it was packed. The lanai next to the boat dock at Whaler Cove Inn looked like a Michelob commercial, the tables filled with young men and women eating nachos and drinking beers and margaritas. In the window of the empty corner space of the strip mall that Burger King apparently had its eye on was a sign that said COMING SOON! TRISHA'S EUROASIAN BOUTIQUE! FABULOUS FASHIONS FROM FRANCE AND THE FAR EAST! That was the store Amber had been so hot on.

I found the small management office on the second floor. A pretty young Chinese lady stopped typing on a computer when I walked in; she looked up and smiled. Behind her a door opened to a private office. Amber's, I assumed. I thought I'd play it cute.

"Hi," I said. "I'm interested in renting a space in the mall here. Could I talk to the manager?"

"We just leased our last available space," she said, looking at me in that friendly way a single woman does when she sees a man who doesn't repulse her. I liked that. I hate to feel repulsive. She continued, "But I'll get Mr. Williams to talk to you just in case something else opens up."

She got up before I could say anything and headed for the private office. In seconds she emerged with a balding, middle-aged haole man in tow who looked like Elmer Fudd. Mr. Williams, I presumed.

"Good afternoon," he said, pleasantly enough.

Why is it whenever I try to play it cute, I run into an Elmer Fudd?

"I'm sorry, sir," I said. "I actually was looking for Amber Kam. I thought she ran this office."

"She did until yesterday," he said. "She's been moved to Four Gates Plaza downtown. Is there anything I can do for you? Miss Lee said you were interested in a space here?"

"I was just sort of kidding around," I said. "Do you have Amber's new number?"

He suddenly went from Elmer Fudd to crotchety Mr. Wilson from *Dennis the Menace*, his hairy eyebrows diving toward the middle of his face.

"Miss Lee, would you provide the gentleman with Miss Kam's new phone number?"

He spun on his heels and returned to do whatever

important strip-mall-related work I had interrupted him from doing.

Miss Lee scribbled on a piece of paper and smiled when she handed it to me.

"He's a little grumpy today," she said. "He was sent down here from the Plaza. Kind of a demotion, I think."

When I got back in my truck, I opened the piece of paper. Along with Amber's new number she had written a phone number for a Beverly Lee. How sweet.

Amber apparently had been kicked upstairs, which probably explained why she had not been able to get back to me. I remember her telling me that Four Gates Plaza was where the action was. I called the new number to congratulate her but got her secretary. She said Amber was in a meeting and took my name and number.

Since I was already practically back on the windward side I decided to return home along Prince Kalanianaole's memorial roadway instead of backtracking to Honolulu and going over the Pali. As I drove past Hanauma Bay, the sky was so clear I could see the island of Molokai across the channel. It was when I passed the Halona Blowhole that I saw the black Cadillac SUV come racing up on my bumper. The highway was twisty and narrow at that point with lava rock walls on one side and cliffs that dropped off into the ocean on the other. If the SUV hit my bumper just right, doing what the police call a "pit maneuver," my truck could be spun over the cliffs or slammed into the lava wall. That seemed to be exactly what Danny Chang was trying to do as he continued to bump and push my truck. We came out of the dangerous section where the highway straightened out past Sandy Beach. I cranked the truck hard right into the Sandy Beach parking area and then slammed on the brakes near one of the restroom buildings. This wasn't exactly what I had in mind when I decided I'd meet Dragon Boy on my terms, but at least it was broad daylight in a heavily used public park and not some dark alleyway.

The SUV slid to a stop on the crushed coral and sand next to my truck, creating a cloud of fine white dust. I looked quickly around the truck cab for something I could use as a weapon. My choices were a dirty beach towel, an empty Starbucks Grande coffee cup, and a Coast Guard booklet with tide charts. Now, Bruce Lee might have been able to defeat a rival karate school with those items, but they didn't do shit for me.

I got out of the truck, walked to the back, and leaned against the tailgate with my arms crossed. There were a lot of people on the beach and others going to and from the restrooms. I figured Danny Chang wouldn't do anything stupid in front of so many witnesses. When he got out of the driver's side and two more young Chinese men emerged from the bowels of the SUV like bad guys in a *Hawaii Five-0* episode, I figured I had figured incorrectly. These guys looked like they were open for business.

I could have run around screaming for help and yelling for someone to call 911. But I would have gotten my ass kicked anyway and would have had to live with the less-than-manly image of me running around screaming for help.

Danny stopped about three feet in front of me with his support staff on each side, slightly behind him. He was wearing black slacks and a black dress shirt with a heavy gold necklace. He slowly pulled off his mirrored sunglasses, folded them, and put them in his shirt pocket. Then he smiled.

"That white guy back at security place," he said. "He don't like you so much."

"Nobody does," I said.

"He said you asking about taro patch."

I had nothing to say to that.

"Some people don't like you ask about taro patch so much. Maybe you go ask about coconut trees or pineapple field," he said. "Maybe more better for you that way."

"Maybe," I said.

"Yes," he said, smiling. "Maybe."

I saw his right leg move almost imperceptibly, just the briefest flutter of his black slacks near his right foot. I thought it might be a good time to duck, but by then it was nappy time.

Chapter Twelve

If I was going to get the crap kicked out of me for asking a few questions about Wai Lo Fat and a taro patch, I wanted to know why. I wanted to know everything I could about Four Gates Enterprises, and I knew a good place to start: Sue Darling, my lawyer. To get to her I wouldn't have to go far.

Sue Darling kept her sixty-four-foot Viking motor yacht, the *Sue Hard*, at the Bayview Yacht Club at the end of A Pier. A finger pier between her boat and her neighbor's led me to the aft deck, where she was sitting on the circular settee near the swim step platform sipping Cristal mimosas with her friend Mary Ann. They were wearing bikinis that if joined together might be able to cover a child of three. On them the fabric, shared appropriately, covered just enough to leave absolutely nothing to the imagination.

She looked up with something like horror on her face when she saw me and said in her thick Slavic accent, "Stryker, my darling! Your face! It is not so perfect!"

There was no denying the ugly purple and black bruise

on the right side of my head, a souvenir from my run-in with Danny Chang the day before. The encounter had left me lying in a state of extreme tranquility in the Sandy Beach parking area for several moments until some good Samaritans came by, stood me up, and dusted me off. A city and county lifeguard was summoned to make sure my head was still completely attached to my body. It was, so that was good. Several witnesses had seen the incident and watched the black SUV speed away. They offered to call the police. I told them that wasn't necessary. The side of my head throbbed; I felt like I had been hit by a train, a train driven by a karate master. I asked how many times he had hit me. They said he had kicked me just once. So I guess I was lucky there. I climbed into my truck and drove off as a few of the spectators argued about what kind of a kick Danny Chang had used on me, a roundhouse or a flying scissor kick. You don't see a guy almost get his head kicked off every day, and they wanted to make sure they had details right.

"Come, sit down, my darling, and let me put some ice on your poor face," Sue Darling said, holding out a hand to help me onto her boat. Mary Ann, a strikingly attractive blond businesswoman I had met several times with Sue Darling, poured me a mimosa, and I acquiesced to their care.

Sue Darling was a Russian émigré who came to the United States to study law and never went home. Her real name was Svetlana Bezdushnaya, but she changed her first name to Sue because it sounded to her like a good name for a lawyer in America. She changed her last name to Darling by marrying Jonathan Darling, the chief justice of the Hawaii Supreme Court. She and Justice Darling had a short, dramatic marriage that lasted almost three months. Svetlana Bezdushnaya, a brilliant, ruthless lawyer referred to by attorneys around the courthouse as "ICBM," proved to be more firepower than the equally brilliant and ruthless Justice Darling could handle.

"I turned him gay and he turned me into a lesbian," she told me once. That wasn't quite true. Everyone in the courthouse knew Justice Darling was gay before she came along. His clerks tended to be vicious, tall blond boys who seemed to have been bred in some secret camp in Brazil. Justice Darling and Svetlana's union was a marriage of mutual enchantment, with neither harboring any illusions that it was anything but a strange, transitory experiment. He wanted to experience the raw, Russian excitement she offered, and she wanted instant, unassailable entrée to the farthest reaches of Hawaii's legal universe. Through her husband, she had access to just about every personal and corporate secret in the state, information that made ICBM one of the most feared attorneys in town. After her divorce from the Supreme Court justice, Svetlana decided not only to keep the name Sue Darling, but incorporate the word "darling" into her everyday speech, either because she liked the way it sounded or to remind those in the legal community of her marital provenance.

The ice didn't make my face feel any better, but a couple mimosas helped. I had come to ask my attorney to do a quick paper chase of Four Gates Enterprises, but that could wait. Despite her reputation as a merciless lawyer, Sue Darling had a tender side, especially when it came to me.

I had met her at the yacht club one hazy afternoon about a year and a half earlier. By hazy, I mean the sky was clear blue but I was a little hazy. I was living in a studio apartment in Kailua and spending my days hanging out in the yacht club bar seeing if I could go from being a semipro recreational vodka drinker to full-time professional.

She sort of adopted me, if not as a pet, then as a pet project. I was in self-imposed hibernation as a result of my meeting with Jake Stane and months of resulting physical therapy. I had developed a nice little case of post-traumatic stress syndrome and was expanding it into an even nicer case of pre-traumatic stress syndrome. Why worry about something bad that has happened to you when you can worry about all the possible horrible things that might happen to you in the future? Pre-traumatic stress syndrome offers many more exciting possibilities for misery.

I was sitting alone on a stool in the Longhouse Bar, your typical tacky nautical-themed yacht club affair with a lot of sailing trophies, brass plaques, and an ancient rusty whaling harpoon hanging over the cash register. Sue Darling sat down next to me.

"They say, Mr. McBride, that vodka corrupts, and Absolut vodka corrupts absolutely," she said.

I looked at her and was smitten. She had dark, dark hair and even darker eyeliner highlighting strikingly blue yet brooding eyes. (I learned later that while she did have brooding eyes, the striking blue was actually due to contact lenses.) She ordered a vodka and clinked her glass against mine.

"Yop tvayoo mat," she said, tossing back the drink in one swig, like a St. Petersburg longshoreman.

"Yoptoo mopetoo," I repeated as best I could, finishing off my cocktail. "To your health!"

"No, my darling," she said, waving for a refill. "Yop tvayoo mat . . . it means in English 'fuck your' . . . well, let's say . . . 'fuck the bullshit.'"

"Well, I'll drink to that," I said.

We tossed off a few more, and I learned some other great Russian lines like "Gavyonnaya blyat," which I think she said means "piece of shit whore." You use that one when the bar service is slow.

She was right about Absolut corrupting absolutely, because it wasn't long before I was corrupted to the point of barely being able to sit on my bar stool. She helped by keeping her arm around me and speaking very close to my ear. It is safe to say that I was completely in love by then with the woman I took to be a real-life incarnation of Natasha from the Bullwinkle cartoons. Lucky for me, there was no Boris around.

"My darling," she said, "you are not so perpendicular."

She pulled me a bit more upright.

"What are you, Mr. McBride, one of those functional alcoholics?"

"Barely," I said.

"Alcoholic?"

"Functional."

I am told we ended up on her boat for several days, although I have no independent memory to verify that. Sue Darling did not believe in self-imposed misery. In her world, misery was something you imposed on your enemies. And with a vengeance. She resolutely went to work drawing me out of my funk. I was her personal recovery project, human recycling. She didn't really care about what had happened to me except to the extent that she could make the people responsible for it suffer.

"The gavyonnaya blyat will pay," I think is how she put

it. And they did. ICBM targeted the parent company of the *Honolulu Journal*, the City and County of Honolulu, and various insurance companies, and in the end I had a three-hundred-thousand-dollar houseboat, enough money in the bank so I would never have to finish the novel I wasn't working on, and my own personal psyche reconstructionist. Sue Darling set out to methodically purge me of self-pity, self-doubt, and self-abuse. She did this partly by making me switch from Absolut vodka to Budweiser.

"No more drinking for you, my darling," she said. "Only beer."

Most of her rehabilitation involved an intensive regime of sexual therapy and exploration. To say Sue Darling kind of liked sex is like saying Carl Sagan kind of liked stars. She had a raging, feral sex drive that contained no emotional element. In her world, sex had nothing more to do with love, guilt, or jealousy than fishing for bass or painting a house. So despite her quips about Justice Darling, he did not turn her into a lesbian. She was an unrepentant "try-sexual" before she met him, with emphasis on the "try."

After my third mimosa I told her about Amber Kam calling me out of the blue and my going over to her house a few times.

"You have met a girl! At last!" she said, as if it were a major breakthrough in my therapy.

"It's not like that," I said. "I'm just doing a favor for an old friend."

"Of course you are," she said, hugging me.

I told her about Wai Lo Fat's death and asked if she could dig up anything on Four Gates Enterprises and who actually owned the Kahala taro patch.

"I will do everything I can for you," she said, "but first, you come to the sandbar with us. We go exercise."

Mary Ann had climbed back onto the swim step after jumping into the water. She picked her drink up off the stern rail and walked up to us, looping her arm through Sue Darling's. I tried not to stare at the rivulets of water streaming down her breasts but failed.

When Sue Darling talked about getting exercise, she really was talking about sex. She liked to take her friends out for exercise on the *Sue Hard*, parking her boat in the middle of Kaneohe Bay near a sandbar that appeared at medium and low tides. The first time she invited me out for exercise with a lovely friend of hers, I was nervous. I like exercise as much as the next guy, but her openness about it kind of rattled me.

"Really, Stryker, it is just a threesome," she had said to me. "And, my darling, a threesome is better than a onesome." And it was. One is the loneliest number, after all.

I would have gladly joined her and Mary Ann that morning, but I was going to give Amber a call and arrange to take a look at her new office in Four Gates Plaza.

"Can I get a rain check? I have something I have to do this afternoon."

"It is Amber, no?" she asked. I just smiled.

"This Amber," she said, turning serous. "She better not hurt you, the gavyonnaya blyat."

When I got back to the *Travis McGee* that afternoon, the message light on the telephone was blinking. I pressed the PLAY MESSAGE button.

"Hey, Stryker," a voice said in a hurried half whisper. "It's Jake Stane. I only have a second. You need to come and see me. It's important."

Chapter Thirteen

There allegedly is an old Indian saying—or perhaps an extremely elderly Montana fly fisherman saying—that if you stand by the river long enough, the bodies of your enemies will float by. The body of my chief enemy, Jake Stane, had yet to float by, he being safely beached in the Halawa High Security Correctional Facility near Pearl Harbor. That's the thing about living on an island: Even bad people, when sent away for the rest of their lives in prison, are really just up the road a bit.

I had done a pretty good job of forgetting about Jake Stane and the events that led up to my shooting. If I had been the only person shot, I probably could have done it. But I felt responsible for Officer Jeannie Kai being killed and thought I always would. No amount of Absolut vodka could erase the image of her dying in my arms as we floated two miles off Waikiki in the dark of night.

Jake was serving a life sentence without the possibility of parole for the murder of his fellow police officer Jeannie Kai. He got a consecutive sentence of twenty-five years for shooting yours truly. So it's comforting to know that after he dies in prison, he still has to serve twenty-five more years for shooting me. How the justice system would pull off this feat, I didn't know.

And now, two years after trying to kill me, Jake Stane wanted me to visit him in prison. Why? Had he found Jesus? Did he want to tell me that God had forgiven him and that we could be buddies now? Maybe he had contracted cancer and wanted to make amends before shuffling off this mortal coil. His message said it was important for us to meet. It must have been important enough for him to somehow manage to get to use a phone, if only for a few seconds. He was in protective custody, locked down in solitary for twenty-three hours a day, allowed out of his cell just to shower and get a little exercise. Cops in prison—even cops who kill other cops—have to be kept in deluxe detainment to keep them from being murdered by other inmates, and they don't get telephone privileges.

Ironically, Jake Stane grew up in Laie, the same Mormon community that later became home to Three Man Stone. The odds that such a tiny, God-fearing village could have produced two stone-cold killers are just off the board.

Laie is home to Brigham Young University's Hawaii campus as well as a sprawling tourist attraction known as the Polynesian Cultural Center, run by the Church of Jesus Christ of Latter-day Saints. Visitors to the center can watch stage shows featuring Tahitian dancers dancing and Maori warriors chanting, and visit replicas of South Pacific villages where the indigenous people of those re-created villages did typically indigenous things. Mormon kids like Jake Stane weren't allowed to drink Coca-Cola growing up in Laie, but they could watch women strip coconut husks with their teeth and guys juggle flaming machetes.

As Puka told me when I spent the night at his house adopting Kane, Lono, and a bad hangover, Jake Stane was a star football player for Kahuku High School but generally known as a punk and troublemaker. He apparently cleaned up his act enough to get an associate degree in exercise and sports science from Brigham Young and join the Honolulu Police Department, where, after twenty years on the force, he had managed to reach only the rank of sergeant.

Although not heavily educated, he had street smarts and cunning and was not hamstrung by things like morals and ethics. He was the right man in the right place when the Honolulu City Council made its most monumental blunder in the city's history: voting to allow off-duty police officers to freelance as security at island bars and nightclubs.

The crime war of 1998 came to an end with Three Man Stone getting blown off the bar stool, but the public was anxious that something similar didn't happen again. Bowing to pressure from their constituents, city council members passed a bill that would cut any potential crime figures out of bar and club security, putting cops in their place. Until then, off-duty cops were restricted to directing traffic around construction sites and road repair. It was boring, dirty work, and the prospect of working in air-conditioned clubs appealed to the rank and file. There were literally hundreds of strip clubs, hostess bars, and nightclubs that would be looking to hire off-duty cops. The city council had the naive idea that having a police presence in the bars would also cut down on the amount of crime associated with those businesses.

And at first, it seemed to work. The new program went

into effect in late 1999, and things were quiet until fall of 2000. Then I started to hear the first rumblings from sources that things were not perfect in the club security world. There were stories of some cops becoming permanently attached to certain bars and not only looking the other way when drug dealing, gambling, and prostitution occurred but actually taking payoffs from the bar owners and managers. This shouldn't have come as a surprise to anyone. The roots of Honolulu bars involved in the sex and drug trade traced back to South Korea, Taiwan, and the Philippines, where paying off law enforcement was a part of the culture and custom. Many Honolulu strip clubs and hostess bars were managed by front women sent to Hawaii by organized crime organizations in those countries.

I began looking more closely at the clubs and discovered that it seemed like a certain clique of cops was in charge of determining which police officers were assigned to work at which bars. I had pretty much confirmed that the police union had fractured into two factions: the small, powerful group led by a sergeant named Jake Stane who controlled the bar security action and a reform group attempting to get support of the rank and file headed by Officer Jeannie Kai. Jake Stane decided which cops worked where. Officers who complained not only didn't get the cushy bar security work but found themselves reassigned in their daily police duties to less attractive beats, like walking patrol on Hotel Street during the midnight shift.

I had decided to reach out to Jeannie Kai but before I could do that, she reached out to me.

She was a patrol officer waiting for her first chance to take the sergeant's exam. She had done her first couple of years as a rookie walking beats, transporting prisoners, and doing all the other scut work that new cops have to do when they graduate from cop school. When I met her she was attached to HPD's Kailua sub-station on the windward side where shoplifting and jaywalking were considered major crimes. She had a college degree in law enforcement but had to put in the mandatory time at various divisions before being allowed to take the sergeant's test. Where Jake Stane flunked the sergeant's exam several times before finally passing it after many years on patrol and then never rising any further, I figured Jeannie Kai would blow through the test on her first try and start studying for lieutenant's exam the next day.

Her goal was to become a homicide detective, which would turn out to be depressingly ironic. She put up with the scut work with good grace, knowing it was a rite of passage. But she couldn't abide by dirty cops. Her efforts to work within the HPD union for reform apparently were going nowhere. Jake Stane's rein on the State of Hawaii Organization of Police Officers (SHOPO) was solid.

Jeannie Kai figured she only had two choices: go to Internal Affairs, which would make her a pariah in the department, or "go off the reservation" and secretly meet with a newspaper reporter and try to publically expose Jake Stane's capers.

It's not a big ego boost to find out you are the lesser of two evils, but when Jeannie Kai began telling me what she knew about Jake Stane's racket, I felt just fine.

Our first contact was surprising. It was the summer of 2000. I had just come out of the tunnels in my little Mazda hatchback one afternoon and was blazing down the Pali Highway at all of about one mile an hour over the speed limit when a tan Ford Crown Victoria slipped up behind me from out of nowhere. It was wearing a tiara of police lights, indicating it was what's called a "HPD subsidized vehicle." In Hawaii, after a few years on the force, police officers can use their own cars for patrol and the department picks up part of the costs. HPD brass figured out that cops were a lot easier on their own cars than the city and county blue-and-whites, which they generally drove the balls off of.

At the beginning of each shift, patrol officers in a subsidized car just strap a rack of blue lights to the roof and they are good to go. If they arrest someone, they call for a blue-and-white to pick up the offender for transportation to the lockup.

Having patrol officers use their own cars saves the city money, but it makes them harder to spot when you're speeding. Which I wasn't. But the blue lights on the Crown Victoria started flashing anyway so I pulled over to the shoulder.

As the female cop walked toward my car in her dark, cobalt blue uniform, I expected the usual, "Do you know how fast you were going, sir?" and had a snappy reply all ready. But she didn't say anything. She just handed me a piece of paper with a phone number and a time of day written on it and then drove off.

I called the number at the appointed time and that was the start of my months of quiet collaboration with Jeannie Kai to determine the scope of Jake Stane's activities.

Jeannie Kai and I arranged to meet at Heeia Kea Pier on the windward side. At the end of the pier were a tackle shop, a plate-lunch takeout diner, and gas pumps for boaters. The pier was located on a lonely stretch of Kamehameha

Highway and frequented mostly by local fishermen and Japanese tour groups going out on the glass-bottom-boat rides to the reefs in Kaneohe Bay. It was a good place to go when you wanted to meet someone and you didn't want the world to know about it.

We talked about Jake Stane and his operation while eating teri-beef, rice, and macaroni salad off paper plates at an ancient picnic table next to the diner service window. She said she was collecting evidence to present to Internal Affairs. She refused my suggestion to go right to the city prosecutor—as a cop, she was expected to keep things on the reservation—but she said if I happened to break the story in the *Honolulu Journal*, that was my business. She only asked that I not quote her and that I give her a heads-up before the story ran.

That was supposed to be the only time we met in person. We decided to communicate by phone from then on.

I was getting close to breaking the story and had been working only with the *Honolulu Journal*'s city editor so that the exposé wouldn't even be talked about in the newsroom. No other editors or reporters knew what I was working on. It was the most dangerous time in an investigation, the days leading up to publication. The last thing I had to do was call Sergeant Jake Stane, introduce myself, and get any comment or denials he had on the record before the story went to print.

About three days before the story was to run in the *Honolulu Journal* a message was left on my telephone answering machine. It was a woman's voice, spoken rapidly in a whisper.

"This is Jeannie. Meet me at Honolulu Harbor at Pier 10 tonight at 11:30. It's important."

It seemed odd. Meeting on the Honolulu waterfront at night was a bit too *Hawaii Five-0* for me, but I figured she had a reason for doing it.

I ran a little late and didn't get to Pier 10 until just before midnight. Jeannie, wearing her patrol blues, was pacing, angry.

"Why'd you want to meet at this fucking pier in the middle of the night?" she asked as I walked up. "I'm working the desk tonight. I've got to get back."

"What are you talking about" was all I got out of my mouth before a man stepped out of the darkness holding a mini-MAC 9 mm machine gun on us. Smaller than a Black & Decker nail gun, the MAC-9 was deceptively menacing. With its short barrel and an ammo clip the length of a baby's forearm, I knew it could spit out twenty rounds in less time than it takes to say, "Ah, shit!"

Jeannie Kai took a step toward the man and said, "What are you doing? Are you crazy?"

"I just like talk to you before things get all jam up," he said in pidgin.

"You know this guy?" I asked, turning to Jeannie Kai.

"Shut the fuck up, bruddah," the man said, turning the ugly little gun toward me.

"Stryker," she said, "This is Jake Stane."

Jake Stane smiled at me.

"Stryker McBride, eh?" he said. "Bruddah, you stay in way over your head this time."

He turned the gun on Jeannie Kai.

"I'll have that gun belt, sista," he said. "Undo 'em. Slow kine."

She slowly unhooked the utility belt containing her handgun, pepper spray, and radio. But instead of letting it drop to the ground, she quickly pulled the Velcro strap releasing the handgun and grabbed the butt.

He took a step forward and slammed her across the face with the MAC-9. She fell to the ground. I made a move toward her and he swung the weapon at me. He held the gun on me as he patted me down with his free hand.

"Why'd you make me do that, you stupid wahine?" he asked. "I just like talk to you guys, that all."

A boat engine grumbled in the darkness. A few seconds later, a commercial fishing boat pulled up to the dock.

"Get on the boat," Jake Stane ordered, waving the gun at me. I helped Jeannie Kai to her feet. Blood was seeping out of a wound near her left temple. She seemed in a daze. I helped her onto the boat and sat her down on a padded bench by the starboard rail.

Jake Stane climbed on board and motioned to a man on the flying bridge. The two big Merc engines gurgled, and the boat moved away from the dock. I sat down next to Jeannie, and Jake Stane sat on the rail bench across from us on the port side. He held the MAC-9 casually in his lap, but the barrel was pointed in our direction and his finger was on the trigger. Once the boat was clear of the dock, the man on the flying bridge increased power and the boat surged into the darkness and out of Honolulu Harbor. I noticed that we had no running lights on.

I looked at Jeannie Kai, who was slumped back against the rail. Her eyes were open, but she just stared at the deck.

I knew then that Jeannie Kai and I had been set up. Somehow Jake Stane had arranged it so I thought Jeannie set up the meeting and she thought I had set it up. And despite what Jake Stane had said, he hadn't brought us out here just to talk. I gave it the old college try anyway.

"So what do you want to talk to us about, Sergeant?" I asked.

"Shut the fuck up," he said, flashing the gun at me. A man of few words.

The boat raced through the darkness, putting out a huge white wake that quickly disappeared into the blackness. There was no moon. The only lights were the Honolulu skyline rapidly disappearing behind us. I knew then we were being taken out to be killed, and I knew our only chance would be to dive off the boat and get lost in the darkness. If I tried to charge Jake Stane, he'd have five bullets in me before I could stand up. Jeannie Kai seemed frozen, dazed. She wasn't going to be any help. The longer we stayed on that boat flying at high speed into the open ocean, the better the odds that we were going to die. So I made a unilateral command decision. I suddenly grabbed Jeannie Kai by her dark blue shirt and pushed us both backward over the boat rail. Jake Stane squeezed off I don't know how many shots. You could hardly hear the gun over the sound of the engines, but what I did hear sounded like a playing card flapping in bicycle spokes. I felt a sting in my upper right leg as I went over the rail. We splashed violently into the water, and the speeding boat quickly left us in the darkness. The mystery man at the controls apparently had not noticed the commotion in the back of the boat.

After tumbling in the boat's wake, I surfaced, still holding Jeannie Kai. I pulled her toward me and wrapped both arms around her. She clung to me, moaning. We had both been shot, but I didn't know how bad. I was pretty sure I was only hit once. I heard the boat slow down somewhere ahead in the darkness and apparently turn. Jake Stane was screaming at the man on the flying bridge. They were coming back to look for us. I adjusted Jeannie Kai so that she was leaning against my hip and I was holding her with one arm across her chest. Using my good leg and one arm, I propelled us ninety degrees to the direction the boat was going. I could see a flashlight beam bouncing off the water a good hundred yards from where we were. Jeannie Kai started moaning louder, and I had to put my hand over her mouth to keep her quiet. The boat moved away from us. The engines went quiet. Jake Stane's voice floated through the darkness, unsettlingly clear.

"Hey, come on, bruddah! That was just an accident! I didn't mean to fire! We're just going to talk. Come back to the boat!"

Then he started cursing.

"That fucking bitch!"

"Do you think you got 'em?" a deep second voice said. Now the boat was just fifty yards from us, and their voices bounced along the surface of the water as clear as if they were in the water with us.

"I hit 'em both," Jake Stane said.

"They won't be able to survive out here. We're a couple of miles out," the other voice said.

"Yeah, you're probably right, but shit!"

Apparently out of frustration, Jake Stane let loose a stream of bullets wildly into the darkness. Some of them zipped into the water just feet from us.

The boat slowly motored away, a lone flashlight beam dancing along the ocean surface as Jake Stane made one last try to find us. The boat got farther and farther away until its engines were an indefinable purr, and finally it was just Jeannie Kai and me alone in the vast liquid night.

She had been hit twice, I later learned. One in the leg

and another in the side that struck her in the lung as we fell over the side. She was having a hard time breathing. She couldn't talk. Holding Jeannie with one arm, I stroked the water with my other and slowly kicked with my good leg toward the lights of Waikiki. We were two to three miles out and the current was against us. That would change when the tide changed at about 2:00 A.M. All there was was about a billion stars overhead, a large, dark ocean, and the lights of Honolulu seemingly a lifetime away.

At about three in the morning, Jeannie Kai died in my arms. She simply quit breathing. I thought about just letting her go. I was worried about sharks. I thought we must be putting a lot of blood in the water. But I figured if a shark was going to get me, he'd get me whether I let go of Jeannie Kai or not. And I had already decided that her death was my fault. The least I could do was die trying to get her body to the beach, back to her family. Jake Stane had intended for neither of us to ever be seen again, and I had to do whatever it took to ruin his plans.

I had once covered a case where two brothers, Maui marijuana growers, had been taken out in a fishing boat several miles from shore by a couple of rival growers, tossed in the water, and shot several times. One of the brothers actually lived, though shot twice, once in the scrotum. He treaded water for two days without ever being bit by a shark and was finally found by a passing fishing boat. So I knew that, in theory, anyway, I might be able to survive several hours in the ocean with a gunshot wound. I also knew that in theory there is no difference between theory and reality, but in reality there is.

At sunrise that morning, an old haole man scanning Waikiki Beach just off the Moana Hotel with a metal detector saw a man he took to be a surfer coming out of the water. He took a second look. It was a man emerging from the ocean with the body of a dead woman in his arms. It had taken me eight hours to make it to shore. The treasure hunter told the *Channel 2 Morning News* reporter the only thing I said before I collapsed was "This is police officer Jeannie Kai. Jake Stane killed her." Then I fell down into the sand and didn't wake up for twenty-one days.

That was about two years ago, and now Jake Stane wanted me to visit him in prison. Why? I didn't know. Would I go? I didn't know that either.

Chapter Fourteen

I had been anxious to see Amber again, but apparently she wasn't that anxious to see me. She hadn't returned any of my calls since the pleasant afternoon we had spent in her bedroom. She didn't return the calls I made to her new number at Four Gates Plaza. Most guys would have been able to read the lotus blossom leaves and just let the matter drop, but I'm not one of those guys. I like things spelled out for me. And who knows, maybe she had just been real busy in her new job and hadn't had time to get back to me. So I decided to put the Jake Stane invitation on the back burner and instead drop in on Amber at her new digs in Chinatown.

After snagging a metered parking spot on Maunakea Street that thankfully wasn't in front of the Coiling Dragon Wushu Academy, I found myself standing outside a massive glass high-rise that I had never really noticed before. When you go to Chinatown, you mainly see the quaint markets at street level with the dead ducks hanging in windows and crates of strange vegetables stacked on the street. You listen to the clangy musical lilt of Chinese merchants speaking actual Chinese to Chinese shoppers, little ancient ladies who seem old enough to have been around since the Chinatown Fire. You are engulfed in the sounds, tastes, and smells of Chinatown. You don't really look up at the tall buildings.

Apparently Four Gates Enterprises had so many enterprises that it needed a huge high-rise just to keep track of them all. That assumption proved wrong when I noticed on the office directory in the lobby that Four Gates Enterprises only occupied the top ten floors of the thirty-five-story Four Gates Plaza building. The rest were leased to lawyers, accountants, dentists, and other professionals who needed office space on the edge of downtown Honolulu.

I took an elevator to the Real Estate Division on the twenty-ninth floor. It was a hot afternoon, and I felt clammy and irritable. Traffic was bad on the Pali Highway, and my truck's air conditioner was broken. So I had been steaming like a Chinese dumpling for the past forty-five minutes on the drive into town, and now my wet shirt clung to my back, turning uncomfortably cold in the building's central air-conditioning. I was a little pissed that Amber had not returned my calls. And despite the kind attention of Sue Darling and Mary Ann, the right side of my face still hurt from where Dragon Boy had kicked me.

The elevator door opened directly into the Real Estate Division's front office, where a mousy secretary with her hair in a bun told me that Amber Kam didn't have an office on the twenty-ninth floor.

"Miss Kam is on the thirty-third floor," she said, looking at me nervously. "Executive corporate offices."

I realized that with my sweaty shirt and black-and-blue face, I didn't exactly look like the typical Four Gates millionaire client.

I thanked her for the information and was headed back to the elevator when the secretary said, "Sir, you have to have a special pass card to access that floor."

"Can I borrow one?" I asked, knowing the answer.

"Let me call Miss Kam's secretary and tell him you are here," she said. "It will only take a second."

It took about forty-three seconds of her whispering into the phone, looking up every few seconds at the side of my head. I thought she might be talking to security, but she eventually hung up, came from behind her desk, and escorted me to the elevator. She quickly swiped the key card that allows mere mortals access to the high country of Four Gates Enterprises, pushed the thirty-third-floor button, and backed away holding the key card in front of her like it was a switchblade knife. I felt a little like the Elephant Man.

Amber's secretary was a young Chinese guy who looked like he knew kung fu. I know that if I worked in the exclusive executive suites of a billion dollar corporation I'd have a secretary that knew kung fu. But she'd have to look like Uma Thurman.

He led me into Amber's office, a spectacular affair with floor-to-ceiling windows that offered a view of the leeward side of Oahu from Pearl Harbor to Diamond Head. The ocean stretched out into the distance, and we were so high up I thought I could see the curvature of the earth. Amber was standing behind a desk the size of an aircraft carrier, talking on the phone. She held up one finger to me in the international "my life is more important than yours" signal. While I was in my time-out, I noticed she was wearing a striking, tight-fitting skirt and dress shirt and jacket that said "You've come a long way, baby!" And she had. In just two days she'd gone from a dumpy second-floor office in a strip mall to the top of the world. I, on the other hand, looked like an escaped felon and was sure I reeked like a horse in the sixth chukka at the Waimanalo Polo Grounds. It would be awkward when she came around the desk to give me a hug.

She hung up the phone, sat down behind her new koa wood desk, and said angrily, "Stryker, why did you tell that security guard firm I was going to sue them over my grandfather's death?"

I guessed the hug was out.

I settled into one of two large beige leather chairs facing her desk, rubbing my wet back into the cushion.

"Comfy," I said. "So, how ya been, Amber?"

"You look horrible," she said. "What happened to your face?"

"Some Chinese guy confused it with a soccer ball," I said. "Funny thing. He started following me all over the island after you told everyone at your grandfather's memorial service that I was working for you."

"Why did you tell that security company I was going to sue them?" she asked. "Their lawyer called my boss, Michael Lee, the CEO of Four Gates."

"Stop it, Amber," I said. "Look, you wanted me to shake up some people, and I did. You said, 'Poke around a little bit more,' and"—holding my arms out to indicate her new posh digs—"voilà, here you are."

"I don't know what you are talking about, Stryker," she said, feigning hurt feelings. "I asked you to look into the death of my grandfather, that's all. I appreciate what you tried to do for me. We had a little fun. Now I think it's time to just move on."

"Well, that might be a little bit of a problem, Amber," I said. "When strangers start kicking the shit out of me on the side of the road and tell me to quit asking questions about something, it makes me want to know why. Makes me want to start asking more questions, like 'Why does a little taro field have to be guarded?' I've seen bigger marijuana patches that didn't have twenty-four-hour security."

"Stryker, it's time to move on," she said with more force. "If you want me to pay you for the work you've done, I will."

I let that hang in the air a few beats.

"That's okay, Amber," I said. "Just happy I could be of service to you."

If she had smiled at that, given some real human response, I probably could have left then and called it a draw. But she couldn't resist the opening.

She looked me in the eyes, all pretence of civility dropped, and said, "You call that service?"

It was a good line. A little obvious. And her intonation of barely concealed disgust was a nice touch. But just so she wouldn't think I was the kind of former lover who, after being dismissed with a well-delivered put-down, went softly into the blazing sun of a hot Honolulu afternoon, I said, "The medical examiner said she was still waiting for some toxicology test results on your grandfather. She's going to call me. I'll let you know how that turns out. And I have an appointment to talk to someone at the University of Hawaii Ag Department about the cultivation of taro. You mentioned that some UH students were helping in the taro field."

She had turned her back to me, but now she spun on her heel, eyes glaring.

"You are to conduct no further discussions on my behalf regarding my grandfather's death. You aren't working for me anymore, Stryker. You understand?"

"Sure, Amber," I said. "I'll have the ME call you directly about the toxicology tests. But as far as taro goes . . ."

I slowly rubbed the bruise on the side of my face.

"Well, I've kind of developed an interest in taro."

Chapter Fifteen

A day after essentially being fired by Amber, I was nursing a Budweiser on the stern deck of the *Sue Hard* while my attorney talked on her cell phone quietly in the cabin. It was about three in the afternoon, and we were a mile or so out into Kaneohe Bay, anchored in deep water away from any boat traffic. Her friend Mary Ann was sunning on the bow, sans bikini top. I knew that because just minutes before, I had been up on the flying bridge making sure that the flying bridge was still there and that Mary Ann was sunning on the bow, sans bikini top. The job of a deckhand never ends.

Mary Ann, who came to Hawaii from England, was one of Honolulu's most successful entrepreneurs. She was founder and CEO of the Honolulu Men's Health and Wellness Academy, an exclusive high-end weight-loss business that catered only to gentlemen. *Honolulu Business* magazine raved about her company, saying she employed a secret proprietary weight-loss method in which men, without being put on any rigid caloric, exercise, or fat-intake regime, lost forty or fifty pounds within six months and kept the weight off with a maintenance program, the details of which also were a closely held corporate secret. Her clients had to sign an ironclad contract—drawn up by Sue Darling—promising to keep all details of the program confidential. The penalty for violating the privacy clause, I was told, was one million dollars or the surrender of homes, cars, boats, or other personal assets matching that amount.

The magazine article quoted Mary Ann as saying, "The key to weight loss with men is motivation. They have to want to take the weight off, and my method ensures that they will want to take it off and keep it off."

The article went on to quote wives of some of Mary Ann's clients raving about their "new husbands" and saying the fee of five hundred dollars a month was a small price to pay to have their husbands in shape again.

"We've been married twenty-eight years and our sex life has never been so good," one wife gushed. "Whatever Mary Ann Morgan is doing to get my husband to lose weight and keep it off is fine with me. She's an angel!"

Mary Ann told me the secret to her success after a boozy afternoon frolicking with Sue Darling and me on *Sue Hard* off Chinaman's Hat.

"Blow jobs," Mary Ann said in her charming British accent. "For every ten pounds they lose, they get a blow job."

"What kind of a program do you put them on?" I asked. "Low carb? Low fat? High protein?"

"I don't put them on any program," she said. "How they lose the weight is their business."

Mary Ann had kind of a wicked sense of humor, so I don't know if she was just "having me on," as they say in England. I asked Sue Darling if it was true and she winked at me and invoked attorney-client privilege. But I have to say, when it comes to motivating men, Mary Ann's alleged business plan was a no-brainer, meaning the brain rarely has anything to do with motivating men.

Sue Darling walked onto the stern deck, closing her phone.

"That gavyonnaya blyat," she said, tossing the phone on a padded seat and pouring herself a glass of Cristal from a bottle on ice near the cabin door. Svetlana only adulterated Cristal with orange juice before noon.

She sat down on the seat and opened her laptop and tapped at the keys.

"Yesterday I looked at state Department of Commerce files," she said. "Public company files open to public. Four Gates Enterprises is private company, private stockholders. All corporate records sealed."

She smiled and took a sip of champagne.

"Except from me."

She read relevant parts of documents she had downloaded the day before out loud. Four Gates was incorporated in 1946. It is controlled by a board of directors. The board appoints a chief executive officer, who currently is Michael Lee. The CEO oversees the corporation's two main divisions: Private Development and Community Outreach. Departments listed under Private Development include Land Development, Commercial Development, Government Partnerships, and Research. Community Outreach falls under the umbrella organization the Blue Lotus Society. The Blue Lotus Society oversees public service projects, educational scholarships, native Hawaiian projects, and the annual Blue Lotus Society Chinese community cultural celebration and beauty pageant.

"There are five people on the board of directors," Sue

Darling said. "According to original incorporation documents, directors are appointed by the corporation's private shareholders. Yesterday, directors were a minor estate lawyer, an accountant, a Blue Lotus Society special events vice chairperson, a seventy-four-year-old restaurant owner, and the CEO's secretary."

She closed the laptop and laid it next to her phone.

"I just talk to my friend in corporate records," she said. "This morning Four Gates filed sealed, amended corporate report. Amber Kalanianaole Kam, that gavyonnaya blyat, is now vice president of commercial property development and a member of the Four Gates board of directors."

I just smiled and took a swig of beer.

"Are you all right, my darling?" she asked.

"I'm fine," I said. "You got to admit, that was a hell of a move. From strip mall manager to corporate titan. And apparently all because of me. The question is, what did I do that scared them so much that they made her a director? Who got the ax, by the way?"

"Old restaurant lady," she said. "These directors are nobody. They are replaced every year. How can CEO's secretary appoint CEO?"

"The shareholders obviously call all the shots," I said. "They appoint the directors. They tell the directors who to appoint as CEO. The shareholders tell the CEO what to do. The corporate structure is a ruse. So the big question is, who are the shareholders?"

"Even I can't find that out," she said.

"Why do I suspect that Amber's grandfather Wai Lo Fat was an original shareholder?" I said. "It would explain how Amber was able to leverage herself into suddenly being named vice president of commercial property development. The seat on the board is bullshit, but Amber probably didn't even know that."

Mary Ann came walking to the back of the boat. Her yellow bikini top, what little there was of it, was back on duty. She slipped her arm through Sue Darling's, took the glass of champagne from her hand, and took a sip. I have to admit it is distracting to see two lovely young women in bikinis sharing a glass of champagne. For some reason, the words of Saint Augustine came to me: "Give me chastity and continence, but not yet."

"Shall I ruin Amber for you, my darling?" Sue Darling asked.

She said it matter-of-factly, as if asking if I wanted her to help me renew my driver's license. I knew she meant it. With her connections, Sue Darling *could* ruin Amber, create a lot of legal mischief for her, perhaps engineer a state tax investigation that would mysteriously become public, or even an indictment.

"No, Svetlana, my love," I said. "We're done with Amber."

"What are you going to do?" she asked.

"I think I'll have a glass of champagne."

It wasn't out of compassion or misguided gratitude toward Amber in memory of our most private moments that I decided not to unleash Sue Darling on her. It was the realization that I no longer had an interest in the Blue Lotus Blossom Queen. As I sipped my Cristal, I realized my only concerns now were finding out who sicced a Chinese thug on me and why Jake Stane wanted to see me in prison.

Chapter Sixteen

It was easier than I thought it would be to arrange to see a convicted killer in prison. There's actually a phone number you call at "Prison Visitation Services," and if the killer you want to visit puts you on a list, you can come and hang out with him. Just like that. I called and left my name, and Jake Stane agreed to the visitation. It was easier getting cleared to enter the prison than it was to get into Kala Lane Estates.

So, on a Tuesday morning, I pulled on a clean polo shirt, some long pants, and deck shoes and headed once again over the Pali.

I found the Halawa High Security Facility without much trouble. There were a lot of big imposing buildings in the industrial park tucked into Halawa Valley, just off the H-3 Freeway. I correctly guessed that the prison was the big imposing building with razor wire atop all the walls. In all my years covering crime in Hawaii, I had never been inside a prison. I had more interest in writing about who should be in prison, not who was already there.

I parked my truck in visitors parking next to a snow

white Mercedes-Benz SLK 320 and a silver Jaguar XK8. Someone inside must have good attorneys, I thought. Or maybe the cars belonged to a couple of the inmates' more successful colleagues. In either case, I hoped they wouldn't ding the side of my beat-up F-150 with their car doors.

In a drab gray front office, an intensely disinterested Hawaiian woman looked at my driver's license, then at me and then at the license again. She typed something into a computer terminal with all the zeal of an anesthetized head-injury patient and said something I couldn't make out into a walkie-talkie circa 1942. I hoped the other "high security" technology from which the Hawaii High Security Facility got its name was more advanced than the communications system.

A few seconds later a Samoan prison guard the size of a Mercedes-Benz SLK 320 came through a locked metal door and said, "Mr. McBride?"

I'm six foot four, but this guy could have dunked on me in basketball on his tippy-toes. He was crammed into a dark blue prison guard uniform that looked like it would shred apart if he lifted a finger to scratch his nose.

I nodded to him to answer his question, and he said, "Come with me."

He led me down hallways that seemed to get more drab and depressing the deeper we went into the bowels of the beast. We went through various locked gates, each one slamming shut behind us with a disturbing clank of finality. We came to a small cubicle with a glass partition that looked like an East German interrogation room from the Cold War. I understand that prisons aren't supposed to be happy places but, man, how does the help show up every day for work without killing themselves in a place like this?

I suspect that prison guards never sing "Hi ho! Hi ho! It's off to work we go!" before their shifts start.

Two equally enormous guards of mixed Polynesian descent brought Jake Stane to a plastic chair on the other side of the presumably bulletproof glass and parked him there. He was wearing a festive orange jumpsuit, and his hands were bound with cuffs and a chain around his waist like a Harry Houdini protégé. That's when I noticed that there weren't the usual intercom phones you see on cop TV shows that allow the inmate to talk to his lawyer or visitors. There was a five-inch square of metal mesh imbedded in the window, which I now suspected wasn't even bulletproof.

The guards on his side disappeared from view. Jake Stane smiled at me and said, "Hey, Stryker, long time, no see."

I didn't know what to think. You meet a guy exactly twice in your life. The first time he tries to fucking kill you, and two years later he says, "Long time, no see?"

"My" guard left the room and shut the door, which caused an involuntary shudder of claustrophobia to go through my body.

I just looked at Jake Stane through the glass. He seemed older than his fifty-plus years. His skin was grayish and, despite his festive party-hearty jumpsuit, he looked like a man about to die.

"I'm gonna die, Stryker." he said matter-of-factly. "Cancer."

"Well, I can't say I'm unhappy to hear that, Jake," I said.

"Yeah, I know," he said with a strange smile on his face. "Can't blame you. But you don't look so hot yourself, bruddah. You run into bus?"

"Karate practice," I said.

"You should try a different sport," he said.

"What do you want, Jake?" I asked. "You could have told me over the phone you were going to die. I wouldn't have sent flowers."

"Do you know how much it cost me just to make that ten-second phone call?" he asked. "A carton of cigarettes—and I don't even smoke. I just buy 'em out of my canteen account to pay for little favors. I didn't call to tell you I was dying. I knew you wouldn't give a shit about that. I wanted you to come here to give you a little warning, and then maybe tell you something you've been wanting to know for a while."

It was his show, so I just waited for him to get on with it.

"How do you like the facilities here?" he asked.

"Real Andy Griffith," I said, tapping on the metal mesh on the glass partition.

"They are in the process of upgrading the whole place, putting in a new visitor center and computerized communications. So they're using these old rooms for visitation. Kind of rustic, but it does provide a little more privacy."

"I'm leaving, Jake," I said.

"Mike O'Brian told me you dropped by Paradise Protective," he said.

"You and Mike buddies, are you?" I asked.

"Members of a kind of exclusive club," he said. "Cops in crisis, you might say."

"Busted cops, you mean."

"Whatever," he said.

"How did he tell you this?"

"We have ways of communicating," he said.

"So what's it to you if I drop by Paradise Protective?"

"Ho, bruddah," he said. "It could mean everything to me. I'm dying but not, like, tomorrow. Unless you speed up the process."

"How would I do that?"

"You know that Paradise Protective is Auntie Kealoha's kuleana, right?"

"I know she runs it," I said.

"Auntie Kealoha and I aren't exactly on friendly terms," he said.

"What does that have to do with me?"

"I don't know," he said. "That's what I wanted to find out. You know the only reason I'm in prison is because I took the fall for all the big shots involved in the Three Palms Security fuckup."

"The reason you're in prison is because you killed Jeannie Kai and almost killed me," I said.

"Okay, let me put it a different way," he said. "The only reason I'm alive is because I took the fall for the big shots in the Three Palms fuckup. If I hadn't pleaded out and agreed to keep my mouth shut, I would have been knocked off deader than Three Man Stone."

"So?"

"So if you suddenly start poking around, digging up the past, things could get ugly."

"I'm not poking around in anything that has something to do with you, Jake," I said.

"If it has something to do with Auntie Kealoha, it has to do with me," he said. "Look, Stryker, do you know why I thought I had to take you out? You and Officer Kai?"

"Because you were afraid I was about to expose your extortion and drug operations in the clubs and bars," I said.

"Afraid of you, Stryker?" He actually laughed. "Bruddah, I wasn't afraid of you. I was afraid of Auntie Kealoha. I was afraid of Tiny Maunakea. Who do you think it was gunned down Three Man Stone at the Paradise Club at two in the fucking afternoon? How many four-hundred-pound Hawaiians are walking around Honolulu with machine guns? You never even know what you were getting into."

"I had the story about you controlling security at all the bars ready to run," I said. "I knew you were running a bunch of dirty cops."

"Bruddah, you didn't know shit," he said. "You didn't know what was really going down. You just knew enough to get me killed. I knew what you had. I had a copy of your fucking story in my hands printed right out of the news-room computer."

That, I admit, stunned me. The only person who knew what I was working on was the city editor, Jack McGlau-phlin. Jack was a stand-up guy, an editor who stood fully behind his reporters. There's no way McGlauphlin would have given Jake Stane a hard copy of my story or allowed anyone else in the newsroom access to it.

"That's the trouble with you reporters," Jake Stane continued. "You think you know everything when you only know a little piece of something. And you know what they say, bruddah, a little knowledge is one dangerous kine thing."

"Who gave you a copy of my story?" I asked.

"That's the something I figure you like know for a while," he said.

My lack of response told him that I had no idea that someone in the newsroom had given my story to him.

"You never know you were betrayed?" he asked. "You more clueless than I thought."

"Who was it?"

"I'll tell you," he said, "but first you have to understand something. Yes, you knew we were doing some bad shit with clubs, but you never understand how it all came down. We started Three Palms Security with the blessing of the police brass because they didn't want hundreds of cops spreading out through the city setting up their own deals with bar owners. Three Palms was supposed to be a straight-up legit security firm. But word got around and suddenly everyone wanted a piece of it: the police union, members of the liquor commission, and even Auntie Kealoha. She had been providing security to the bars and clubs in Honolulu in an off-the-books capacity, if you catch my drift. I think that was Tiny Maunakea's responsibility. When she heard about Three Palms she wanted part ownership. And Auntie Kealoha gets what she wants in this town. Lawyers drew up the papers, and everyone got some of the action, although their names didn't end up on the incorporation papers. They used front men, like lawyers, accountants, and even secretaries."

I noticed, his pidgin came and went depending on how excited he got on a certain subject.

"That would have been at the end of 1999," I said.

"Yeah, and it ran like a charm," he said. "Every cop who wanted work was getting work. Then the shit start coming down. Some of the guys were getting kickbacks from the drug, gambling, . . . prostitution. They wanted to be assigned to certain establishments, the ones making the most money. For a cut of the action, I put them where they wanted to be. We were making a ton of money, Stryker. I mean, sick money. That was all off the books, but what we were bringing in on the books was enough to keep all the

Three Palms partners happy. Then people started getting greedy. I admit, I let it get out of control. I was just a little guy from Laie and all of a sudden I was King Shit. I ran my own crew of headmen, cops I could trust. We called ourselves the Touchables because there was no piece of the bar and club action we aren't getting a taste of. Then some cops started to complain that they weren't getting their fair share of off-duty assignments. Some knew about the payola and wanted it stopped. That's where Jeannie Kai came in. The union election was coming up, and she was going to run for business manager."

"She didn't know about all the criminal activity," I said. "She just wanted all the cops to be treated equally when it came to working off duty."

"I didn't know that," he said. "All I knew was that she was causing trouble. Then I found out you were talking to her. If this thing blew up, we—the Touchables—weren't going to jail, we were dead men. We were ripping off Auntie Kealoha. I wasn't afraid of you, Stryker, I was afraid of Tiny Maunakea showing up at my house one night with a machine gun. So, I decided that you and Jeannie Kai needed to disappear to give me a little breathing room. That plan didn't work out so well."

"No shit," I said.

His pidgin was completely gone at this point. I realized he was smarter than I gave him credit for.

"You know where I was when Channel 2 did that live shot from Waikiki Beach with the old haole dude with the metal detector looking right into the camera and saying, 'Jake Stane killed police officer Jeannie Kai?' I was in Major Takahashi's office having a cup of coffee, our usual weekly morning meeting. Two assistant chiefs were in there. It was what you might call an awkward moment. The only good thing, and don't take this the wrong way, was that you were in a coma. Police Chief Kanahele met with someone from the mayor's office, the city corporation counsel, and the state attorney general's office, and they came to the conclusion that Officer Kai's death was the result of a limited, rogue police operation that went no higher than me. They knew that was bullshit, but if they moved fast they might be able to contain the problem. It was suggested to me that I quickly plead guilty to killing Jeannie Kai and shooting you, fall on my sword and avoid a scandal that would have destroyed HPD, the liquor commission, the police union, various high-ranking politicians, and Paradise Protective Association and all of Auntie Kealoha's contracts with the state—and do it before you either died or came out of your coma. I was told through back channels that although there is no official death penalty in Hawaii, there is an unofficial one, and if I tried to fight the case I likely would end up like Three Man Stone, whether I was in custody or not."

"So when I woke up twenty-one days after coming ashore, the case was closed," I said.

"Yeah, and the funny thing is, while you were almost dying, your newspaper ran the story you had written, and your story supported the version that a small corrupt group of cops were on the take from local bars," he said.

"That's funny?"

"Okay. Not funny. Ironic, I guess," he said. "Now, two years later, I hear you are on the street again. It gets me thinking . . . maybe Stryker's pissed off at the way things turned out. Maybe he wants to start poking around in shit again . . . maybe get the whole story out this time. The story that would bring down a lot of big people in the state and get me killed."

"All of that just because I stopped by Paradise Protective Association? You've got too much time on your hands."

"Not that much," he said. "Doctors say about a year. What I have left I'd like to spend in peace."

"I'm working on something that has nothing to do with you, Jake," I said. "I'm not interested in reliving the Three Palms debacle. But I would like to know who it was who gave my story to you."

"Fair enough, Stryker," he said. "I believe you."

And he actually did look a little relieved.

"There was a night city editor," he said. "Burl Morse. A drunk, and a degenerate gambler. Every night after work he hung out at one of our clubs near the news building. At the time it was called Club Moondance, but everyone called it Free Air and Water because the name and management changed so often. Everyone parked behind the club at Lex Brodie's Tire Service, next to the FREE AIR AND WATER sign. Burl owed a lot of money on bad sports bets. We wiped them out in return for a printout of your story."

Burl Morse? I barely remembered the guy. He was one of those morose has-beens on the night desk, burnout cases that newspaper management couldn't fire because of the guild. But it made sense. As night city editor, he probably had access to the city editor's story files.

He watched me turning things over in my mind.

"You going to look up this guy Burl?" he asked.

"Why should I?"

"I don't know, just to have a little chat," he said. "After all, if it wasn't for Burl I wouldn't have shot you."

The two guards on his side appeared and lifted him up.

He leaned over toward the little mesh opening and said, "Good talking to you, bruddah. Don't be a stranger."

On the drive back to the windward side I thought about the meeting with Jake Stane. I'd thought I'd want to break through the glass partition and strangle him, but I felt no overt anger toward him. Getting shot by someone elevates your mental state beyond mere anger, the anger you can dredge up in a second when some idiot cuts you off in traffic. Did I want him dead? Sure, but that wasn't my department, and it looked like he was doing fine in that respect on his own. I'm no doctor, but I wouldn't put money on him living out another year.

I was feeling a little different toward Burl Morse. It really pissed me off that he would hand my article over to known criminals. It pissed me off that I had no clue that he had done it. It pissed me off that I could barely pull up a visual memory of him. He had been a complete nonperson to me. I wondered if he was still around. It sounded like he was in pretty bad shape two years ago with his drinking. He had to know that he was responsible for Jeannie Kai getting killed and me getting shot. I kind of hoped it made his life just a little more miserable.

When I got back to the yacht club I spent some time in the bar, knocking back some beers and watching a football game on the big-screen TV with the grumpier old salts. Kane and Lono finally came loping into the bar through the open sliding wood and glass doors to remind me it was dinnertime.

After I put out their gruel on the aft deck, I noticed the voice message light blinking on the phone. I hit the button.

"Stryker, you cost me another carton of smokes."

It was Jake Stane.

"An hour after you left, Tiny Maunakea dropped in to see me. Looks like he's close to some of the guards here. He wanted to know what we were talking about. I didn't tell him anything. I just thought you ought to know."

Chapter Seventeen

The average human lifespan is about 530,000 hours. For some reason, after the human body has held together for that length of time, the atoms decide to wander away. Nobody knows why. But whatever force of nature holds the atoms together in the various bones and organs and muscles that make up the human body just suddenly decides not to hold them together any longer. The organs malfunction. The body dies. The atoms begin to disperse through decomposition. Some of the atoms are released into the air as gases, some into the ground. While the body ceases to be, the atoms that once constituted the human vessel, the container that provided mobility to that elusive thing called a soul, are redistributed, becoming parts of the air, water, and plants and even other animals. The decomposition process isn't so much "dust to dust," as the Bible alleges, but the recycling of atoms from the human body back into the cosmos.

Some people live not only the entire 530,000 hours—which is about sixty-three years—but a lot longer. Many aren't so lucky. As one philosopher brutally put it, "Life is short and almost always ends messily."

I was thinking these cheery thoughts about a hundred miles northeast of Hawaii as the sailboat I was driving, a forty-foot Lapworth named *Merde Incendie*, flew down the face of a twenty-foot wave during a rain squall that was pushing the boat along at better than fifteen knots. The sails were flapping from the acceleration as we raced down the wave, and I knew that when we hit the bottom we would slam into the breach of the trough where the wind was blocked and the boat would screech to a stop. Then the sails would suddenly fill with wind from the squall, making a sound like a cannon going off, and the boat would shoot forward. Hopefully forward. Doing these kinds of surfing maneuvers in a forty-foot sloop-rigged sailboat was dicey. If I wasn't able to keep the wind behind us, there was a good chance the boat would "round up," or lay over on its windward side, the mast actually digging into the water, turning the boat back into the wave we just surfed down. To make things a tad more exciting, it was midnight, but the moon was full and I had pretty good visibility. If I looked backward and upward from my position at the tiller, I would see the top of the wave. But I was more interested in keeping the boat pointed straight down the face and holding on to the tiller with both hands. If the boat rounded up, the wave could actually break it in half, and I'd come up short on my allotment of 530,000 hours of atom cohesion.

But the *Merde Incendie* charged through the trough like a champ, and after its sails refilled, we raced forward, waiting for the next wave. These trade wind squalls only happen at night within a day or two of Hawaii. They come through like freight trains, strengthening until dawn. You actually can see them coming in the moonlight. They block out stars. The trick is to jibe in front of them and catch the converging winds on their leading edge. Then you are in for a great ride.

Jacques Devereux was in the cabin sleeping, missing all the fun. We both were getting only about three hours' sleep a day. It had been thirteen days since we passed under the Golden Gate Bridge, one of forty-five boats taking part in the biennial Pacific Cup sailboat race from San Francisco to Kaneohe Bay. So, even though *Merde Incendie* was behaving more like a bucking horse than a sailboat, Jacques was fast asleep. He'd be up at 3:00 A.M. to relieve me.

I had crewed for Jacques on his various sailboats when he visited the Islands, and we became good friends. When you sail with someone, particularly in the extreme conditions Jacques enjoyed, you become either good friends or former friends.

Jacques was forty-five and had made himself a multimillionaire before he was thirty. He developed some piece of proprietary software when the Internet was still an obscure computer network used by scientists and college researchers to trade data. His company, Unincorporated Incorporated Inc., went public and was suddenly worth millions of dollars. He was smart enough to sell the whole damn thing before the dot-com bubble burst and spend his time sailing, flying his private jet, and doing other expensive things that people with a lot of money can do. I often ask myself, even with all of his toys, all of his money, jetting with his beautiful Hollywood-blond model wife between

Paris, New York, and Hawaii . . . is *Jacques Devereux happier than me?* And the answer always comes back, *Hell yes.*

We had sailed in the Pacific Cup previously, but that was in a bigger boat with a crew of five people. This year Jacques wanted to sail the race two-handed, meaning we would be the only two people on board. The Pacific Cup bills itself as "the Fun Race to Hawaii," but with only two crew members, the trip can become a nightmare, especially on a "vintage" boat like *Merde Incendie*, first christened in 1961. The trip can take anywhere from twelve to twenty days, but after just six or seven days without much sleep, you're so dopey you're chatting it up with passing marlin. I knew we wouldn't win the Pacific Cup or even beat other boats our size, but it wasn't going to be a social cruise, either. Jacques was a man who bored easily. He wanted to push the *Merde Incendie* to its limits for the sheer joy and terror of it. And so did I. After dealing with Amber Kam, Jake Stane, and Dragon Boy, I needed the kind of psyche cleansing that only being physically battered across an angry ocean for a couple of weeks can provide. The boat might be a little old, but it was a stallion. As it roared like a roller coaster car out of control down the face of another giant wave in the moonlight just a hundred miles shy of Oahu, while I clung to the tiller with all my strength, I understood how it got its name. In French, *Merde Incendie* means "Shit Fire."

Chapter Eighteen

We radioed in our fifty-mile check to the Pacific Cup communications center after the sun came up. The squalls had disappeared with the daylight, and a nice trade wind breeze was pushing us in the general direction of Hawaii at about nine knots. At this rate, we should cross the finish line outside of Kaneohe Bay early in the afternoon.

Before I flew to San Francisco for the start of the race, there was one bit of business I wanted to take care of. It wasn't hunting down Burl Morse, the night city editor who betrayed me to Jake Stane. That could wait. And I still had to think about how I was going to handle that meeting. I didn't want to do something stupid and end up being fellow inmate to Jake Stane at the Halawa Correctional Facility and Snack Bar. Since it seemed Danny Chang had clearly been dispatched from someone worried about my interest in the taro patch, my ego and bruised face insisted that I look further into the whole taro issue.

To that end, I found myself on the Waianae Coast at Makaha, the famous big-wave surfing beach, to meet the only other person I knew personally who had been shot. It's a fairly exclusive club.

Blue Ho'okane was a retired cop who had been part of a special police department crime reduction unit called the Metro Squad. Members of the Metro Squad were said to be the toughest on the force, trained in judo and known to bust heads on the street when needed. "Ho'okane" means "manly," in Hawaiian and from what I had heard, Blue was the Man when he was on the streets. He retired in the early 1970s when the old-school physical form of law enforcement went out of vogue, thanks to soft judges and personal injury lawsuits. But because of his great contacts on the street, he allegedly was brought back onto the force, apparently on a special contract, to help track down a terrorist supposedly out to blow up a dirty nuke off Waikiki. When discussing this operation the words "allegedly," "apparently," and "supposedly" are sprinkled liberally around because nobody really knows what happened. No bomb ever went off in Waikiki, so the alleged plot apparently was thwarted. Blue Ho'okane went back into retirement with a bullet wound in his leg. That was not hypothetical. I've surfed with Blue for years, and I've seen the scar. He claims he accidentally shot himself while cleaning his service revolver. He doesn't seem like the kind of guy who would accidentally shoot himself.

He now spends his days surfing at Makaha and running a nonprofit community farming program in Waianae. I called to let him know I was dropping by. I parked my truck in a dirt driveway and walked up the broad wooden steps to his covered porch. He lived in a beachfront plantation house, and when I knocked on the door, there was no answer. I looked out at the small waves breaking near the point and recognized his goofy-foot stance as he rode a wave nearly to the beach. He saw me walking toward the water and paddled in.

"Stryker, howzit, brah?" He gave me the "hey, bruddah" local-style handshake.

"Good to see ya, Blue," I said. "How's the leg?"

"It's fine. And your okole, still sore?"

"Nah," I said.

"You want to catch a few waves?" he asked. "Pretty small but not crowded."

"I actually came all the way out here to talk to you about taro," I said.

"One of my favorite subjects!" he said. "Come on, let's get a beer."

A few minutes later, with his longboard stashed on the lanai and beers in hand, he led me down a sandy lane and across Kamehameha Highway to a field where I could see rows of plants, mostly corn. A hand-painted sign on a wooden-post fence read WAIANAE AGRICULTURAL YOUTH PROJECT. VOLUNTEERS WELCOME. POACHERS WILL BE SHOT. ALOHA!

"The fence is mainly to keep the pigs out," he said as we went through the gate. "Those buggahs can wipe out a crop of yams in a few hours. We grow corn, sweet potato, melons, cucumbers, and some different types of greens."

"And taro?"

"We're trying."

We walked past the melons and cucumbers to a sunken field of water containing some sickly-looking taro plants with yellow wilted leaves.

"That's what's left of our kalo," he said. "Sad, yeah?"

"What's the matter? Is it the heat?" I asked.

He yanked one of the plants out of the water. The root was skinny and knotty looking.

"Not the heat," he said. "And we've got plenty of water. It's a virus. No taro is growing anywhere on the island. All the poi and luau leaves sold in the stores are coming from Kauai. But it won't be long before the virus reaches Kauai and the other islands. Then there'll be no taro growing in the whole state."

"What if I told you I knew about a taro patch on Oahu that has healthy green plants about this big?" I asked, holding my hand waist high.

"Where?"

"In Kahala. Smack in the middle of the Kala Lane subdivision," I said.

"A taro patch in Kahala? And the taro is healthy? That sounds weird, brah," he said.

"An old rich Chinese guy named Wai Lo Fat put the taro in a long time ago to honor his Hawaiian wife," I said. "She died some time ago, and Lo Fat drowned in the taro patch about a week ago."

"And you say the taro looks completely healthy?"

"I'm no expert, but it didn't look like this," I said, holding up one of the yellow leaves. "Apparently the patch is connected to the University of Hawaii. Maybe they've found a strain of taro that is resistant to this virus."

"Maybe, but I doubt it," he said. "There are two viruses on the island that wipe out every known strain we have— Hawaiian, Indonesian, Chinese, Vietnamese, it doesn't matter."

"This taro looked pretty healthy to me," I said.

"That high?" he asked, holding his hand about three feet above the ground. I nodded.

"I think I better go take a look at it," he said.

"When?" I asked.

"When" was sunrise the next morning. I met Blue at Kewalo Basin in Honolulu, where boats from the commercial fishing fleet already were making their way through the narrow channel between the surf spot Kewalos on the left and the bodysurfing spot Point Panic on the right. The chartered deep-sea fishing boats wouldn't go out until the tourists woke up. Half an hour after parking the truck, I was standing with Blue on the flying bridge of the *Pearly Shells*, a thirty-five-foot Bayliner flying toward Diamond Head.

"Why the boat?" I asked through the wind and salt spray.

"We're going to take a little side trip to Molokai after we raid the patch."

"Raid the patch." I said. "I thought you just wanted to look at the taro plants. See why they were growing so well."

"I'm pretty sure I know why they're growing well, but I need evidence. We'll park the boat at the beach park across the highway from Kala Lane Estates, jump the wall, grab a couple of plants, and get the hell out of there."

"Did I mention that Paradise Protective Association apparently is providing security for the taro patch?" I asked.

He looked at me, suddenly interested. "No, you didn't," he said.

"PPA is owned by Auntie Kealoha," I said.

"I know," he said.

"Isn't she supposed to be the Godmother of Organized Crime in Hawaii?"

"Something like that," he said.

"Won't she be upset if we raid her taro patch?"

"You said the patch is connected to the UH." he said. "Right?"

"Yeah."

"Paradise Protective provides security for the university. It probably keeps a night watchman out there to keep the tools from being stolen," he said. "Auntie Kealoha probably doesn't even know PPA has a man out there. Even if she does, I bet she doesn't really know what's going on in that patch."

"What do you think is going on?" I asked.

"Genetic engineering," he said. "That's the only way those plants could be healthy while all the rest of the taro on Oahu is dying."

I looked at Blue as he gunned the engine and the boat raced forward even faster. The fact that the taro patch might be guarded seemed to invigorate him. Blue had a reputation on the police force as being a man of action. He reportedly broke the back of a German shepherd attack dog over his knee when raiding a Maunakea Street gambling den once. I was hoping the night watchman didn't have a dog.

As it turned out, the raid was anticlimatic. After running the boat up onto the sand at the beach park and tying it up to a coconut tree, we ran across the highway, climbed over the stucco wall into the subdivision, ran past a few houses, and each yanked a plant out of the muck. The guard apparently slipped out of the subdivision before sunrise to do a little fishing every morning. We spotted him down the shore, fishing off a small pier. He dropped his fishing pole when he saw us dragging the plants across Kalanianaole Highway and ran toward us yelling. But we were

halfway across Kahala Bay before he reached where we had
tied up the boat. And we'd be halfway to Molokai before he
could report the incident to headquarters, if he did at all.
How was he going to explain what he was doing when we
were inside the property grabbing the taro?

"There is a twenty-year moratorium on growing genetically altered taro in Hawaii," Blue said as we cruised
through the Molokai Channel at a more reasonable speed.
"It's a crime. If we can show that someone at the university
was in cahoots with that dead Chinese guy to develop
Frankentaro, the shit is going to hit the fan."

"Why Molokai?" I asked.

"There's a pakalolo grower over there," he said. "Well,
former pakalolo grower. I busted him years ago. He's a
plant expert, a PhD from some big Mainland university.
He's gone legit, trying to find better ways to grow plants
indigenous to the Islands. He's helped us with our ag project in Waianae. He'll be able to get these plants tested to
see if they are Frankentaro."

We delivered our mystery plants to a hippie-looking
haole guy standing on the docks at Kaunakakai Harbor.
Later that night I was on a plane to San Francisco for the
start of the Pacific Cup race. I had gone out to Waianae
thinking I was going to have a little chat with Blue while
we surfed and ended up committing Grand Theft Taro.
Maybe it wasn't a good idea to get two guys together who
have been shot. Their outlook on life might be a little
skewed. For all I knew there'd be an arrest warrant waiting
for me when I crossed the Pacific Cup finish line. In fact,
what happened was even more surprising than that.

After fourteen days of hard sailing, we were all beat—me,
Jacques, and the *Merde Incendie*. The venerable old boat

had performed magnificently. It creaked and groaned during the bad weather, but nothing broke. Our only problem was losing our best spinnaker during a surprise gust. It got ripped off the bow and dragged under the hull. Jacques turned the boat into the wind so I could dive off and cut the sail away from the keel.

I figured I had had a total of about forty hours of sleep during the entire race. I was exhausted, but I felt good. We passed the Pacific Cup finish line at 1:30 in the afternoon, slipped through the Sampan Channel into the bay, and parked the boat at the Kaneohe Yacht Club, host of the event and just a half mile from the Bayview Yacht Club. Many of our friends from the Bayview were at the KYC docks to greet us. We did all the champagne squirting and drinking that is mandatory on such occasions. Officially, we had come in second in the double-handed sailing category. The fact that there were only two boats in that category didn't dampen our spirits. If they had a category in the race for Fastest Time by an Old Boat with a Naughty Name, we would have taken first. I was punchy from lack of sleep, so the champagne hit me pretty hard. But not as hard as what Sue Darling whispered in my ear when she hugged me as I climbed off the boat.

"My darling," she said. "Jake Stane is dead."

Chapter Nineteen

Incapacitated as I was by champagne and fatigue, the twenty-four hours following the Pacific Cup finish were pretty much a blur. I woke up at about one in the afternoon on the *Travis McGee*. To borrow a line from Jimmy Buffett, how I got there I haven't a clue. But I felt good. Completely relaxed. Drained of any physical or emotional tension. I was just lying there in bed when I heard someone stomping along the stern deck. Then there was some pounding on the door. This was against all boating protocol. You aren't supposed to go onto someone else's boat without first asking permission, even if that boat is up on blocks and not in the water. I knew it must be a friendly because the gods weren't ripping whoever it was to shreds.

"Get your fat ass outta bed, you lazy bugger!" came a loud bellowing. It belonged to Fleetwood Richardson, the burly ex-marine commodore. I had asked him to take care of Kane and Lono while I was gone.

I got out of bed and padded toward the stern and opened the door. The gods rushed in, almost knocking me over. They kind of pinned me against the couch, jumping all over, barking and smiling in that way that dogs can do when they are really happy. If I didn't know better, I'd think they'd missed me.

Fleetwood came in, beer in hand, and made himself at home in the recliner.

"Hell of a party yesterday," he said. "Great finish for you guys. Can't believe that piece of shit boat of yours made it all the way from the Mainland without falling apart. Amazing performance for an ancient tub like that."

I fought off the dogs, went to the refrigerator, and took out a bottle of orange juice.

"The *Merde Incendie* is not ancient," I said, taking a swig. "It's just a little older than I am."

"Yeah, well, I'm surprised you made it all the way across without falling apart, too, you old fart," he said.

That's about as close as Fleetwood got to a compliment. He considered being loud and crusty as charming. He was seventy-two years old and had sailed between Hawaii and California no more than ten or twenty times, and he looked like he could do it tomorrow if he had to.

"How were the boys?" I asked.

"Real sweethearts," he said. "I slept on my boat while you were gone, and they hung out with me. They scared the living shit out of a couple of kids who paddled up to the end of A Pier one night in a skiff. They were just some neighborhood kids paddling home from a party down the way. Drunk probably. Kane and Lono let 'em get real close to the pier and then they raced at 'em like mad dogs, barking like Kingdom Come. Shit, that little skiff lit outta here like it had jet engines. I doubt they've stopped paddling yet."

I sat on the couch and petted the dogs, who clearly knew they were being talked about and liked the attention.

"Is Jacques still around?"

"Yeah, he moved that old boat down here from the Kaneohe Yacht Club. It's out there at the end of the A Pier. How married is that guy, anyway?" he asked.

"Pretty married," I said.

"Yeah, well, he didn't look too married last night. I think he had about ten gals on that boat when he pulled in."

"Admiral Nelson said every man's a bachelor once out of sight of Gibraltar," I said.

"Yeah, I know. And Kaneohe Bay is shit outta sight of Gibraltar."

He took a slug of beer.

"Here are your keys," he said, tossing them to me. "I never bothered to lock anything up. With those monsters around, nobody would dare climb on this boat. Bunch of those TV news weenies showed up for a coupla days after that guy killed himself in prison. I ran 'em off. And this big Hawaiian guy came by looking for you."

"Big Hawaiian guy?"

"Big freakin' Hawaiian guy. Four hundred pounds at least. Mean looking. Talked funny. Old-fashioned like. Formal, you know. Didn't leave his name."

I recognized the description immediately. There aren't many four-hundred-pound Hawaiian guys on Oahu who speak Victorian English. It had to be Tiny Maunakea.

The Pacific Cup party had kind of knocked Sue Darling's whispered disclosure about Jake Stane's death out of my head until the commodore mentioned it.

"Jake Stane killed himself in prison?" I asked.

"That's what the papers say," he said.

Jesus, I thought. *Jake Stane kills himself and then Tiny*

Maunakea comes looking for me. That couldn't just be a coincidence. And it couldn't be good.

"Well, I gotta get going," Fleetwood Richardson said. "Takin' a herd of Filipinos out to the Sandbar in my boat."

"Herd of Filipinos," I said, smiling at him. "Real culturally sensitive."

"Hey, they're my wife's family. I can call 'em whatever the hell I wanna call 'em."

I walked him out to the back of the boat. The dogs went running off behind him. Guess they hadn't missed me that much. I went back inside and looked at the telephone answering machine. The display said there were twenty-five messages. That would be the whole cassette. I know I was gone for two weeks, but I've never had that many calls. I hit the PLAY button.

"Mr. McBride. This is Sandy Morita at Channel 2 News. We wanted to get your reaction to the death of Jake Stane. Can you call me back? It's ten, Tuesday morning. Thank you."

All the rest of the calls were in the same vein, from every TV and radio station in Hawaii and a few from the Mainland. I hit the button to hear the last message, which would have been the first one recorded, and the hair seemed to stand up on my neck. I mean, I've heard the cliché before, but the fucking hair on my neck actually began to tingle. The voice on the tape was Jake Stane.

"I'm getting real popular all of a sudden," he said. "A Chinese guy named Danny Chang managed to get in to see me. I don't know how, maybe through the Chinese gangs in here. So much for high security. Wanted to know something about a taro patch. I told him to fuck off."

He chuckled a bit.

"If he was your karate teacher, I'd stay out of his way," he said.

The call had come in just a day before he killed himself. He didn't sound suicidal. He sounded kind of happy he could still shake things up from behind bars.

Chapter Twenty

I could tell I had lost a few pounds during the Pacific Cup race. Those twenty-hour days, pulling on lines, struggling with the tiller, and wrestling sails up and down, were better exercise than you can get in the best health clubs. And we never actually had a real meal the whole time. We just grabbed handfuls of cereal or opened a can of turkey chili and ate it cold. It was too much trouble to heat up anything. I even ate the freeze-dried fruit desserts without adding water to them. It was like eating sweet Styrofoam.

I was lean and burned brown by the sun, and I thought I was probably in the best shape I had been in for years. Then I went out on my regular run and realized I had no legs anymore. Just two weeks without running seemed to have turned them to stumps. And after all that time on a boat, where the deck seems to give when you walk on it, the land was unreasonably hard and unforgiving, especially running on it.

After a mile, I felt a little better. I almost had my first wind.

After the commodore dropped by my boat that morning,

I spent an hour at the Longhouse's trading library, going though the stack of old newspapers, trying to read up on Jake Stane's death. There wasn't much. The *Honolulu Journal* had a front-page story with a photo of Jeannie Kai and an old head shot of me. The headline read COP KILLER KILLS SELF IN PRISON. A subhead read WAS SERVING LIFE FOR KILLING POLICE OFFICER AND WOUNDING JOURNAL REPORTER. There weren't a lot of details on his death, only that he was found slumped by his bed, a strip of sheet tied around his neck and to the metal bedstead. Most people think that when someone hangs himself in prison, he actually hangs himself from the rafters or a light fixture, the way they hanged people in the Old West. But most inmates who kill themselves in prison know they only have to tie a strap of sheet around their neck and onto a chair or desk or bed frame and sort of just lie down. The pressure of the sheet will cut off the blood to their head and they'll just fall asleep and die lying there. From what I could gather from the newspaper accounts, that's what happened to Jake Stane.

The other thing about prison suicides is that a lot of them are actually murders. It's fairly easy for a couple of guys to overpower a man, choke him out, and then make it look like he killed himself. For that to have happened to Jake Stane, another prisoner would have had to persuade the guards in the solitary detention wing to let him into Jake's cell and then disappear while he did the deed. Or it could have been some guards themselves. They aren't all college graduates. Many prison guards have ties to crime outside the prison. Danny Chang and Tiny Maunakea didn't seem to have a problem arranging a face-to-face with Jake Stane without his consent.

But who would want him dead? I mean, other than myself and a few members of Jeannie Kai's family. I couldn't believe he would be killed simply for talking to me. I like conspiracies as much as the next guy, but that didn't seem plausible. If he had been murdered, maybe it was because he pissed off Tiny Maunakea. Tiny doesn't seem to be the kind of guy you just tell to fuck off. After considering all the possibilities, I decided Jake Stane might have just had enough of life and decided to exit on his own terms, the way Dr. Lew Eden had.

I ran past the marine base entrance and up the on-ramp to the H-3 Freeway. As I ran along the freeway, I thought of Burl Morse, the *Honolulu Journal*'s night city editor. I didn't have the same intense desire to beat the shit out of him that I did when Jake Stane first told me of his betrayal. I guess fourteen days on the high seas had mellowed me some. If I decided to hunt him down, it would be just to let him know I know what he did. I don't want him living the rest of his life thinking he got away with it.

I was running along the right side of the mostly empty town-bound lanes, when I noticed a long black limo parked at a scenic overlook pullout. It struck me as a little strange. Tourist limos are usually white. And there usually are tourists lining the scenic lookout wall, looking out, so to speak, at the scenic view. No one was looking out at the lookout. I was thinking it might be Danny Chang, but when I was about twenty feet away, the driver's door opened and the largest human being I have ever seen in person got out of the car. He wore an aloha shirt that, if erected with tent poles, could have provided shelter for a homeless family. He was dark complexioned, Hawaiian apparently. He was, I knew, Tiny Maunakea.

He walked around the back of the car and into my path between the car and the lookout.

"Pardon me, Mr. McBride," he said, "Might I trouble you for a moment of your time?"

He opened a passenger door and with a beefy paw the size of a baseball mitt directed my attention toward the vast, dark interior.

"If you please," he said.

I stood panting in the heat of the early afternoon, looking back and forth between the darkened interior of the black stretch limo and the deceptively passive face of Tiny Maunakea. I didn't know if Tiny Maunakea was an actual family name or a nickname, but it suited the man mountain before me. The Big Island's Mount Mauna Kea is the highest volcanic peak in Hawaii and considered the tallest mountain in the world if measured from the ocean floor to its top. Tiny Maunakea, if measured from the H-3 freeway pavement to the top of his head, would certainly be about the biggest man in Hawaii.

"Mr. McBride, allow me to offer you a ride," he said.

Since his request for me to get into the car came in the form of an invitation, I decided to test the edges of it for wiggle room.

"What happens if I don't get in the car?" I asked.

"I daresay the second half of your run perhaps would not be as delightful as the initial half," he said, deadpan.

The statement carried some interesting implications, most of them painful. The bruise on my face caused by Danny Chang's right foot was gone after my fourteen days at sea. I didn't want to collect any similar souvenirs from Tiny Maunakea. Other than getting in the limo, my only choice was to bolt. I knew I could outrun him, but he obvi-

ously knew enough about me to know my habits and movements. He or someone working for him eventually would
show up at the yacht club or catch me in Safeway or someplace else. Unless I wanted to move to Irkutsk, I didn't
have many options—and, frankly, the cool air pouring out
from the air-conditioned limo felt pretty damn good. I got
in the car.

He started the engine and pulled onto the freeway heading for the Koolau Mountains. I sat back in cool, luxurious
comfort. Chamber music, Canon in D by Pachelbel, I think,
sifted softly through several invisible speakers.

The tinted glass partition between the driver's compartment and the several acres of couches in the passen-
gers' lounge lowered is if by magic.

"Mr. McBride, Auntie Kealoha requests the pleasure of
your company," he said. "For your comfort during our short
trip to Portlock Point, there are iced beverages in the refrigerated compartment to your left."

"Why don't we swing by the yacht club and I'll take a
shower and change into something likely to be a little less
offensive to Auntie Kealoha than these running clothes?"
I suggested.

"A noble sentiment, sir, but, I assure you, quite unnecessary," he said. "Auntie Kealoha's capacity to interact with
persons of less than ideal deportment has been honed to an
impressive degree."

I opened the refrigerator and found it filled with sodas
and beer. I pulled out an icy Budweiser, wondering if he
had known it was my brand. After several minutes of air-
conditioning and most of a beer, I began to relax. I was
pretty sure he wasn't going to kill me. At least not until
after my meeting with Auntie Kealoha. I finished the first

beer and cracked open another. Tiny didn't seem at all the homicidal terror I had imagined him to be. The Rev. Franky Five Fins had told me that Tiny Maunakea was the only man on earth he was afraid of. And for a stone-cold killer like Franky, that was saying a lot. But this guy seemed like a dignified gentleman. He left the glass partition down, so I took it as a sign further conversation was allowed.

"I mean this with all due respect," I said, "but you are probably the biggest Hawaiian I have ever met."

"Hawaiian-Chinese," he said, "and it is true that the fates have favored me with an expansive physique. I find it aids me in my line of work."

I didn't press him on his line of work. There was ample anecdotal evidence of what that was. We drove on in silence for a few minutes while I considered how a gigantic Hawaiian-Chinese man born and raised in the Islands managed to channel the ghost of Jane Austen in his manner of speech, and why. Maybe Tiny Maunakea figured out that the best way to intimidate the less than sophisticated assortment of criminals his job required him to ride herd on for Auntie Kealoha was to speak weirdly and carry a big fist. I daresay his overly polite invitation to me to get in the limo fairly scared the shit out of me. It was like being kidnapped by a deranged Polynesian Charles Dickens.

As we turned off the freeway onto Kalanianaole Highway heading toward Makapuu, he said, "I should think you heard about the unexpected passing of Mr. Stane by his own hand while in prison. I hardly suppose you are grieving because of it."

"You suppose right," I said. "How sure are you that it was by his own hand?"

"Why, sir, it certainly was by his own hand, if not literally, then by considering the premise in its widest possible context."

Man, this guy had a way of packing his remarks chockfull of intriguing possible meanings. Had he just taken credit for killing Jake Stane?

"I don't suppose you would tell me, then, why you went to see Jake Stane in prison," I said.

"Now, that, sir, was strictly a personal visit," he said. "I simply inquired about the gentleman's health."

I imagined how I would feel if Tiny Maunakea dropped by and inquired about my health.

"His health wasn't so good after your visit, apparently," I said.

"It would seem so," he said.

"Did you know him? I mean, before you went to see him in prison?" I asked.

"I do not wish to speak unpleasantly of the departed, but I rejoice to say I never suffered the discomfort of knowing the gentleman. His notorious activities as a police officer distressed Auntie Kealoha remarkably. I assure you she grieves from the knowledge that had she divined Mr. Stane's nefarious business dealings earlier, you and that young female police officer would not have been subject to his murderous scheme."

"Well, I'm sorry she grieves over my shooting, but if she wanted to talk to me about it she could have just called. Is that what this trip is all about?" I asked.

"I should think Auntie Kealoha is in the best posture to disclose the purpose of your visit," he said.

"I guess I should, too," I said, cracking another beer. I was kind of becoming fond of this guy. The Victorian dialogue, the string quartet humming in the background—it was kind of like a road trip sponsored by PBS.

"I don't suppose, Mr. McBride, you would disclose the purpose of your meeting with Mr. Stane in prison," he said.

There was no point asking how he knew about that visit. I figured in his line of work, he kept up a pretty good intelligence network within the prison, both with inmates and guards.

"He called me and asked me to come by," I said. "He wanted to tell me he was dying of cancer, and I didn't mind sitting on the free side of that bulletproof glass in the visitation room as a reminder that I was alive and well. Sometimes survival is the best revenge."

"True," he said. "Survival is often spoken of with favor."

He paused a few seconds, probably not to link the two lines of thought, then he said, "Have you any idea why an individual named Danny Chang would also visit Mr. Stane in prison?"

We just happened to be driving past Sandy Beach Park, where I had had my date with Dragon Boy. Talk about timing.

"I don't," I lied. I didn't know why Auntie Kealoha wanted to see me, but I figured it had something to do with Blue Ho'okane and me raiding the taro patch. I was going to call Blue after my run and find out if he had talked to Auntie Kealoha about our little operation, but my abduction preempted that call. So I nudged the focus away from Danny's meeting with Jake Stane.

"Who is this Danny Chang, anyway?" I asked.

"Alas, I know little of Danny Chang," he said. "Other than that he was born in Hong Kong and came to Hawaii about three years ago. He has connections to certain criminal organizations in Hong Kong and is a member of the Hung Bang Kongsi."

"What is the Hung Bang Kongsi?" I asked.

"One of the many ancient societies that go back thousands of years in China. Some call them secret societies, but I daresay they are no more secret to the Chinese than the Brotherhood of Freemasons is to the West."

He looked at me through the review mirror. "Do you know Danny Chang?" he asked.

I inadvertently rubbed the side of my face.

"I've met him," I said. For some reason, I had a hunch that Tiny Maunakea knew all about my run-in with Dragon Boy.

"I daresay that Mr. Chang's path will cross with mine eventually," he said.

I thought, *I'd like to be at the junction of those paths when they cross. That's going to be something to see.*

We went past Hanauma Bay and turned left into the neighborhood of Portlock, which is set on a peninsula across the highway from Hawaii Kai. We continued on Poipu Drive until we were at the end of Portlock Point, at the ornate gates of Auntie Kealoha's sprawling waterfront villa. I was a little disappointed to see that the entrance to her compound wasn't guarded by cigar-chewing goombas holding shotguns like at Don Corleone's house in *The Godfather*. If Auntie Kealoha was the Godmother of Organized Crime in Hawaii, she was pretty relaxed about security. Or maybe she had her best marksmen from her Paradise Protective Association hidden in the coconut trees with sniper rifles.

Tiny Maunakea drove the limo up a long, winding

driveway that lead to the huge double koa front doors of a white adobe mansion. An elderly Hawaiian woman in a white muumuu came out of one of the doors holding a plumeria lei in her hands. At first I thought it was a housekeeper or what passes as a butler for rich folks in Hawaii. Tiny Maunakea stopped the car and walked around to open the door for me. As I got out of the limo, I realized the kindly-looking old lady putting the lei over my head onto my shoulders and kissing me sweetly on the cheek was the legendary lady herself, Auntie Kealoha.

"Aloha, Mr. McBride," she said. "Welcome to my home."

Chapter Twenty-one

Auntie Kealoha led me into a grand entranceway where hundreds of orchid plants formed a sort of botanical gauntlet. I thought I might need a machete to get through them. We continued through the house via a wide polished white marble hallway that opened up to an enormous concrete patio that could have come from the Hearst Castle. Beyond the lanai a lawn stretched to black lava cliffs that dropped twenty feet into the ocean. You could hear the waves pounding on the base of the cliffs like the rumble of distant cannon fire. A guava tree heavy with fruit and a raised white pagoda framed the view from the right, and a small grove of coconut trees on the left counterbalanced a scene that could easily have graced a Waikiki postcard. The term "Shangri La" came to mind. Not too surprising considering the deceased tobacco heiress Doris Duke's Islamic-style manor named Shangri La was just two mansions down the street.

With Tiny Maunakea behind me, I followed Auntie Kealoha across the lawn and up the steps into the pagoda. From there, looking back you could take in the entire snow-white residence, whose size rivaled a small hotel. Auntie Kealoha settled in a high-backed wicker chair surrounded by baskets of plumeria, orchid blossoms, and other flowers. Several completed leis hung on pegs built into the pagoda railing. Tiny Maunakea wandered over to a koa desk on which sat a couple of telephones, a computer terminal, some stacks of paper and—apparently in honor of Tiny's Victorian sense and sensibilities—a Tiffany lamp that that likely cost more than my truck. He sat on a padded chair big enough to hold his bulk comfortably. My guess would be the chair had been built just for him.

"Please sit down," Auntie Kealoha said to me, motioning to a wicker chair of less grand proportions near hers. As I sat down, she picked up a nearly completed lei and began stringing flowers on it, the way some women on the Mainland might take up their knitting needles in front of a fireplace. This clearly was her spot in the world, a place where she spent a lot of time. Looking at Auntie Kealoha stringing flowers and Tiny Maunakea at his desk, I had the feeling that not much happened on Oahu that Auntie Kealoha didn't know about from this center of operations.

She seemed in no rush to get to the point of this meeting, humming to herself as she finished her lei. I felt a little embarrassed that I had not immediately recognized her when we arrived. For thirty years Auntie Bernice Kalakaua Kealoha headlined a Polynesian show in the Hibiscus Room of the Waikiki Sands Hotel at the foot of Diamond Head. She regularly performed with Don Ho, who treated her like a sister. When he popped into her club, they'd sing the "Hawaiian Wedding Song" together and then joke with the audience.

"In Hawaii," she'd tell the tourists, "I'm known as the female Don Ho. Actually, he's Don and I'm just a ho."

Like Don, Auntie Kealoha was politically connected, a friend of governors going back to the territorial days and all the power players in government and business. During campaign season, Auntie Kealoha provided free entertainment for all the major Democratic political fund-raisers, there being only about three Republicans in the whole state. At one fund-raiser in Aloha Stadium, thirty thousand people came out to support two candidates for Congress and the party nominee for governor. Actually, they came for the free concert set up by Auntie Kealoha featuring every major stage performer in Waikiki. All of the entertainers "volunteered" their services at these events because when Auntie Kealoha asked you to be someplace with your guitar, ukulele, or twenty-five-piece band, you were there. Or else you would find yourself entertaining on Guam.

But she hadn't performed in public regularly for years and I guess most of the photos or snippets of video you saw of her on TV were from the earlier days, usually when she was dressed for the stage. In person she looked like a generic sweet little old Hawaiian grandmother, her gray hair pulled back in a bun. It was hard to believe that she could also be the Godmother of Organized Crime. According to local legend, when two Las Vegas organized crime figures came to Hawaii in the early 1960s to collect gambling debts and perhaps get a operational foothold in the Islands, Auntie Kealoha had them killed, stuffed in a trunk, and returned to Vegas with a note that said, "Delicious. Send more."

A lovely dark-haired Asian woman in a flowered muumuu

came across the yard with a tray of refreshments. She put a cup of tea on the table at Auntie Kealoha's elbow and then poured a Budweiser from the bottle into a frosty mug and put it on the table beside me. Tiny Maunakea reached into a small refrigerator at his side that I hadn't noticed when we sat down and pulled out a can of Coke. A big man has to have his nutritional supplies close at hand. He went back to work tapping at the computer.

"There," Auntie Kealoha said, tying together the ends of the pink orchid lei. She hung it on a hook on the railing with several others and gave them all a spritz of water from a spray bottle. "It seems some days all I do is make lei, Mr. McBride."

She put the water bottle down and directed her full attention to me.

"I have fourteen grandchildren, seven great-grandchildren, and the children of too many nephews and nieces and hanai family to count," she said, "and they all seem to be graduating from something all the time. High school, elementary school, hula class . . . Why, did you know that they actually have ceremonies now for children graduating from kindergarten? Then there's outrigger canoe races, singing contests, birthdays, weddings—I'm surprised there are any flowers left on my estate."

"You make all your leis by hand?" I asked, feeling stupid as soon as I said it.

"Lei, Mr. McBride," she said. "The plural of lei in Hawaiian is lei. And, yes, I make them all myself. I couldn't imagine presenting a Chinatown lei or airport concession stand lei to friends or family. Some things are sacred to Hawaiians."

I lifted up the lei she had given me from my chest and smelled the yellow-tinted plumeria blossoms. I couldn't remember the last time someone put a lei over my head.

"Those flowers came from that tree over there. One of my favorites, more than sixty years old," she said. "I think plumeria trees get better with age. Their blossoms become more fragrant. I have a ranch on the Big Island with plumeria, hibiscus, ginger, protea, orchid, gardenia . . . it is glorious."

I wondered if everyone who visited her got a lei or just people of less than ideal comportment who had been jogging for a half hour in the hot sun before being kidnapped off the street. I also wondered when she was going to get around to telling me what I was doing there. I decided to push the issue.

"I appreciate your hospitality," I said, "but you really didn't need to send someone to, uh, pick me up. A phone call would have done the trick. I've got a driver's license and everything."

"Oh, I see, Mr. McBride," she said. "Was Mr. Maunakea less than civil in his invitation?" She looked over to the big man in question. He looked at her and then turned his head toward me with an expression that said he was extremely interested in hearing the next thing that came out of my mouth.

"He was a perfect gentleman," I said. "It's an honor to meet you. I only wish I could have been more presentable. And please call me Stryker."

That seemed to satisfy Tiny Maunakea. He went back to his computer, but I knew he was listening intently to everything we were saying. It was part of his line of work.

"Stryker, the next time I invite you over, I will give you time to don your best tuxedo," she said, "but time is something of the essence, and I thought we should meet. As you know, I am a businesswoman as well as an entertainer. I'm not ashamed to say that over the years I have managed to accumulate not only some wealth but a certain amount of, well, let's say . . . influence. With influence comes responsibility, and I'm sorry to say that some of the most distressing parts of my life have been when I have failed in that responsibility. In the Jake Stane affair, for instance. As a partner, though a silent partner, in Three Palms Security Services, it was my responsibility to make sure the operation was run correctly. I should have known about Jake Stane and his band of criminal associates, but I didn't. As a result, things got out of hand. People were hurt. Careers ruined. An innocent young woman was killed. While I think that in the aftermath, things were handled as best they could be considering all the various and diverse political, public, and law enforcement interests involved, I see the disgraceful Jake Stane episode, in a large part, as my fault. I have great resources at my disposal, and after the Three Palms fiasco I resolved to use them more proactively, to use my influence to try to stop unnecessary, shall we say, unpleasantness before it happened."

"Ma'am," I began, "I appreciate your feelings, but I don't hold you in any way accountable for what Jake Stane did to me. I—"

"Stryker," she interrupted. And when Auntie Kealoha interrupts you, you stay interrupted. I shut my mouth. She obviously had a monologue in mind, not a dialogue.

"One thing about you I find charming is your utter lack of self-awareness," she said. "You truly have no appreciation for how the public views you. Although you may have chosen to withdraw from society, to not capitalize on any celebrity that could have come from the Jake Stane affair, you weren't forgotten. In fact, your disappearance only heightened interest in you. You have become a reclusive man of mystery. A crime fighter struck down in his prime. A tragic hero."

I was going to kick my instep and say "aw shucks, ma'am" but wisely decided against it.

"Did you really think you could suddenly reappear in public and start asking questions at the medical examiner's office and the police station about a dead man and no one would notice?" she asked. "Did you think you could meet Jake Stane publicly in prison and it wouldn't get around? That people would not be interested? Did you think you could just walk into the main office of the state's largest private security firm, my company, and I wouldn't hear of it? That I and others wouldn't wonder why Stryker Mc-Bride is suddenly investigating the death of an old Chinese man in a taro patch? You have made a lot of people suddenly very nervous, Stryker."

It occurred to me that making people nervous was precisely what Amber Kam had wanted me to do. Her self-interest was moving up in Four Gates Enterprises, and a good way to do that would be to agitate the board of directors and the CEO by having a former fairly well known investigative reporter knocking around town asking questions about her grandfather's death. I understood what Auntie Kealoa meant about my lack of self-awareness. I thought having a tumble with Amber would balance out whatever her motive was for reaching out to me. Man, talk about not knowing the value of your brand.

Auntie Kealoha had paused for a few moments, as if to give me time to figure this all out. Then she continued.

"I knew Wai Lo Fat," Auntie Kealoha said. "He was respected among the Hawaiian people for his love of our culture. His wife was Hawaiian. His taro patch was a tribute to her. Four Gates Enterprises has financed a number of native Hawaiian projects and made educational scholarships available to Hawaiians. I was sad to hear of his death."

She took a sip of tea, but I knew it wasn't so I could get a few words in. She had the pagoda floor.

"I know Mr. Lo Fat's granddaughter asked you to investigate his death," she said. "Her grandfather, although a founder of Four Gates, did little to help her rise in the company. She knew that with his death, she would have even less influence. So she used the last bit of leverage she had to cause a stink so she could get a promotion within Four Gates. Which she did."

I suspected that Tiny Maunakea's access to sealed information and government records from his command center a few feet away rivaled Sue Darling's and that he, too, had examined the Four Gates incorporation documents.

"I don't want to hurt your feelings, Stryker, but now that Miss Kam has what she wants, I would not be surprised if any infatuation she had with you has evaporated."

How true, I thought. But I did get to leave a big sweat stain on the new leather chair in her office, so that was good.

"Now," she said sweetly, "let's talk about the visit you and Blue Ho'okane made to the taro patch."

I almost choked on my beer.

"Relax," she said. "I've talked to Blue about it. I've known him for twenty years. We've worked together on, you might say, projects of community interest from time to time."

It was rumored that some law enforcement agencies sometimes reached out to Auntie Kealoha when they were having a problem with certain criminal elements. It's said that after she allegedly sent those two Las Vegas gambling collectors home in a box, Mainland organized crime did not make another attempt to infiltrate Hawaii.

"Blue is impulsive," she said. "I can understand that when you told him about the taro thriving in Kahala while it was dying everywhere else on the island, he'd take immediate action. However, raiding the taro patch was unnecessary. If he had asked me, I would have let him take all the plants he wanted."

"He was afraid that if we started asking permission, the plants would have disappeared overnight," I said.

"The reason Blue Ho'okane was forced out of the police department was because his theory of running a criminal investigation was that it is always easier to ask for forgiveness than ask for permission," she said.

"I haven't talked to him since I finished the Pacific Cup sailboat race," I said. "What were the results of the tests on the plants we, uh, harvested?"

"They were a genetically modified species," she said. "Technically illegal. As a Hawaiian, I don't want to see our sacred kalo genetically manipulated, and I certainly don't want someone to claim legal ownership of taro. I had assumed that the University of Hawaii was merely using the Kahala taro patch as an agricultural laboratory, testing legal strains of taro. We provided a guard to the patch only for liability reasons because of our security contract with the university."

"What happens now?" I asked.

"You, Blue, the gentleman on Molokai who tested the

plants, and I currently are the only people who know that it is illegal taro growing in Kahala," she said. "That is, other than the people growing it. Blue wants to keep it that way for now, and I agree. There is a question of who was in charge of the genetic modification program. Was it someone in the university? Four Gates? Was it a partnership? Blue will make some . . . discreet . . . inquiries."

I guess she considered my bursting into the PPA offices and threatening lawsuits if my questions about the taro patch weren't answered being indiscreet.

"Stryker, are you satisfied with that course of action?" she asked.

"Sure."

"Are you satisfied that the death of Wai Lo Fat was accidental?"

"Pretty satisfied," I said. "There are still some toxicology tests that have to be completed."

"Are you planning to do anything to annoy Miss Kam because she hurt your feelings?"

"She didn't hurt—" I began and then checked myself. "No. Amber and I are no longer an item."

"You understand that you are not as anonymous as you thought? You understand that when you ask questions around town about dead people and that when you meet with prison inmates who later kill themselves, that makes people nervous?"

"I do now," I said, although I didn't like the way she insinuated that Jake Stane killed himself because of our meeting.

"It was a pleasure meeting you, Stryker," she said. "If you ever need anything, please ask. Mr. Maunakea will give you a contact number. Please don't share it with others. And if you intend to continue to associate with Blue Ho'okane, please try to pick up his good habits. He does have a few."

"Blue and I mainly just surf together occasionally," I said.

"Good," she said. "The thought of you two scamps running around town together is frankly unsettling."

Tiny Maunakea stood up, an apparent signal that the meeting was over. Since we all had been getting along so well together and my inhibitions had been somewhat suppressed by Budweiser, I thought I might try to pin down one urban legend before we broke up.

"Could I ask you one question before I go?"

"Yes, of course," she said.

"I really hope this does not insult you in any way, but the story, the myth really, about the two Las Vegas gangsters who came to Hawaii and got sent back in a trunk with a note that said, 'Delicious. Send more' . . . Is that true?"

She smiled sweetly at me, a kindly Hawaiian grandmother smile.

"Of course not," she said. "Don't be silly."

Then, as I began to walk down the pagoda steps, she said, "Two gangsters? My word! There was just the one, dear."

Chapter Twenty-two

I helped myself to another beer in the back of the limo. I had to say I was enjoying myself. Hanging out with Tiny Maunakea and Auntie Kealoha was a lot more fun than a kick in the head. At least, so far.

On the ride home I sat up closer to the driver's compartment so I could chat with Tiny Maunakea without a megaphone. He wasn't such a scary guy once you knew he wasn't going to kill you. And I could get used to this kind of transportation. If there was another passenger, we could have played tennis back there.

"Auntie Kealoha is an amazing woman," I said. "Have you worked for her long?"

"Alas, I am restrained by internal company policy from discussing my employment with Auntie Kealoha," he said.

"Can you tell me a little more about the . . . Hung Bang Whatsit Society?" I said.

"Hung Bang Kongsi," he said. "It goes back to ancient China, when warlords ruled and treated the populace with undo cruelty. These societies developed as underground 'self-help' organizations. They provided food, medical care, financial aid, and a limited amount of security to the peasant class. When Chinese came to Hawaii, the Hung Bang Kongsi acted as something of a shadow government, providing services not provided by the territorial government and private businesses."

"It's still around today?"

"Yes, but more as a social and cultural organization," he said. "The Blue Lotus Society is the cultural face of the Hung Bang Kongsi, with its annual pageant and various public service activities."

"The pageant?" I asked. "You mean the one Amber Kam won to become the Blue Lotus Blossom Queen in high school?"

"Alas, yes," he said.

"You know Amber?" I asked.

"Only to abhor her from afar," he said. "Waianae High School was my alma mater. A cousin of mine entered that pageant in that particular year. I suspect the judges perceived my cousin's blood to be too heavily tainted with Hawaiian, rendering her unfit to wear the Blue Lotus Blossom tiara."

"But Amber Kam is part Hawaiian," I said.

"No doubt, but it is a matter of degree," he said. "Also, to be sure, in the history of the Blue Lotus Blossom pageant, no winner has ever come from the ranks of rural public schools. I rejoice that my cousin failed in her quest. I find the winners of all such contests to be strange, offensive creatures, and Amber Kam one of the most offensive."

Amber Kam certainly wasn't going to be named Miss Congeniality in this particular limousine.

"So her grandfather Wai Lo Fat must have been part of the Hung Bang Kongsi," I said.

"Yes, he was one of the venerable elders of the society," he said. "He is the second venerable elder of the Hung Bang Kongsi to pass away recently."

"What?" I asked, suddenly stunned. Two elders of this ancient secret society died recently? "What was his name?"

"Chin Chen Yu," he said. "A great man in the Chinese community in Hawaii, but one with some somewhat, I daresay, controversial aspects to his life. His funeral service was attended by the governor and other dignitaries."

"What was controversial about his life?" I asked.

"I'm afraid our trip will not be long enough to allow me to elucidate the details of his various interests," he said. "Chinese culture has been likened to an onion with its many layers. I will just say that he was reputed to be involved in the Chinese underworld both in Hawaii and in Hong Kong, and he had some associations other than with the Hung Bang Kongsi that the U.S. government apparently found useful."

I suspected that the Chinese enjoyed weaving elements of mystery and secrets into stories about their culture just to annoy Westerners. American society is pretty fucking complicated itself, with secret rules and alliances. How else do you explain how people from the same freakin' families keep getting elected president every four years? There has to be a wider pool of potential presidents than Adamses, Roosevelts, and Bushes.

"You said Danny Chang is a member of the Hung Bang Kongsi," I said. "Is he high up in the organization?"

"I have been attempting to ascertain that myself," he said. "He seems lately to have achieved an increase in influence. I daresay it is possible that with the deaths of Wai Lo Fat and Chin Chen Yu, there may be some opportunities for advancement of enterprising individuals within the organization."

"So you're keeping an eye on him?"

"As Auntie Kealoha related to you, she believes she has a responsibility because of her stature and influence in the community to endeavor to keep situations from getting out of control. Danny Chang is new to Hawaii and not as sensitive to the nuances of life on a small island as he might be. His meeting with you at Sandy Beach, for instance, was ill-advised and somewhat rash."

"You know about what happened between Danny and me?"

"Just that it was a rather short, dramatic meeting," he said. I think he was trying to be funny.

"Are you Hung Bang Kongsi?" I asked.

"No, my Asian antecedents came from northern China," he said. "Most Chinese immigrants to Hawaii came from southern or central China. Still, the Chinese community is relatively small in Hawaii, so it would be quite unusual if I did not have associates within the Hung Bang Kongsi."

A tennis tournament on the two Bayview Yacht Club courts came to a complete standstill when Tiny Maunakea drove the massive black limo through the gates. The geezers on the courts stood with their rackets at ease and gaped as I emerged from the beast. Before I shut the door, Tiny leaned back and handed me a business card through the partition to the passenger cabin.

"Now that you no longer have an interest in the taro patch, I suspect Danny Chang no longer has an interest in you," he said. "However, if you feel he represents some manner of continuing threat to you, call me at that number any time of the day or night. As I stated before, I suspect my path inevitably will cross the path of Mr. Chang. With people of his temperament and questionable wisdom, it always does—and Auntie Kealoha does not want you put in harm's way anew."

Chapter Twenty-three

When I got back to the *Travis McGee* after my forced audience with Auntie Kealoha, there was a message from Dr. Melba McCall on the answering machine. She'd decided to take me up on the invitation to drop by for a drink. She'd be here at about three that afternoon. That seemed kind of odd. When I asked her to drop by and have a drink with me, we hadn't spoken of a specific day or time. Now she was just assuming that I had nothing going on and would be available at three. I mean, I would. I had more than an hour to get ready. Still, it's kind of rude to just assume a guy doesn't have other things happening in his life. Maybe I'd get kidnapped again if I stepped off the property.

As I washed off in the small shower stall in the master bedroom bath—only cold water, since it came from one of the club's lawn hoses attached to the master external water hookup on the side of the boat—I thought about Tiny Maunakea's remark that his path inevitably crosses with people like Danny Chang, people of questionable temperament and wisdom. Was that what happened with Three Man Stone? Had Tiny monitored Three Man Stone's activities as he blundered around on the periphery of the Honolulu underworld until the giant Tongan caused a crime war and Tiny had no choice but to take him out? From what I knew years after the events, my main suspect in the murder of Franky Five Fins was Three Man Stone. Would the order for the hit on Three Man Stone come explicitly from Auntie Kealoha? Probably not, I thought. Watching her humming to herself while stringing orchid lei on the pagoda while Tiny tapped away contentedly on his computer at the koa desk, I sensed that the two of them had developed such a close symbiotic relationship over the years that they knew each other's thoughts. Three Man Stone had fucked up and so he had to go. Was Danny Chang headed down that same dead-end road?

I appreciated Tiny's offer of help should Dragon Boy show any further interest in me. I had no desire to be put in harm's way anew, as Tiny put it. Danny Chang had gotten the upper hand—or at least an upper foot—on me at Sandy Beach. He had chosen the time of that encounter, and I had prepared no contingency plan for such an attack. I ended up just having to take my lumps. Although I wasn't particularly looking forward to it, I knew I'd run into Danny Chang again. Now that I had Tiny Maunakea's business card stuck to the cork board over my desk, there seemed to be a number of pleasant possibilities.

I told myself that Dr. McCall's visit wasn't a date or anything. But it would be the first time a member of the fairer sex had dropped by to have a drink with me for, well, probably since the premed students graced my vessel. I wasn't expecting that Dr. McCall and I would end up in the hot tub, but I did spiff up the place a bit and make sure there was no dirty underwear hanging from the light fixtures and things like that; Make it look less like a Bangladeshi jail and more like a three-hundred thousand dollar houseboat.

By 3:00 P.M. she hadn't shown up, and I was on the couch watching Geraldo Rivera on TV. Geraldo had thoughtfully invited to his stage members of a radical black activist organization and a group of Ku Klux Klan members. The KKK guys were wearing red robes instead of white for some reason. Maybe those were their "away" jerseys, like visiting football teams wear. I was pretty sure someone was going to be severely injured for the sake of TV ratings, and I was hoping it was Geraldo. I had read somewhere that around A.D. 160 the Roman Emperor Commodos filled the Coliseum with cripples, dwarves, and freaks and made them fight to the death with meat cleavers. Emperor Commodos was sort of the Geraldo Rivera of his day.

Before the battle began on *Geraldo*, I heard the gods yapping at the bottom of the stairs that lead to the *Travis McGee*'s rear deck. I turned off the television and walked outside. Kane and Lono were dancing all around the doctor, who was holding a laptop computer in one hand and a small silver-colored metal case in the other.

Dr. McCall apparently had been around boats enough to know that you just don't trudge on board a boat, even if it is landlocked, without asking first.

"Permission to come aboard, big fella?"

"Come on up," I said. "Need a hand?"

"Nope, I'm good," she said, ascending the stairs. When I'd realized that the *Travis McGee* might be stuck on land for quite a while, I'd built a nice wide set of wooden steps leading from the lawn to the deck. The gods beat her up the stairs and headed for a cool spot under the aft deck awning.

Melba McCall was wearing khaki slacks and a yellow knit shirt instead of the blue pajamas I last saw her in. I guess this was her "away" uniform. Instead of her dark hair being pulled back in a ponytail, it had been set free. She looked amazingly fetching. I had forgotten what a knockout she actually was.

"Welcome, Doctor," I said. "Can I get you a drink?"

"Only if you call me Melba instead of Doctor," she said. We walked into the day room.

"What will it be, Melba, beer, wine, gin and tonic?"

"Whatever you're having," she said, putting her gear on the coffee table. "I didn't mean to barge in like this. I hoped we could have met at my office."

That sounded like this was more business than pleasure. And it explained the computer and luggage. I had called her a few days earlier and told her to forward any toxicology reports directly to Amber, that I was no longer involved in anything to do with the death of Wai Lo Fat, but it looked like she had brought the reports with her, anyway.

I poured two nice chardonnays into a pair of my better wineglasses at the wet bar and carried them over to the couch. She had opened the silver metal case, revealing a digital microscope that she was busy plugging into the laptop. I handed her a glass of wine and said, "Cheers."

She clinked glasses with me, took a sip, and put the glass on the coffee table.

"Now, stick out your hand," she said.

Before I could ask her what this was all about she had poked my index finger with some hellishly sharp object that made a bubble of blood on the tip. She sucked up the blood with a little glass tube and transferred it onto a microscope slide. Then she put the slide in the microscope and fiddled with the computer mouse until an image came on the screen. She fiddled with the mouse some more until the picture became clear. It was my blood. I'd recognize it anywhere.

"Do you always test the blood of men you drop by to have a drink with?" I asked.

"We can't get great magnification with this microscope, but it should be all right," she said, ignoring my comment. I watched the screen as she increased the magnification until we could see the red and white blood cells.

"I'm sorry," she said. "What did you say?"

"I said, is this how you screen your dates?"

"Just want to make sure there's nothing funny going on in your blood, Stryker," she said looking at the screen. Then she turned to me and said, "There isn't."

She took the slide out of the microscope and placed it and the glass tube in a small envelope with the universal HAZARDOUS MEDICAL MATERIAL icon on it. Then she put that in the metal box with the microscope and sat back.

"Good," she said.

"Yeah, I didn't cry or anything," I said.

"No, I mean the wine is good," she said, taking another sip. "I'm no wine aficionado, but I like it."

"Safeway's Best," I said. "What's all this blood test stuff about?"

"You did visit the site where Mr. Lo Fat died, right?" she asked.

"Yeah, in the taro patch. Why?"

"I was worried there might be some bacteria or virus there that could be picked up and end up in the blood," she said. "Are you familiar with viruses, how they work, how they travel, and all that?"

"I was in the Peace Corps in Sierra Leone in 1984," I said. "I think there were some cases of Ebola in some of the outlying villages, but most of the health problems were just dysentery and worms, that kind of thing."

"I was in the Congo for a year with an international health organization," she said.

"Coroners Without Borders?" I asked.

"Something like that," she said, smiling. "Forensic pathologists looking at Ebola and some of the other viruses that seem to come out of the jungle from time to time."

"Wai Lo Fat had Ebola?" I asked.

"No, but in my preliminary workup, I noticed some kind of virus in his blood," she said. "Not enough to kill him. So I stuck with my preliminary findings that he had died of asphyxia due to drowning in the taro patch water."

She went on to say that she sent some of Lo Fat's blood off to a friend of hers, a doctor who specializes in viruses.

"It took a while, but he just got back to me and said the virus cells in Wai Lo Fat were Asian bird flu," she said. "The Asian bird flu has never been documented in the United States. It's been confined to Vietnam and Southeast Asia. Some in China. The weird thing is that the Asian bird flu cells were broken and deformed. My associate said they were dead."

"So, in other words, Wai Lo Fat did drown," I said.

"No, that's what so amazing," she said. "My friend did a whole workup on the blood I sent him, and it turns out that Mr. Lo Fat died from a cytokine storm."

"A what-kinda-storm?"

"Cytokine storm," she said. "It gets kind of complicated here. Kind of sci-fi. Cytokines are small proteins that are secreted by certain cells in the body's immune system.

They are signaling cells, alerting other cells in the immune system that the body is under attack by a virus. Cytokine proteins tell immune cells, like T-cells and macrophages, to travel to the site of the infection. It's part of the body's normal defensive mechanism. But in some cases, the signals to the immune cells create a massive feedback loop, causing the creation of more cytokine cells, which cause an exaggerated response to the danger, sending even more immune cells into battle. It creates what they call a cytokine storm. If the cytokine storm takes place in the lungs, fluids can eventually block off the airways, resulting in death. Initial symptoms of a cytokine storm are high fever, extreme fatigue, nausea—something you might think is a flu bug."

"Wai Lo Fat might not have known he was that sick and gone for his usual walk in the taro patch," I said.

"Yep. Then, when his airway was blocked, he fell into the water," she said. "I was looking for asphyxia from fluids blocking the air passage, and I found it. Unfortunately, I thought it was the taro water that killed him."

The gods were feeling left out, I guess, because they started panting at the screen door. I let them in and then topped off our wine.

"The strange thing is that Mr. Lo Fat's immune system went to war with a threat that didn't exist," Dr. McCall said, continuing her story. "There weren't enough avian flu virus cells to hurt him. Another strange thing was that the dead bird flu cells looked like they had been genetically altered."

"That's interesting, because it turns out that the taro in that field had been genetically altered," I said.

"That wouldn't have anything to do with the bird flu

virus," she said, thoughtlessly quashing my "Aha!" moment. "Genetically modifying viruses has to be done in a quarantined lab under carefully controlled clinical conditions. It's the kind of very expensive research and development that can only be done by a government-sized program. These might have been specifically engineered on the sub-DNA level—and when a government starts genetically modifying viruses, they are doing it for only one reason."

I was afraid to wade again into the conversation for fear of another rebuke, but I gave it a shot.

"Biological warfare?"

"Yep. My buddy thinks those avian flu cells might be weaponized. That's pretty interesting."

I understand the stoic nature of the scientific mind, but I thought the doctor was being way too nonchalant about all this weaponized avian flu business.

"Uh, Melba, don't you think you should call somebody besides your doctor buddy? The Centers for Disease Control in Atlanta, for instance? The FBI? Eli Lilly?" I asked. "I mean, if this is the first Asian bird flu seen in the United States and it looks like it's been designed to kill people, isn't that kind of a big deal?"

"Maybe. Maybe not," she said, taking a sip of wine. "Like I said, all the cells were dead, broken. There's no way to tell how long they were in his system. Or how they got there. Maybe lots of people have them."

"So you tested me," I said.

"I tested myself, too," she said. "And others at my office. I thought maybe there had been an accidental release of a weaponized virus on the island from one of the military labs. I know the military in Hawaii has some nukes stashed; maybe they've got labs here working on viruses. Heck, they didn't even have to come from Hawaii. Up at Johnston Island the U.S. military has a facility to destroy Agent Orange, nerve gases, and probably biological weapons left over from the Cold War. They burn them up in fancy incinerators up there. It's only seven hundred miles southwest of Oahu. There could have been an accidental release of dead pathogens that carried on the winds here. If so, it wasn't a major accident, because we didn't have a lot of people here getting sick or dying. I'm not ready to announce a public health emergency."

"So you just came out here to tell me not to worry about something that I didn't even need to know?" I said.

"Yep. Well, I wanted to see your boat, too" she said, standing up with her wine and walking to the galley and then looking down the hallway to the bedrooms. "Nice. It's huge. What's the thing with men about boats and penises? Why are they so hung up on size?"

Many witty retorts didn't come to mind, so I was happy when she smiled at me and I realized her question had been rhetorical in nature, a jest. There just aren't enough funny medical examiners out there.

"At my office, you said it was Mr. Lo Fat's granddaughter who asked you to look into his death," she said. "Did she take you on a tour of the taro patch? Show you where he died?"

"Yeah. Amber Kam is her name," I said.

"I'd like to test Miss Kam just to ease my mind, and maybe take a sample of the water from the taro patch itself," she said. "Make sure this isn't something connected to that specific area."

"It would take more than weaponized pathogens to stop Amber Kam," I said flatly.

"Ooooh, someone sounds a little bitter," she said. "She break your heart or something?"

"Or something," I said.

"Like I said, I don't want to turn this into a big health crisis, but I would like to test Amber's blood. Can you tell me how to get hold of her?"

"Sure," I said. "And when you poke her with that sharp needle thingie, tell her I sent you."

Chapter Twenty-four

Dr. Melba McCall may have a stoic, scientific mind, but I don't suffer from that affliction. I was blessed with a hyperactive imagination that enables me to metastasize a common insect bite into a cancerous lesion in two seconds flat. I was the guy who invented *pre*-traumatic stress syndrome and then engrossed myself in it for the better part of a year. So it was a good sign that after Dr. McCall departed, I wasn't bedridden for the rest of the afternoon with visions of weaponized viruses dancing in my head. Had the chief city medical examiner made a personal house call a year and a half earlier, taken my blood, and filled my brain with images of Ebola, bird flu, Agent Orange, and something-kine storms . . . well, I might have locked myself in my tiny shower stall with a bottle of Absolut vodka for a few weeks.

As it turned out, all it took was another bottle of chardonnay to put me into a relaxed, philosophic frame of mind. I decided maybe hypochondria was a young man's game and I simply didn't have the energy anymore to engage in it.

I wasn't ready to give up on thinking that there was more to Wai Lo Fat's death than a drowning or even the result of a bizarre, yet apparently natural, immune system gone wild. The thing that kept coming back to me was Tiny Maunakea saying that Wai Lo Fat was just one of two elders of the Hung Bang Kongsi who had died recently. I like coincidences as much as the next guy, but I like conspiracies even better. Or at least connections. I didn't think it would be going against Auntie Kealoha's wishes if I kept a low profile and out of trouble while I found out about the other old Chinese guy who died, Chin something or other.

After going through three weeks' worth of the obituary sections from *Advertiser*s and *Journal*s in the Longhouse newspaper stacks and the online edition of both papers, I finally came across a feature obit for Chin Chen Yu online. He was described as a wealthy Chinese businessman who had passed away quietly in his sleep at the age of ninety-two. He had died exactly two weeks before Wai Lo Fat. His obit was longer than Wai Lo Fat's and also contained a photo taken at the memorial service, apparently at the same Chinese temple. Nowhere in the obit did it mention the Hung Bang Kongsi or even hint that Chin Chen Yu might have been involved in some criminal activity, as suggested by Tiny Maunakea. The memorial service photo on the computer was too small to make out all the people in it. Like Wai Lo Fat's memorial photo, it was a shot of a huge group of people standing looking directly into the camera, like just about any high school yearbook football team photo. There was a huge banner behind the group with Chinese characters that I suspected did not read NOTRE DAME FIGHTING IRISH, 1963.

I decided I'd like to get copies of both memorial service photos in higher definition and take a look at exactly who was in them. Tiny Maunakea had said there were some dignitaries at Chin Chen Yu's funeral, including the governor. I looked on the masthead of the *Journal* and saw that Leanne McMillian, who had been an assistant managing editor when I was at the paper, was now the full-blown managing editor. We had always had a good relationship. I thought I'd give her a call, see if she could get me copies of the photos and at the same time maybe tell me if Burl Morse still worked at the paper and how I could get hold of him. My mellowness toward him following the Pacific Cup race was still intact, but I decided I needed to have a face-to-face with him anyway.

I arranged to meet Leanne that Friday at a Starbucks well away from the news building, which is to say about fourteen Starbucks away. I didn't think marching into the newsroom could be considered keeping a low profile. I knew Leanne McMillian would keep our meeting at Starbucks to herself. I was told she actually visited me in the hospital a few times when I was taking the long nap.

She was already in Starbucks when I arrived. I parked out front and instinctively looked up and down the street for a black SUV. I hadn't seen it since Sandy Beach, so Danny Chang apparently had lost interest in me. Leanne was a heavyset lady of about fifty who looked like everyone's auntie, provided everyone's auntie looked like Ethel Merman. She had a husky voice honed from the days when reporters not only could smoke cigarettes at their desks, but I think it was mandatory. I knew she had also been a big fan of good whiskeys. Leanne had left her cigarette and whiskey days behind her, but the gravelly voice was still there.

"Stryker!" she said, hugging me like a trained bear. "You look great! How are you? I was so happy to hear from you!"

I hugged her back and mumbled that I was good. Like I've said, I'm not used to people being happy to see me.

We made small talk for a few minutes while we drank our coffee. She could see I didn't want to talk about the old days, and she seemed undisturbed that I was pretty vague about what I had been up to lately. I congratulated her on her promotion to ME, a post she was born for. She's a natural leader and an excellent editor with a track record as a reporter that included a string of national writing awards just short of a Pulitzer Prize.

"Here's the eight-by-tens of the photos you wanted of the two Chinese memorial services," she said, sliding a manila envelope across the table. Being a reporter at heart, it was not surprising that she asked me why I wanted them. She had been so good to me over the years that I did what gratitude compelled me to do: I lied.

"They're for friends of the families," I said.

She knew I was lying and understood my lie to mean, "Look, I'm working on something, but I can't tell you about it right now. Don't bug me."

I was more forthcoming when I brought up Burl Morse.

"Is he still working at the paper?" I asked.

"No. After your . . . your . . . I'm sorry, Stryker, I don't even know what to call what happened to you," she said.

"It was just a thing," I said.

"Okay, after your, uh, thing, we had to let Morse go. His drinking got worse. He was really a mess," she said. "When he showed up for work he usually screwed something up. Then he got arrested for DUI. We had a photographer down at the cop shop to grab a photo of a guy arrested for murder. You know how they handcuff all the prisoners together when they lead them out of the police station to go to court in the morning? Guess who was unlucky enough to be handcuffed to the murderer on the day the *Journal* had a photographer down at the cellblock?"

"Burl Morse?" I asked.

"We had to crop the photo to keep him out of the paper," she said. "After that he was done here. Stryker, did Burl have anything to do with what happened to you?"

"Leanne, this is just between us. Okay?" She nodded. "It was Burl who gave the cop who shot me a copy of the story I was working on. That's how the cop managed to set Jeannie Kai and me up."

"Oh, no!" she said, putting a hand over her mouth. "My God, Stryker, I'm so sorry."

"You have nothing to be sorry for."

"But the newspaper was responsible for—"

"I got a good settlement from the paper, and Burl's name never even came up," I said. "It's in the past. Or almost. I just want to see him so I can put the . . . thing . . . completely behind me."

"The last I heard he was living at the YMCA on North Hotel Street," she said. "He was going downhill fast. Now I know why."

There was a silence that lasted just a little too long while we showed unnatural interest in our coffee. Then Leanne suddenly laughed quietly to herself. I looked up.

"What's funny?"

"Just now when you asked about Burl, after I gave you the photos of the Chinese funerals, I thought you wanted to find Burl in connection with those," she said.

"Why?"

"Because, in his early days at the paper, before he became a drunk, he was kind of our expert on the Chinese community," she said. "He wrote some amazing pieces about life in Chinatown. He even speaks Chinese."

"I didn't know that, and I'm not looking for Burl's help on anything," I said. "I just want to let him know I know it was him who set me up. I don't want to give him the pleasure of going through the rest of his life thinking I was clueless."

Leanne and I went through some pointless chitchat after that, both of us wanting to get out of Dodge. I'm sure she felt that as assistant managing editor at the time of the shooting, she should have known more about what the staff was up to. Now she felt embarrassed, even though she didn't need to. I had purposely kept the higher-ups at the paper out of the loop on the Jake Stane investigation, assuming that only the city editor had access to my work.

Leanne and I hugged again outside the coffee shop and promised to see each other before too long. But I had the feeling that—just from the little I told her about Burl—Leanne McMillian was pining for a cigarette and a shot of Makers Mark and was hoping I wouldn't bother her again anytime soon.

Chapter Twenty-five

The YMCA was located in an old, refurbished three-story Honolulu office building. The building was kind of a landmark with its graceful colonial architecture and a large swimming pool in an open courtyard. I had never been inside, but I assumed it would be a kind of seedy flophouse place, the way YMCAs are portrayed in old movies.

So as I entered I was surprised to find it was clean and modern, with a large, open ceramic-tiled lobby and granite-topped registration counter. It was more like a hotel than a flophouse, and the lobby was not littered with creepy old men trying to make friends with young boys looking for a cheap room for a few nights.

The lady behind the counter, a perky young surfer girl with blond hair, told me that Burl Morse had not lived at the YMCA for several months. She leaned forward conspiratorially and in a low voice said, "He stopped paying his rent, and people complained because he didn't bathe."

The last she had heard he was living in a homeless shelter down on Dillingham Boulevard. I climbed back into my truck, wondering whether a whole "Where's Waldo" search for Burl Morse was worth it. How far are you expected to go to tie up loose ends?

But the homeless shelter was only about a mile away, so I continued my quest. This particular homeless shelter was well known and one of the first in Honolulu. It was referred to as the Spam and Eggs Ministry because it was run by an Anglican minister and was a place where anyone down on their luck could at least get a hot meal and a mattress to sleep on until they were on their feet again.

I got there just at lunchtime, apparently. There was a long line of people standing with trays waiting to be served cafeteria style.

"Are you hungry, brother?" a small, bent white-haired man asked, touching my elbow. "The line moves along rather quickly, you'll find."

I recognized him from his pictures in the papers. He was Father McGreggor, founder and proprietor of the Spam and Eggs Ministry.

"No, I'm fine," I said. I appreciated his kindness but wasn't real happy with the implication that I looked like I needed to be fed. It's somewhat disheartening to be confused with people who sleep under bridges and drink Old Overcoat for breakfast. I sleep on a boat and I'm a Bud man.

I looked around the room. There must have been a couple of hundred people sitting at long school-cafeteria-type tables, eating lunch. Off in a corner at the end of one table, I noticed the hunched-over figure of Burl Morse. I walked over and sat opposite him.

"How you doing there, Burl?" I asked.

He looked up slowly from lunch, which, appropriately, turned out to be a couple of Spam slices and scrambled eggs. He looked sickly yellow—what doctors in the old days might have called "liverish"—with about three days' worth of stubble on his sunken cheeks. I figured he was only a couple of years older than me, but he looked like an old man.

"Stryker," he said hoarsely by way of acknowledgment, taking a sip of milk from a small carton. If my appearance was a surprise, he didn't show it. "You here to beat me up or something?"

"I've thought about it," I said.

"Will you let me finish eating first?" he asked.

He was wearing a plaid long-sleeved shirt that was glossy from being lived in continuously. The smell of stale alcohol radiated from him.

"I'm not going to hurt you, Burl," I said. "I just wanted you to know that I know what you did. That you gave Jake Stane a copy of my bar security story. From that he was able to lure Jeannie Kai and me to the waterfront and get us out on that boat. You know what happened after that."

"I never meant for you to get hurt, Stryker," he said, "and I was awful sorry to hear that the lady cop got killed. That was pretty much the end of my life, too, right there. Officer Stane had his claws into me . . . he forced me to . . . well, I let him."

"You know that Jake Stane is dead?"

"I saw that he died," he said, straightening up. "I still read the papers."

He took a bite of eggs and chewed slowly. I felt kind of sick. I don't care how bad a man is, when you see him eat, it reminds you that he's just another human trying to survive. From the looks of Burl Morse, he wouldn't be around much longer. I had come ready to hate him, and now I felt nothing but pity. It seems kind of unfair when villains rob you of your chance to hate them. I wasn't sure what else to say. There was nothing I could do to make Burl Morse's life any more miserable than it was right then. I didn't even want to. Not anymore.

He put down his plastic fork and looked at me with sad, watery eyes.

"I was a hell of a newspaperman once, Stryker," he said. "I broke some big stories before you came to the *Journal*. I should never have gone on the desk. You go on the desk and everyone forgets that you were a good reporter. I hit the bottle pretty hard. Still do when I can get it. I admit that I was a little jealous of you. You came on like gangbusters from the Mainland, breaking big stories all over the place. You never saw me in my prime."

He looked around the room slowly.

"And this isn't it," he said, with the smallest of smiles.

I realized that the whole time I worked at the newspaper I never really had a discussion with Morse that wasn't about work. When he was an assistant city editor on the desk, I usually tried to go around him and work with the city editor directly. When he became night city editor, he became a nonperson, like all night desk men. I had had absolutely no interest in him as a person. That didn't give him an excuse to do what he did, but I did understand our different perspectives. I decided I needed to say something to make him feel, I don't know, relevant. I remembered what Leanne McMillian said about him being kind of an expert on the Chinese community.

"I've been looking into the death of an old Chinese guy, Wai Lo Fat," I said.

"The guy who drowned in Kahala," he said.

I was impressed. He did still read the papers. And carefully. There were only a few places in the coverage of Wai Lo Fat's death that mentioned he had drowned.

"You know what was interesting about his death?" he asked. "Just two weeks before that, another old Chinese man died. His name was Chin Chen Yu. They were both members of the Hung Bang Kongsi."

That threw me. This asshole nearly got me killed, but he knew his Chinese stuff.

"You know about the Hung Bang Kongsi?" I asked.

"I wrote a huge piece on the Chinese community on the hundred and twenty-fifth anniversary of their arrival in Hawaii," he said. "I interviewed a lot of people. Lived with them, practically. That's the way I did things back then. The Chinese had these so-called secret societies, going back to their home country. When they got to Hawaii, they continued membership in them."

He sat up a little straighter. He could see I was legitimately interested in what he was saying. And it made him feel better.

"Everyone in the Chinese community knows of the Hung Bang Kongsi. The Hung Bang Kongsi was made up of a core group of immigrants from the same part of China. Southern, I think. Elders of the Hung Bang Kongsi settled disputes among the Chinese in Hawaii. Arranged marriages. Oversaw investments. They formed companies and banks and even their own newspapers. Anything the white establishment kept them from doing, the Hung Bang Kongsi did for the Chinese in the Islands."

"A Chinese-Hawaiian guy was just telling me about the Hung Bang Kongsi just the other day," I said.

"Here's something I bet he didn't tell you," he said,

leaning forward. "Inside the Hung Bang Kongsi is another organization. It's called the Lodge of the Inner Eight. I'm probably the only haole in Hawaii who knows about it. An old Chinese woman told me. The Lodge of the Inner Eight was eight members of the Hung Bang Kongsi, formed just after World War II. They are the real power behind the Hung Bang Kongsi and the real power behind any commercial activities the Hung Bang Kongsi is involved with in Hawaii."

I thought about what Tiny Maunakea had told me about there being Chinese groups within groups, like layers of an onion.

"Wai Lo Fat worked at a company called Four Gates Enterprises," I said. "It developed all of Kahala."

"The Lodge of the Inner Eight developed Kahala," he said. "Four Gates was just the front company, along with many others."

"So you think Wai Lo Fat was a member of the Lodge of the Inner Eight?" I asked.

"I know he was," he said, "and so was Chin Chen Yu. Now, here's an interesting thing: Unlike the Hung Bang Kongsi, the Lodge of the Inner Eight does not accept new members. When lodge members die, they're gone and nobody takes their place."

"How many are left now?"

"For the past fifteen years, there were only three members of the Lodge of the Inner Eight left," he said. "Wai Lo Fat, Chin Chen Yu, and So Young Hee. Now there is only So Young Hee."

"Do you know him?"

"No, all I know is what the old Chinese lady told me a

long time ago," he said. "That the lodge exists and who its members are. Or were."

"Do you think Wai Lo Fat and the other guy, Chin Chen Yu, might have been killed on purpose?" I asked.

"Why? Was there anything suspicious about Wai Lo Fat's death?"

"I can only say that there is an odd twist to his death that I just found out about yesterday," I said.

"Wai Lo Fat and Chin Chen Yu were both very old," he said. "They probably just died from old age. Now they're walking Kahala Road."

"What does that mean? Walking Kahala Road?"

"It's just an expression among the older Chinese in Hawaii. It means death. Walking Kahala Road. It's like crossing the River Styx."

He stood up unsteadily and picked up his tray.

"Look, Stryker, I've got stuff to do," he said. "If you aren't going to beat me up, I've got to go."

I could see his pants now; they were dirtier than his shirt, crusted with oily grime, almost like they were made of plastic. He saw me looking at them.

"My other suit is at the dry cleaner's," he said, again with almost a smile.

He shuffled away toward a bank of rubbish cans at the back of the hall. I almost called out, "Take care of yourself," but I could see it was too late for that.

Chapter Twenty-six

That night I walked the piers with Kane and Lono, feeling depressed after finding Burl Morse at the homeless shelter. Depressed and a little put out that I was cheated out of being able to hate the guy who almost got me killed. The man had fallen and fallen hard. I gave him just a few months to live, if what he was doing was called living.

I was impressed by his knowledge of the Chinese community, but there was even something depressing about that. He wanted to show off how much he knew about the Hung Bang Kongsi, as if simply knowing something I didn't automatically conferred some dignity and respectability upon him. I had brought up the death of Wai Lo Fat because I wanted him to feel relevant, and in the end, he felt superior, even to the point of cutting off our conversation and saying he had something else to do. Then he stood up and saw through my eyes how pathetic he looked in his filthy shirt and plastic pants.

What he had said about there being a subgroup of the Hung Bang Kongsi called the Lodge of the Inner Eight was interesting. With the death of Wai Lo Fat and Chin

Chen Yu, there was only one member of the Lodge of the Inner Eight left. Since I wasn't taking notes, that gentleman's name went right out of my head. But if it was true that there was a Lodge of the Inner Eight and it controlled Four Gates then the one remaining lodge member was solely in charge of a billion-dollar enterprise. The members of the Lodge of the Inner Eight must have been the private shareholders who appointed the Four Gates board of directors and the chief executive officer, the people that Sue Darling had not been able to find on the incorporation documents.

When I had gone to find Burl, I hadn't taken the two photographs of the Chinese funerals with me. I bet Burl could have told me some interesting things about the people in the pictures.

The photos looked almost identical, two large groups of mostly Chinese men standing in front of an ornate mausoleum at one of the oldest Chinese cemeteries in Honolulu. It was the same big banner with the Chinese characters behind both groups. One difference was that at Chin Chen Yu's memorial there were more people in the picture, including Governor Joshua "Kimo" Anderson and a middle-aged haole man in some kind of military uniform. The main difference between the two pictures was that at Chin Chen Yu's memorial, there were two elderly Chinese men seated in chairs in the middle of the picture. They were obviously guests of honor. In the photo of Wai Lo Fat's memorial, there was only one elderly Chinese man sitting as a guest of honor. My guess was that the missing old Chinese man in that picture was Wai Lo Fat himself. Meaning the guy sitting in the chair at Lo Fat's memorial had to be the last remaining member of the Lodge of the

Inner Eight. The governor had not bothered to show up for Wai Lo Fat's service. And the mystery military man wasn't there either. The only other person I recognized in both pictures, standing among several younger, stern-faced Chinese men directly behind the elderly man in the chair of honor, was Danny Chang. I'm no forensic photograph examiner, but whoever the man in the chair was, he didn't look comfortable. He reminded me of prisoners of war who are forced to appear in videos shot by their captors and try to blink out coded messages to their families. To me it looked like the man in the chair of honor was surrounded by Danny Chang and his Coiled Dragon kung fu students.

I could call Tiny Maunakea and ask him to look at the photos and give me his impressions. But he'd probably tell Auntie Kealoha—or she would know by osmosis—and they'd just warn me again to quit fucking around in other people's business. Or I could just go find Burl Morse again and see what he thought of the photos.

The next morning, I called Dr. McCall, in part because I wanted to know what happened with Amber's blood test and in part because I just liked talking to her. I'd like to have her back on my boat again but I was worried she might take more of my blood or remove an organ or something. I also liked her because she didn't screen her calls. She picked up the phone on the second ring.

"How'd your visit with Amber Kam go?" I asked, trying to sound innocent.

"Grand," she said. "She said she was thinking of having you arrested for harassment."

"You told her I sent you?"

"Of course not," she said. "You didn't send me. I explained that I was just following up on my investigation into the death of her grandfather, but she didn't believe me. She's sure you put me up to it."

"Fantastic," I said.

"The house looks great from the outside, but inside is a complete dump," she said.

"She had it cleaned up for me," I said. "Guess it was part of the charm offensive."

"I don't want to know about whatever weird relationship you two had. But trust me, she's not playing hard to get. She really hates you."

"How was Amber's blood?" I asked.

"Blue. Very blue."

"I mean, other than that."

"I can't tell you, Stryker. Privacy issues, you know," she said.

"I might have another customer for you," I said.

"Another old girlfriend you want me to poke with a needle?"

"Two weeks before Wai Lo Fat died, another old Chinese man died. I can't go into details—privacy issues. But they were members of the same exclusive club. If he has any of those dead weaponized germs in his blood, then you might have to change the cause of death on both of them."

"What's his name?"

"Chin Chen Yu."

"Not my customer."

"What do you mean?"

"I mean, I didn't chop him up. That means he must have died under medical supervision, either in a hospital or at home under a doctor's care."

"You sure you didn't see him?"

"Stryker, if a Chin Chen Yu came through the doors and two weeks later I sliced and diced a Wai Lo Fat, I'd remember."

"Can you just check out how he died? Don't the hospitals have to file a report with you or something?"

"I'll try if I get time," she said. "You caught me on a coffee break. In the other room I've got a knifing, an unattended death, and a three-car pile-up to deal with. I'm up to my elbows in elbows."

"What about the water you tested from the taro patch? Is that privileged information, too?"

"There is no taro patch," she said.

"What are you talking about?"

"There's a pond with koi fish in it and beautiful plants with blue flowers, water lilies, I think. A lovely little path runs through the whole thing, and there's a little thatch-roof hut on one end. Looks like a postcard."

"No taro?"

"Nope."

Blue Ho'okane had said he wouldn't be surprised if the genetically altered taro disappeared once someone started looking into it. That was the whole point of our amphibious landing. Whoever took out the Frankentaro didn't bother to replant regular taro because they knew it wouldn't grow. So they turned it into a lily pond. Smart. Except Blue still had a sample of the Frankentaro that was growing in there. I'd have to call him and let him know of this development. It would make his day.

Chapter Twenty-seven

It was several days before I could go back on the Burl Morse hunt. My truck came down with a bad case of mechanical indifference. When I turned the ignition key it coughed dryly like a little kid who doesn't want to go to school. I opened the hood and looked at the engine. It was just as complex and nasty-looking as I knew it would be. I don't know shit about the internal combustion engine, but I believe it's a rule that a man has to stand and look at it for a certain amount of time when the car or truck refuses to run.

Luckily, there is a deep bench of engine mechanics at the Bayview Yacht Club because if you own a boat with an engine or motor and don't know how to repair them, your vessel becomes a huge hole in the water into which you shovel cash.

Any work party at the club involves a lot of drinking, so there were a certain number of hours spent in the parking lot with Football Mike, Pilot Bill, Julie's Bob, Annie's Bob, and Mai Tai John standing by the disgruntled truck, drink in hand, fiddling with the engine and discussing all the various mechanical disabilities from which it might suffer. One of the first things I learned upon joining the club was that just about all the men were named either Bob, Bill, Mike, or John, and the only way to identify them in conversation was by what their job had been when they had jobs, who they were married to, or what they drank. I was the only Stryker at the club, so I didn't have a nickname, although I thought I heard someone refer to me as "the vodka guy" during my Absolut days.

While the Bobs, Bills, Mikes, and Johns were working on my truck, Blue Ho'okane came by to talk about the Frankentaro and look at the two photos of the Chinese funerals.

"Hey, let them try to cover up that they were growing genetically altered taro," he said. "We've got the evidence, and those plants will be a great bargaining chip when we sue Four Gates and the University of Hawaii and start talking settlement."

"What kind of settlement?" I asked.

"I don't know yet," he said. "We could use an infusion of cash into our Waianae youth agriculture project, but it will go farther than that. People's heads are going to roll over this, Stryker. Careers are going to end. The entire direction of diversified agriculture in the Islands is at stake. Bruddah, this is huge."

I still didn't quite grasp the hugeness of it, but I deferred to his expertise. Putting aside the unpleasantness of experimenting on plants that could be your ancestors, I thought genetically modified plants could be a great help to countries that have been suffering from droughts for decades or voracious pests for even longer.

I showed him the Chinese funeral photos and, other

than the governor, he didn't recognize anyone in the pictures. He had been off the police force for twenty years, so even the presence of Danny Chang didn't interest him when I pointed him out.

"There's always pricks like him hanging around," he said. "On the Metro Squad we used to just beat the shit out of them on the street, and then they behaved until we had to beat the shit out of them again."

I told him that Dragon Boy was a mixed martial arts expert who had tried to run me off the road at the Blow Hole before almost kicking my head off at Sandy Beach.

"Well, let's go have a talk with the bruddah," he said. "I don't know karate, but I know Smith and Wesson. It's all about physics. If you explain the difference between the speed of a roundhouse kick and the muzzle velocity of a hollow-point bullet, they catch your drift."

Auntie Kealoha had asked that I try to pick up Blue Ho'okane's good habits, and I think she was talking about situations like this. So I changed the subject to the mystery military officer in the Chin Chen Yu photo. Blue had been in the army and had gone to Vietnam, so he had some knowledge of uniforms and ranks. He looked at the photo closely.

"He's army," he said. "Looks like he has a lot of decorations. Looks like a colonel. That's a strange insignia there. Can't make it out. He's not regular army, I can tell you that. Make me a copy of this photo and I'll get back to you. I know some guys at Schofield Barracks. They still do some live fire exercises in the Makua Valley. I'm an official community observer. I can get on base and everything. I watch the firing practice and make sure they don't miss their target and lob a live round into the Waianae 7-Eleven."

After the various Bobs, Mikes, Johns, and Bills got my truck going again, I headed back to the Spam and Eggs Ministry to find Burl Morse. Father McGreggor told me he hadn't seen Burl Morse for a few days. He said that usually meant Burl was on a bender. The last time I had seen Morse, it didn't look like he had too many benders left in him.

"We don't allow consumption of alcohol by our clients who sleep here," McGreggor said. "So the drinkers find places to stay on the street and only show up for meals. They don't stray far. Burl's probably somewhere sleeping it off within a few blocks of here. Some of our clients prefer the freeway underpass because it's dry."

So I drove around the neighborhood slowly, eyeballing clumps of homeless people hunkered under trees or behind businesses drinking bottles of beer or wine hidden in brown paper sacks. The street drunks keep their booze in brown paper sacks on the mistaken presumption that if a cop can't tell what's in the sack, he doesn't have probable cause to arrest you. That's a dumb urban myth. The reason cops don't arrest street drunks is that they pee in the back of their patrol cars.

My plan was to find Burl Morse and take him back to my boat. I'd get him cleaned up and let him stay with me for a few days and get himself together while I picked his brain on all things Chinese.

I reached the freeway, and Father McGreggor was right, the underpass was a great place for homeless to hang out. Roomy, covered, fairly clean. As I approached the underpass, I saw Burl Morse walking kind of unsteadily along the road. I drove past him and then pulled over. I got out and opened the passenger door. He was almost at the truck before he recognized me. There was a strange look on his face. He looked scared.

"May I offer you a ride, Mr. Morse?" I asked.

"What if I don't get in?" He was looking right and left for some manner of escape.

"Perhaps the rest of your walk won't be as enjoyable as the first part," I said in my best imitation of Tiny Maunakea.

"Fuck it," he said. "The first part wasn't that swell to begin with."

He walked toward the open passenger door, but as he approached, the sickening stench of stale alcohol and rancid sweat almost knocked me over.

I shut the door and said, "Uh, would you mind riding in the back?"

Chapter Twenty-eight

I thought about driving through one of those automatic car washes off Dillingham Boulevard to give Burl Morse a sort of precleaning in the back of the pickup truck before we got to the Bayview Yacht Club. Then I realized he might get sucked up into those huge spinning brushes and killed and the brushes would get all jammed up and I'd get sued by the car wash and, well, it was just a thought.

Instead, after we drove through the gate of the yacht club, I parked by the locker room and showers.

"Wait here for a second," I told him. The trip over the Pali in the back of the truck had actually aired him out a little. He wasn't so aromatic. It was the middle of the day on a weekday, and the lockers and showers were empty. I stuck my head out of the locker room's back door, which faced the parking lot, and yelled for him. He still had no idea what was going on but seemed to take orders well. He climbed out of the truck with some trouble and came to the locker room. I grabbed a large black plastic bag out of the maintenance closet.

"Take off your clothes and put them in here," I said.

"Why are you doing this to me?" he asked.

"I'm just trying to get it so that we can sit down together and talk without me losing my lunch," I said. "I hate to break it to you, Burl, but you don't exactly smell like an Irish spring morning."

He took off his clothes and put them in the bag. I noticed his skin was dark with grime, like he had just climbed out of a coal mine. He noticed me noticing.

"There are no bathing facilities at my current place of domestic accommodation," he said.

"Yeah, they're behind at installing showers under the freeways," I said.

I motioned him out onto the lawn and hosed him off, getting the nastier bits of filth off him. Then I handed him a bar of soap and pointed to the showers.

"Get to work in there," I said. "I'll be back with a razor, clothes, and towels."

That afternoon, as we sat by the swimming pool at a round metal table shaded by a big blue canvas umbrella, overlooking the boat basin, Burl Morse looked like a new man; a shaved, cleaned man; the kind of man I'd have an easier time hating. I was sorry his life had fallen apart, but not that sorry.

The first thing I did was get him off that rotgut fortified wine he'd been drinking.

"As long as you are here, you drink beer, no booze," I said. He took a sip of Budweiser, looked at the tall bottle as if he were a sommelier, and said, "Not bad. For a kid's drink."

After another sip he said, "What am I doing here, Stryker?"

"I want to know more about the Lodge of the Inner Eight and Chin Chen Yu," I said.

"Why?"

"There's a certain young Chinese punk who's been dogging me," I said. "I've already had one run-in with him that put a win on his scorecard. He told me to quit asking questions about a taro patch in Kahala, but I think it's more than that. I think the taro patch and Four Gates and the deaths of Wai Lo Fat and Chin Chen Yu are all tied together somehow. And when people try to scare me away from looking at something it usually has the opposite effect."

"You think someone killed those old Chinese guys?"

"I don't know. The medical examiner found remains of engineered pathogens in the blood of Wai Lo Fat. She'd never seen anything like it before, but she can't say it killed him. She's trying to find out if there were any in Chin Chen Yu."

"Engineered pathogens," he said, finishing off his beer in a long pull. "Sounds real James Bondian."

"If someone killed Wai Lo Fat and Chin Chen Yu, then the last remaining member of the Lodge of the Inner Eight could be in danger," I said. "What did you say his name was?"

"So Young Hee," he said.

I opened a folder and pulled out the two Chinese funeral eight-by-tens. He glanced at the photos and then looked at his empty beer bottle.

"Okay, wait here," I said.

I walked up to the Longhouse Bar to get a few more beers. You can drink store-bought beers on your boat, but you have to buy yacht club beers to drink on the lawn or around the pool. It took longer to get the beers from the bar, and Burl apparently took advantage of the extra time to study the photos.

When I sat down he placed the photos in the middle of the table, the way a prosecutor might present photo evidence to a witness on the stand. He seemed to be warming to his role as my China expert. His posture was straighter, his manner more authoritative. I reminded myself that I'd have to smack him down from time to time to keep him from getting too uppity.

"This is the Chin Chen Yu memorial," he said, pointing to the photo on the right. "You know the governor. I think this guy's a state senator. I don't know who the guy in the uniform is. You see the two guys sitting in carved high-back chairs? The one on the right is Wai Lo Fat. The other guy is So Young Hee."

"What does the banner in the back say?"

"It says 'Hung Bang Kongsi,'" he said. "The men in the photo are probably the most prominent members. Like the Mafia, they only get together at weddings and funerals. As the last two remaining members of the Lodge of the Inner Eight, Wai Lo Fat and So Young Hee get to sit in the special chairs. Those chairs are from China. Now, look at Wai Lo Fat's funeral photo. Mostly the same group of people, all Hung Bang Kongsi, but only So Young Hee has the seat of honor. You notice any other changes?"

I felt like we were playing the "What's Different in These Pictures" game in a *Highlights for Children* magazine. I was going to say there's no giraffe in the Wai Lo Fat photo but decided against it.

"No governor, no outside dignitaries."

"Yes. That means that Chin Chen Yu had more pull in the overall island community than Wai Lo Fat. He had connections not just to state government but apparently to the military as well. But look at this."

He pointed to Danny Chang and his group of young toughs in the Chin Chen Yu photo.

"Everyone else is wearing a black armband," he said. "These guys are wearing red armbands. At the Chin Chen Yu service they are standing on the far side of the group, there, on the left. At Wai Lo Fat's service they are standing around So Young Hee."

"That's Danny Chang," I said, pointing at the man standing directly behind So Young Hee in the photo. "He runs a martial arts school in Chinatown. He's the guy I had the run-in with. What's with the red armbands?"

"That would identify them as sort of the marshals-at-arms of the Hung Bang Kongsi," he said. "The muscle of the group when needed."

"I thought that in this photo with Danny Chang and his buddies around him, So Young Hee doesn't look so happy," I said.

"Yeah. I thought at first that maybe So Young Hee had engineered some kind of coup, getting rid of Wai Lo Fat and Chin Chen Yu to take control as the sole member of the Lodge of the Inner Eight with the help of the red armbands," he said. "But you're right, he doesn't look happy. Besides, he shared control of Four Gates Enterprises with Wai Lo Fat and Chin Chen Yu for forty years. Longer than that if you want to go back to the beginning after World War II when the Lodge of the Inner Eight was intact. Why at his age would he suddenly turn against his brothers?"

"Maybe it's Danny Chang who's attempting a coup," I said.

"Maybe," he said, reaching down to pet Lono. The dogs had sacked out in the shade at our feet. Kane and Lono are pretty good about knowing which humans are assholes and which ones aren't. So I was a bit disturbed that Lono let Burl Morse touch him without ripping off his arm.

I decided Burl had cleaned up enough to go on the *Travis McGee*, so we broke up the lawn party and headed inside.

"Wow," he said, looking around the dayroom. "This is some boat! It must have cost a bundle. Where'd you get the money?"

It was a tactless question. Or was he being droll? Either way, it was smack-down time.

"Look, Burl, I thought you could use a few days off of the streets," I said. "We're not buddies. There's not going to be any personal chitchat. You can stay here, but you are going to stay clean, and by clean, I mean take showers, wear clean clothes, and don't pee in your pants. My pants, actually."

"Gotcha," he said, appropriately smacked down. "Look, I don't know what's going on with the Hung Bang Kongsi, but I can make a few calls if you want. My sources would be pretty old by now, but I might find out something."

I pulled a beer out of the refrigerator for him.

"Thanks," I said, handing it to him.

Burl spent the rest of the afternoon on the phone, mostly speaking Chinese. I gave him some space, moving to the Longhouse Bar to hang out with the Bobs, Mikes, Johns, and Bills. When I got back to the boat later that evening, the door to the bedroom I had assigned to Burl was shut. I guess the novelty of sleeping in an actual bed was too much for him, so he turned in early.

When I got up for my swim the next morning, he was gone. There was a handwritten note on the galley counter.

Stryker, thanks for the place to stay and the beers, it said. *The only way I'm going to be able to help you is to go to Chinatown. I'll be in touch. And thanks for the clothes. Real roomy. You're a bigger man than I am.*

Chapter Twenty-nine

The day after Burl Morse left the sound of chimes woke me up before dawn, a gentle clanging and tinkling. I had hung the chimes, made of small metal pipes and seashells, on the leeward side of the boat, protected from the trade winds, so they would only chime when the Kona winds were blowing. If the chimes weren't enough of a clue that we had Kona winds, I also felt the slight burning in my eyes and minor nasal congestion that happened when traces of vog blew over from the Big Island. Kilauea Volcano had been continuously erupting since 1983, but unless winds blew from the southeast, from the little Big Island coastal town of Kona, we never knew it on Oahu. The gaseous emissions are called "vog," which is short for "volcanic fog." It may sound cute, but vog actually is a concoction of sulfur dioxide and other nasty particles spewed into the air when the earth burps. The good thing about Kona winds is that they clean up the surf on the windward side of the island, making a number of "secret spots" that are unridable during most of the year perfect for surfing.

I called Blue Ho'okane before the sun came up, knowing

that the same Kona winds that were making surf spots on my side of the island good were wrecking the waves coming in at Makaha. He had some information about the mystery military guy at Chin Chen Yu's memorial, so he drove over to Kaneohe and picked me up in his tan Gran Torino. With his official military "community observer" pass he got us on the Kaneohe Marine Base just a mile from the yacht club, and we paddled out into excellent six-foot waves off of Pyramid Rock just as the sun peeked over the horizon. The sky and water were stained with reds and yellows and oranges.

As we bobbed in the Martian water between sets of waves, he told me what he found out about the army guy in the funeral photo.

"You're going to love this," he said. "First off, get a load of his name. Richard Gustavus Beauregard. I'm not shitting you, bruddah. Army Colonel R. G. Beauregard. Full bird."

"Why, Colonel Beauregard, didn't we meet at the Battle of Shiloh?" I said in my best southern accent.

"Here's the interesting thing," he said. "Colonel Beauregard's not regular army, he's a spook."

"Army intelligence?"

"An oxymoron, but correct," he said. "A very spooky guy, apparently. My buddies at Schofield Barracks are pretty tough bruddahs—they've all been to either Iraq or Afghanistan—but even they didn't want to talk about Colonel Beauregard. It's like he's Heinrich Himmler or something. I'm surprised he even let himself get photographed in public. He's not covert or anything, but all these intelligence dudes are camera-shy. He must have had to have been there."

"Tiny Maunakea sort of hinted that Chin Chen Yu had been involved in some kind of criminal stuff and may have had some other connections that made him useful to the U.S. military," I said.

"I know that when I was with HPD he was rumored to be in charge of Chinatown criminal activities," he said. "We never could bust into the Chinatown rackets. I mean, the rackets connected to specifically Chinese individuals. It was a closed society. There were regular criminals like Mongoose Pacheco who were involved in shit on Hotel and Maunakea streets like ice and pakalolo, but that was just for the locals. The old-school Chinese had their own thing going."

"What kind of activities would Chin Chen Yu have been running?"

His answer was interrupted by a five-footer attempting to scoot by us unnoticed. Blue was riding one of his longboards, so it took only a few strokes for him to catch the wave and disappear as he dropped down the face. I took the next wave, angling left and getting covered up in a nice tube just as Blue kicked out of his wave in front of me. He hooted as I raced by him still covered up in the red, watery cave.

"Gambling, on mahjongg mainly, opium, prostitution," Blue said, answering my question as if it were just asked when we got back to the lineup. "That stuff had been going on since World War II in Chinatown. The dope supposedly came right from Hong Kong. We didn't have trouble with the Chinatown rackets. They policed themselves."

"What do you think his connection with the military was?" I asked.

"Who knows?" he said. "Has to be something spooky if this Colonel Beauregard was involved. Maybe Yu had contacts in China that were useful during the days China was our enemy, not our trading partner."

Another set came in, and I took the first wave. The top of the wave feathered scarlet with the sun behind it as it jacked up on the reef. It was big, and I took off too late. I was airborne as the board dropped away and I plummeted into the wine-dark pit, a free fall in crimson. I instinctively hugged myself tightly with both arms during the wipeout so as not to suffer another shoulder dislocation. The self-body grab had become my default wipeout position.

We got in another good hour of surfing before even the Kona winds petered out and the waves became mushy. After Blue dropped me off at the club, I called Dr. McCall to see if she had found out anything about Chin Chen Yu.

"This is completely off the record since my office was not involved," she said. "Mr. Chin Chen Yu died quietly in his sleep at Queen's Hospital at the age of ninety-two. According to the treating physician, he died of congestive heart failure, common for gentlemen of his age. He died of what in the old days we'd just call natural causes."

"No weird germ thingies in his blood?"

"They didn't do a tox screen on him at the hospital because he had been under a doctor's care. He's entombed in one of those big Chinese mausoleums now, and there's no way I'm going to order them to crack that baby open and pull him out. Sorry, Stryker, you're just going to have to build your conspiracy theories without Mr. Chin Chen Yu. Or at least without his blood."

"Why don't you drop by after work for a glass of wine," I said. "I never showed you the hot tub on the top deck."

"I guess your fling with Amber Kam really is over, huh?" she asked, laughing. "You had your beauty queen and, what? Now you're going for Miss Congeniality."

"You? Miss Congeniality?"

"I'm one of the most congenial body-cutter-uppers you'll ever see, sweetie," she said.

"So? Cocktails on the bridge at four?" I asked.

"If I turn you down I'm afraid you'll become suicidal and just make more work for me. I have that effect on men. So let's say five o'clock."

"Sounds good," I said, "and I'll try to stay away from any sharp objects until you get here."

Chapter Thirty

It's amazing how little Americans know about China. For instance, most Americans know that in our bloodiest war, the ironically named Civil War, about six hundred thousand Americans died. Few know about the same time the American Civil War was raging, a war was going on in China—the Taiping Rebellion—that killed twenty million people. Twenty *million*. At the time of the Civil War there were only twenty-seven million people in the entire Not-So-United States.

At the time of the Taiping Rebellion, Abraham Lincoln was president. You'd think he might have thrown a line into his Gettysburg Address just to put our Civil War into context. Like, "Now we are engaged in a great civil war, testing whether this nation, or any nation so conceived and so dedicated, can long endure. But if you think it's bad here, man, you should hear what's happening in China! Twenty freakin' million people killed!"

I had never heard about the Taiping Rebellion. It turned out the Chinese started coming to the Islands just when the Taiping Rebellion was getting cranked up. Coincidence? If twenty million people were being killed in the United States, I'd start thinking about moving to Costa Rica.

So I wasn't surprised when Burl Morse suddenly appeared on my doorstep with more stuff about China and Hawaii I didn't know.

It was two days since Burl had left my boat and I hadn't heard a peep from him. Then he simply showed up at the front gate of the Bayview Yacht Club and asked the girls in the office to buzz him in. In an amazing disdain for security, they did. Then he walked right up to my boat, where Kane and Lono not only failed to maul him but greeted him like a lost pack member. I was really beginning to question their tastes. I heard them licking someone to death at the bottom of the stairs, so I stepped outside.

"Hi ya, Stryker!" Burl said. "I've got some information for you."

Not only had Burl Morse not drunk himself to death as I thought he might, but he looked quite hale, hardy, and far less liverish. He was even wearing new clothes, slacks and a button-up aloha shirt that, unlike the clothes I gave him, actually fit him.

I invited him up, and he sat down on the couch in the dayroom. I offered him a beer.

"No, I'm good," he said. "I'm off the sauce for a while."

I handed him a can of Coke and sat on the recliner.

"Sorry I left without talking to you," he said. "After those phone calls I made from your boat, I realized that I probably could get some of the information you were looking for, but I'd have to do it in Chinatown. I found the family of the old lady who had told me about the Hung Bang Kongsi years ago, and they remembered me. It still took a while before they'd loosen up. They liked that I speak Cantonese, but we drank a lot of tea and played a lot of mahjongg before they accepted me."

Burl seemed energized. Fully engaged in the world. Who knew what a shower and clean sheets would do?

"So Young Hee apparently has gone underground," he said. "The old-school Chinese are worried. Most don't know anything about the Lodge of the Inner Eight, but they know that Wai Lo Fat, Chin Chen Yu, and So Young Hee were the most powerful Chinese in Hawaii. There are a lot of interlocking personal and financial interests in the Chinese community, and a lot of people are worried about the impact of losing three major figures in such a short time. It would be as if the heads of Exxon, General Motors, and Bank of America suddenly disappeared on the Mainland."

"What do you think is going on?" I asked.

"There might be some kind of power struggle within the Hung Bang Kongsi," he said. "You asked about a possible coup. It could be happening. Danny Chang and his red armbands have everyone on edge. Everyone in the Hung Bang Kongsi is looking for So Young Hee, but I think the red armbands want to find him first. So Young Hee is probably still around, just hunkered down somewhere trying to figure things out. He probably doesn't know who to trust right now."

"What power does Danny Chang have?"

"It goes back to Chin Chen Yu," he said. "Yu was the head of Chinese organized crime in Hawaii, going back to World War II. After the bombing of Pearl Harbor, prostitution was legalized in Honolulu by the military government, and Chin Chen Yu ran several brothels featuring

Chinese ladies. He also was a member of the Jade Dragon Society, a Hong Kong triad hundreds, maybe thousands of years old. He apparently formed a relationship with the military government in Hawaii to provide intelligence about Japanese activity in Hong Kong and southern China using his Jade Dragon connections. The government didn't care that he was a criminal. Lucky Luciano protected the New York waterfront during the war, and his Sicilian network helped gather intelligence on the Nazis."

"That explains why an army colonel showed up at his funeral," I said.

"Oh, his military connections didn't stop with World War II," Burl said. "After the war, he continued to gather intelligence for the United States on the rise of China as a world power, during the Cold War and probably even until recent times during China's shift to capitalism. I was told the Jade Dragon triad arranged for some Chinese dissidents to get out of China after the Tiananmen Square crackdown, and some may have come through Hawaii. Chin Chen Yu would have been involved if that happened."

"So where does Danny Chang come in?"

"Well, I'm guessing here, but I think whoever in the government was handling Chin Chen Yu recognized that when he died they might lose an intelligence conduit to China. Danny Chang is also a member of the Jade Dragon Society. He arrived in Hawaii about three years ago. I wouldn't be surprised if Chin Chen Yu had been asked to bring in someone like Danny as a protégé. Danny's about the same age that Chin Chen Yu was in World War II."

"So after Chin Chen Yu died, Danny Chang started feeling his oats," I said.

"That's what I think," he said. "He may have some

powerful connections with military intelligence, but he has no legal entrée into Four Gates Enterprises, which is the financial backbone of the Hung Bang Kongsi. If the Lodge of the Inner Eight legally owns Four Gates, that means So Young Hee now legally owns Four Gates."

"We need to find So Young Hee," I said. "Where do we start looking?"

"I might have a line on where he is. Discussions are in a delicate phase right now," he said.

The phone rang. I picked up the handset from the coffee table. Whoever it was was speaking Chinese.

"I think it's for you," I said.

Chapter Thirty-one

At about midnight, the phone on the *Travis McGee* rang, waking me up from a dead sleep. It was Burl Morse. He talked just above a whisper, sounding tired. I thought he must be drunk.

"It's all about Kahala Road," he said.

I could hardly hear him.

"What?"

"Stryker, it's all about Kahala Road."

"What is?"

"Wai Lo Fat dying, Danny Chang scaring everyone, the attack on you," he said. "It all has to do with Kahala Road."

"Have you been drinking, Burl?"

"Listen, I'm in a phone booth. I'm being followed. Just listen. I talked to this old Hung Bang Kongsi member who was at Chin Chen Yu's funeral. He was a friend of Wai Lo Fat's. He said Wai Lo Fat told him that now that Chin Chen Yu was dead, the truth would come out about Kahala Road."

"I thought you said Kahala Road was a myth. Like the River Styx."

"I thought it was, but it isn't. There is a Kahala Road. The old man said Wai Lo Fat seemed at peace. Wai Lo Fat kept telling him that now people would know about Kahala Road. Then he said that haole military guy came and took Wai Lo Fat aside and they talked for a while by themselves. After the military guy left, Wai Lo Fat looked scared and didn't say anything else. Some younger members of the Hung Bang Kongsi came up and escorted him away. They were probably the red armbands."

"Where are you, Burl? I'll come get you."

"Oh, shit!" he said. He started talking real fast. "Someone's coming. Take this down, 225B Plumeria Lane. That's where So Young Hee may be. You got it? 225B Plumeria Lane."

"I got it," I said. "What's going on?"

"It looks like Danny's guys—"

The phone went dead.

Chapter Thirty-two

I thought about calling the police to see if they could trace Burl Morse's call to the phone booth he had called from. It must be somewhere in Chinatown. It sounded like he was in trouble. Then again, maybe he was just back on the booze. What he had said didn't make much sense. But if he wasn't drunk, he knew what he was doing. He knew his way around Chinatown.

So I didn't call the police. I called Blue Ho'okane, and he wasn't too thrilled to be bothered at one in the morning. I gave him the *Reader's Digest* version of what I knew about the possible coup within the Hung Bang Kongsi, the danger to So Young Hee, and the ascension of triad boss Danny Chang. I left out all the gibberish about Kahala Road. As an ex-cop, he quickly understood the situation.

"See?" he said. "We should have beat the shit out of that Danny Chang the other day."

I had looked up the Plumeria Lane address that Burl had given me as a possible location for So Young Hee. It was near the top of Tantalus, a mountain that overlooks Honolulu inhabited by some of the richest people on the island.

Blue agreed to meet me at the beginning of Round Top Drive, a narrow serpentine road that winds through a series of hairpin turns up to the summit.

We were to meet at 2:00 A.M., but I got to the rendezvous point a half hour early and backed my truck under some trees so I could see anyone going up Round Top Drive. I figured if Burl Morse had been able to get this street address, other people could, too. I sat with my lights off waiting.

I always considered the people who lived on Tantalus to be kind of smug and snooty, airborne versions of those smug and snooty rich people who lived in Kahala. The higher they lived on Tantalus, the snootier they got. It was as if they were Greek gods looking down on the rest of Honolulu the way the gods looked down from Mount Olympus, which is ironic since Tantalus actually is named after a Greek demigod banished to Hades for all eternity for killing his son and secretly feeding him to the gods of Olympus for dinner. Not exactly an Olive Garden moment.

Blue Ho'okane drove up fifteen minutes early and stopped at the intersection of Round Top Drive and Makiki Street. I flashed my headlights. I backed my truck even farther into the trees and then climbed into Blue's Gran Torino.

We made our way up the narrow blacktop as it wound back and forth through a series of switchbacks, some places completely dark because there were long stretches of road between streetlights. It wasn't a road I'd like to try racing down on a dark night.

About halfway to the lookout at the top of Tantalus, we came to Plumeria Lane, a long dead-end street that disappeared in the darkness.

"Let's park it here just in case somebody's already up there," Blue said.

He backed the Torino up behind some bushes, pointing downhill. He left the keys on the floor and the door unlocked. He didn't have to tell me that was in case we had to make a fast retreat.

We walked up the long driveway in the dark, even though we both had brought flashlights. The number on a mailbox in front of the first house we came to, a sprawling one-story brick ranch-style, said 225A. Our house, 225B, had to be down a dark gravel driveway running beside the ranch-style house. We crunched along on the gravel until we decided it was making too much racket, then stayed on a grassy area on the right side of the driveway. We reached a smallish bungalow with an empty carport. It wasn't a bad choice for a safe house, tucked as it was into a wooded area. It was a small house for Tantalus, probably the servants' quarters for whoever lived in the big ranch-style.

Blue motioned for me to go to the door by the carport, and he walked toward the bungalow's front door. I heard him knock on the front door but didn't see or hear any response inside. A few seconds later I saw a light dancing inside the house through the window of the carport door. The door opened and Blue said, "Nobody's home."

I walked into the kitchen and scanned it with my flashlight. Some roaches darted out of the kitchen sink where a pile of dirty dishes sat. There were a few more used dishes on the kitchen table, service for one. In the living room, there were signs of habitation: some clothes strewn on a couch and an ashtray with some cigarette butts in it. Of the two bedrooms, only one looked like it had been lived in. The bed was unmade. There was a suitcase on the dresser that was open and partially packed.

"Looks like someone left here in a hurry," Blue said.

There was another ashtray by the bed and a half pack of Dunhill International cigarettes, probably one of the most expensive cigarette brands in the world.

"Yeah, he left his Dunhills," I said.

I was about to turn to go when I noticed something on the floor by the bed. It was a cellular phone. I picked it up and was about to mention it to Blue when we both heard a car coming slowly but noisily up the gravel driveway. We turned off our flashlights simultaneously and ran to the living room picture window. The blinds were closed, so we each took a side of the window and peeked out.

The car turned out to be a black SUV. I couldn't read the license plate, but I didn't have to.

"It's Danny Chang or some of his boys," I whispered to Blue.

Whoever it was wasn't as interested in stealth as we had been. They left the headlights on and got out of the car talking in loud cling-clang Chinese. There were two of them, and they were arguing about something. One finally approached the front door and knocked on it. He yelled something back to the other one when no one answered. He tried the front doorknob and seemed surprised when it opened. I hadn't seen Blue pull a revolver out of somewhere, but he had, and when the guy walked in he slammed the gun down on the back of his head and the man fell to the floor like a load of laundry.

Blue motioned to me, and I dragged the guy away from the door. The man outside yelled something in Chinese. Then something else in Chinese, angrier. Then he came hoofing it toward the door. When he was within ten feet Blue stepped into the doorway and leveled the gun at him.

There was enough ambient light for Danny Chang to see that Blue had the drop on him.

"You crazy man," Chang said. "You know who I am?"

I stepped out from behind Blue and said, "You know who I am?"

Danny Chang actually laughed.

"I know you," he said.

"Yeah, know where I can get some coconuts or pineapples?"

"You not funny so much, man," he said.

Blue must have seen some twitch or something I didn't see because he pushed the gun forward and said, "No, no, no. Keep feet on ground or gun go boom. Now, turn around."

Danny turned toward the SUV, his back to us.

"Throw your keys toward the car," Blue said.

The keys landed with a clink halfway to the car.

"Link your hands behind your neck."

Danny did but wasn't happy about it.

Blue looked around the front patio quickly. He nodded his head toward a brown ceramic planter with a dead bougainvillea in it. I picked it up and tested its heft. About twenty pounds. It should do the trick.

"You going die one day I think," Danny Chang said.

"Yeah, but not today," I said.

Chapter Thirty-three

I drove Danny Chang's black SUV down the driveway to Blue's Gran Torino. Then he followed me down Round Top Drive to where my truck was parked. I backed the SUV under the trees so it was well hidden. Blue climbed in the SUV on the passenger side, turned on the interior lights, and pawed through the glove compartment and other alcoves. He found a piece of paper with the 225B Plumeria Lane address on it. I wondered if Danny Chang had gotten it from Burl Morse when they caught him in the phone booth in Chinatown earlier that evening. I'd like to think they had to pry it out of Burl's cold dead hand, but I have a feeling when they grabbed him he just handed it over and said to keep an eye out for me while they were up there. It was a horrible thing to think, but the man had fucked me over once, and he sounded pretty drunk on the phone.

Blue found a pen in the glove compartment and wrote *Thanks for the good time fellas!* on the back of the slip of paper and left it on the dashboard. He grabbed a bunch of papers from the glove compartment, which I figured were the car registration and such. I assumed Danny had a cellular phone to call for help. Otherwise, it was going to be a long walk down that mountain.

Blue and I left Round Top Drive in our separate vehicles and drove to a Zippy's drive-in on Nimitz Highway to discuss our adventure. I don't know if knocking a couple of Chinese triad members unconscious in the middle of the night was what Auntie Kealoha would consider one of Blue's bad habits, but it seemed like the right thing to do at the time. And I didn't feel bad about clobbering Danny Chang with the potted plant on the back of the head, either. He didn't see it coming just like I never saw his foot coming at my head—and he had *two* guys as backup.

We grabbed a booth inside the dining room at Zippy's. Everything cost about fifty cents more in the dining room than from the drive-in window but, hey, we were big-time vigilantes fighting evil while the rest of the city slept. And it wasn't too hard to grab a booth since the dining room was empty at three in the morning.

We ordered breakfast. I had a Super Saimin, noodles in a broth with thin slices of fishcake, pork, and onions with an egg stirred in. Blue ordered a Loco Moco, an island concoction of a bowl of sticky rice topped with a hamburger patty, a fried egg, and brown gravy.

"The trades are back," Blue said, going at his Loco Moco with wooden chopsticks. "We should hit Makaha Point at sunrise."

For Blue, who was shot allegedly while saving the island from a terrorist trying to set off a dirty nuke bomb in Waikiki and who broke a German shepherd over his knee during a gambling raid, what we had just gone through was merely another night out.

"We've still got to find So Young Hee," I said. "He had been at that house on Tantalus but got spooked by something and bugged out, leaving his clothes, dirty dishes, and expensive cigarettes."

"Don't we have to wait to hear from your buddy who gave you the street address?" he said.

"I'm afraid Dragon Boy might have gotten to Burl while he was calling me," I said. "The call was cut off while he was giving me the Tantalus address."

"Sorry to hear it," he said.

"We might still be in the game," I said. "Looks like So Young Hee left this behind when he fled."

I put the cell phone I had picked up by the bed on the table.

"Hey now, bruddah," he said. "Good police work."

He took the phone and flipped it open. He punched some buttons. Then he held the phone to his ear.

"No thank you, sorry, wrong number," he said into the phone, then hung up. "I think he was planning to relocate before he got spooked. His last call was at 11:00 P.M. to the front desk of the Moana Hotel."

"Hide in plain sight," I said. "Not a bad idea. Let's go see him."

"Let's finish eating," Blue said, picking up some gravy-covered rice with the chopsticks.

"You know the haole colonel in the funeral photo you identified? Colonel Beauregard?" I asked. "Burl Morse found out that Chin Chen Yu had been working with military intelligence since World War II. He thinks he used his membership in a Hong Kong triad to gather information about Japanese activities and pass it on to the U.S. government. After the war, he may have continued working for military intelligence monitoring what was happening in China during the Mao Zedong days and right up to the change to capitalism. That would explain why Chin Chen Yu had a free hand in Hawaii to run his Chinatown rackets without interference. It would also explain why Colonel Beauregard was at Chin Chen Yu's funeral."

"Makes sense," Blue said, unimpressed.

"He thinks that as Chin Chen Yu got into his eighties, the military intelligence people realized they needed another Hong Kong triad guy in Hawaii, so they had Yu bring over Danny Chang," I said.

"There's a big difference between the way Chin Chen Yu handled business and Danny Chang," Blue said. "Yu kept a low profile in Hawaii and didn't bother the civilians. Danny Chang thinks he's Jackie Chan. That's probably that Colonel Beauregard's fault."

"Why?"

"Because Colonel Beauregard couldn't have been Chin Chen Yu's military handler all those years. He's too young. He must be new. He doesn't know Hawaii, and he's making mistakes."

"Like what?"

"Like sending Danny Chang to try to intimidate you when you were looking into the death of Wai Lo Fat," he said. "Dumb move. Shit, bruddah, if Danny hadn't kicked you in the head you would have forgotten all about Wai Lo Fat and that taro field. Now Colonel Beauregard's got Danny Chang stalking one of the richest, most influential businessmen in the state. What does that have to do with military intelligence?"

"Burl Morse told me the whole thing about Wai Lo Fat's death and the taro field is all about Kahala Road," I said.

"What does that mean?"

"I don't know," I said. "Apparently the Chinese have a hangup about Kahala Road. It's synonymous with death. The Chinese say that when their old people die, they are walking on Kahala Road."

"There is no Kahala Road," he said. "There's a Kahala Avenue, but no Kahala Road. I used to patrol that area."

"I think they mean it in a metaphorical sense," I said.

"Are we going to go find So Young Hee or sit here all day?" he asked. Blue was done with his breakfast.

Chapter Thirty-four

Blue Ho'okane apparently knows everyone on the island personally. And they all owe him favors. We walked into the grand entrance of the Moana Hotel at about 4:00 A.M., and the front desk clerk, a Hawaiian man in a suit and tie, greeted Blue like a brother.

"Hey, bruddah! How you stay?" he asked. "So what, brah? You still living out Waianae side? Still surfing?"

"Shoots, bruddah, every day," Blue said. "Waves been kine good, brah. Sick, I no shit you."

The pidgin conversation went on until a drunk haole tourist approached the front desk unsteadily and the front desk man slipped into flawless English.

"Good morning, Mr. Williams!" he said. "How are you tonight, sir?"

The man said something incomprehensible, and the desk man said, "I understand completely." He waved for a bellhop, and a kid in the kind of uniform an organ grinder's monkey wears came up briskly.

"Jonathan, here's the key card to Mr. Williams's suite on the fourteenth floor. Be so kind as to escort the gentleman up and see to any needs he may have. Have a wonderful night, Mr. Williams. Don't miss our Sunday island buffet on the lanai later this morning!"

As Mr. Williams lumbered unsteadily toward the elevators, the clerk continued the pidgin conversation as if it hadn't been interrupted.

"Yeah, bruddah," he said. "The waves here stay cranking last week, but then the Kona winds come and, da kine, make them all funny kine. Bummas, brah."

Blue eventually got around to telling his buddy that we needed to see So Young Hee. Without even asking why, the desk clerk gave Blue a key card to Hee's room.

"If you guys like food or, da kine, beer, l'dat sent up, just call down. I send 'em up, bruddah. Anything, brah."

"Thanks, brah," Blue said, giving him the "hey, bruddah" handshake. "We need one thing. If anyone ask about So Young Hee, you say he no stay. He not here."

"Got it, brah, Hee no stay," he said.

So Young Hee had booked himself into a Howard Hughes–sized room overlooking the same beach I had walked up two years earlier with Jeannie Kai in my arms. Blue didn't knock on the door; he just used the card key to let us in. We assumed Hee would be asleep in bed, so we were surprised when it turned out he was sitting at a koa wood dining room table covered with documents of some sort and smoking what I assumed was a Dunhill International cigarette.

"Mr. Hee," I said when he stood up looking terrified. "We are friends. We're here to help you."

He was eighty-nine years old, but he was not frail. He was wearing slacks and a golf shirt, no shoes, just socks. Smoking expensive cigarettes apparently doesn't shorten your life.

"I'm Stryker McBride," I said, "and this is my friend Blue Ho'okane, a retired Honolulu police officer. We had some cause to think that you might be in danger."

I knew how I'd feel if two fairly large strangers suddenly appeared in my hotel room at four in the morning. I wouldn't be anywhere near as composed as So Young Hee.

"You are Mr. McBride?" he asked. "You are the one that Amber Kam paid to investigate the death of my friend Wai Lo Fat."

I was going to argue the "paid" point, but then I realized it was just a matter of semantics whether she had paid me or not.

"Yes," I said. "Miss Kam asked me to look into her grandfather's death. I know now that she had ulterior motives, and I apologize for any trouble it has caused you."

"Aw, Amber was always trouble," he said, waving his hand dismissively in the air. He lit another cigarette and walked over to a couch by the open sliding glass doors to the lanai. It was dark outside, but you could hear the gentle rumble of the surf somewhere in the distance.

"Please, sit down," he said. "Would you like something to eat? Something to drink?"

We said no, thanks. I sat on the couch, and Blue sat on a chair upholstered in a tropical theme, apparently comfortable to let me take the lead with Hee.

"Amber was always pushing her grandfather to move her up in the company," he said. "She wanted the deed to her house. She wanted another house on the beach. She wanted a big salary. She just wanted, wanted, wanted. She didn't have the maturity to be given more responsibility. She had no *zhi hui*, what the Chinese call wisdom."

"Are you in danger, Mr. Hee?" I asked.

"I believe I could be," he said. "I just need some time to meet with my lawyers and get affairs in order. They are in New York and will be here in two days. I don't know who to trust."

"We were worried that Danny Chang is trying to take over the Hung Bang Kongsi and Four Gates Enterprises," I said.

He laughed and shook his head. "No, Danny isn't trying to take over Four Gates or the Hung Bang Kongsi," he said. "He couldn't do it even if he wanted to. The Hung Bang Kongsi is an ancient cultural association that has no officers, directors, or official structure to be taken over, and Four Gates Enterprises is a privately held legal entity. I am in the process of creating a trust to oversee the operation of Four Gates, but there are many legal complications to deal with."

"What is Danny Chang trying to do, then?" I asked.

"He is working for that army officer who came to Chin Chen Yu's funeral," he said. "I don't even know his name. He took over for General Johnson, who was Chin Chen Yu's military handler since World War II."

"Colonel Beauregard," I said. "He's the army officer who was at Chin Chin Yu's funeral."

"Yes, well, the name doesn't matter," he said. "His job is to keep me from talking publicly about Kahala Road. He has Danny Chang trying to find me. Mr. Chang doesn't even know why. I believe the colonel is a dangerous man, Mr. McBride. I believe he had something to do with the death of my dear friend Wai Lo Fat."

"Why would he want to kill Wai Lo Fat?" I asked.

"It's all about Kahala Road," he said. "I will tell you everything if you can get me to a safe place where I can stay until my lawyers arrive."

Chapter Thirty-five

Blue and I decided that the safest place for So Young Hee would be at Auntie Kealoha's Portlock Point estate. Blue thought Auntie Kealoha would agree once she heard what was going on. I wasn't so sure. So I let him make the call.

I heard him talking to Tiny Maunakea while I stood on the lanai, just as the first rays of sun were hitting a cloud bank on the horizon of the South Shore. From the lanai, I could see the spotlights from the Moana's pool deck lighting the beach where I had almost gone on what novelist Raymond Chandler called "the big sleep." I was happy to find that seeing that stretch of beach induced no great rush of anxiety for me. In fact, I was kind of hoping the old dude with the metal detector would walk by. I'd yell down to him, "Hey, man, how ya doing? Remember me?"

I don't know what Blue told Tiny Maunakea exactly or what Tiny told Auntie Kealoha, but it was decided that Tiny would meet us in front of the hotel with his limousine at exactly 5:00 A.M.

At 4:55 A.M., Blue stepped out of So Young Hee's suite with his revolver covered by a Moana bath towel and made sure there were no surprises waiting for us in the hallway. Blue preferred we take the stairs to the lobby, but in consideration of So Young Hee's age, we'd use an elevator. I pushed the button. The doors to one of the several elevators opened. I made sure the car was empty.

"It's good," I said, motioning to Blue. He quickly escorted So Young Hee into the elevator, looking up and down the hallways one last time before the door closed.

Blue stepped out of the elevator when we reached the lobby. He scanned the area. His buddy at the front desk looked at us from across the room. Blue put an index finger to his mouth in the international "shhhh" sign. The clerk smiled and held up his right hand with his thumb and pinky extended and middle three fingers closed, the island "shaka" sign, which means, "no worries, brah."

We walked briskly through the lobby, Blue and I on each side of So Young Hee, and reached the valet station at the bottom of the hotel entrance steps just when Tiny pulled up in the limo. I opened the door to the passenger compartment and ushered So Young Hee inside while Blue stood by, looking right and left, still holding the handgun under the towel. I climbed in, followed by Blue, and then Tiny Maunakea pulled the limo out onto Kalakaua Avenue. The mile-long limousine attracted little attention, Waikiki being the home of a few hundred of them.

We were getting ready to turn left out of Waikiki and head through Kapahulu to the H-1 Freeway when So Young Hee said to Tiny Maunakea, "Sir, can you go straight?"

We all looked at him. If we continued past Kapiolani Park along Waikiki Beach, we would end up going around the ocean side of Diamond Head crater and end up in Kahala.

"I'd like to go to the taro patch," he said.

"Mr. Hee, please, let us get you to Portlock where you'll be safe," I said.

"Mr. McBride, the taro patch is the last place anyone would expect me to go."

Blue nodded his head toward Tiny, and we continued on past the zoo through Kapiolani Park toward the foot of Diamond Head.

We pulled up to the Kala Lane Estates gate, and Tiny Maunakea lowered the tinted driver's side window. Brad the Gate Nazi bent over to talk to the driver.

"Be so good, sir, as to open the gate" was all Tiny Maunakea said. Brad looked like he was going to say something but thought better of it and said, "Yes, sir." Both the gate and the tinted window went up.

Tiny Maunakea apparently knew the neighborhood pretty well, because he found a little access road I hadn't noticed before, a few houses past Amber Kam's, that took us down to the fields. Or rather, the ponds. The taro patches were gone, and in their place were two glorious shallow ponds ringed with blue flowering water plants. The pea green leaves floated on the water, some of them four or five feet wide. Blue and purplish spiky flowers erupted from long stems in the middle of the plants.

We parked at the inland end of the former taro patches, at the head of the broad dirt path that separated the two ponds. Tiny Maunakea got out of the car, barely concealing what looked to be a mini machine gun under his aloha shirt. He stood at the front of the limo, scanning the rows of houses and the dry brown ridges behind them. Blue Ho'okane headed down the dirt path between the ponds toward the thatched hut on the ocean side.

So Young Hee got out of the limo and stood up, taking in the ponds. We walked down the raised path a short way.

"I always wanted the sacred lotus to grow here," he said, "but Wai Lo Fat wished to honor his dead Hawaiian wife by planting taro. Since he was to live here and look at the field every day, we agreed taro would be grown. I haven't been here for thirty years."

"These are lotus plants?" I asked.

"Yes, blue lotus," he said.

We walked a little farther. I could see foot-long brightly colored koi swimming among the lotus plants.

"The scholar Zhou Dunyi said, 'I love the lotus because while growing from mud it is unstained,'" So Young Hee said. "The lotus shares a lot with taro. Both are planted in the mud but rise above the muck and erupt through the surface of the water clean and beautiful. Like the taro, all parts of the lotus are edible, from its roots to its leaves to its flower petals. The Chinese revere the lotus in the same way the Hawaiians revere the taro plant, and the blue lotus is the most revered of all. In China, the blue lotus also is known as the sacred lotus and is the symbol of purity and elegance. So I let Wai Lo Fat plant his taro, but I insisted the symbol of the Hung Bang Kongsi in Hawaii be the blue lotus. That is how our public service organization became the Blue Lotus Society."

"And that's how the stunningly beautiful yet needy Amber Kam became Blue Lotus Blossom Queen," I said.

"Sad, but true," he said.

I looked up toward her house. She probably was sleeping. I could only imagine what she would think if she looked out those windows and saw me walking in the fields with So Young Hee, if she even knew who he was.

"I did not know Wai Lo Fat had allowed the university to test genetically altered taro here against the laws of the state," he said. "This was his project, this field, although the land is owned by Four Gates Enterprises."

He looked down the path at Blue Ho'okane.

"I assume that gentleman was your accomplice when you raided the patches for specimens of the taro," he said.

"Yeah, he runs a youth outreach farming program on the west side of the island," I said. "As part of that project, he grew taro until all the taro on Oahu came down with a virus that killed it. When I told him I had seen healthy taro, he didn't believe me. Then when I brought him here, he knew exactly what it was."

"Your investigation into Wai Lo Fat's death and stealing the plants could have brought unwanted attention to the taro patch," he said. "Danny Chang told me that the army officer wished me to do everything I could to stop your investigation. He said it was my duty as a patriotic American citizen to stop you. I knew Amber was just using you to cause trouble. So against my better judgment I had her promoted, given an office in the Plaza and a seat on the board of directors. Then I ordered the taro removed and ponds constructed for the blue lotus."

"Why would it be your duty as an American citizen to stop my investigation?"

"I told you, Mr. McBride, it is all about Kahala Road," he said.

"There is no Kahala Road," I said.

"There is, sir," he said. "You are standing on it."

I looked down the raised dirt path that ran about a hundred yards to where Blue Ho'okane was standing. So Young Hee followed my gaze.

"This path is what is left of Kahala Road," he said. He pointed toward the mountains. "It ran a mile that way, joining up with what would become Waialae Avenue."

He turned toward the ocean.

"It was to run that way all the way to Kahala Bay. It would be the only access to Kahala Bay back when all of Kahala was marsh and there was no road along the ocean. In 1942, seven of us were paid ten dollars a day to build Kahala Road. The fill dirt came from military construction sites after the attack on Pearl Harbor. Building the road wasn't an important defense project, like the kind that were being constructed all over the island at that time. After Pearl Harbor the military built heavily fortified gun batteries on the sides of Diamond Head and along the cliffs all around the island. They were worried Japan might attack again. They also wanted land access to Kahala Bay for shore watchers, people who looked for strange ships and submarines. Kahala Road was to provide that access."

"You said there were just seven of you?"

"Yes, just seven," he said. "We were all born in Hawaii, all about the same age, and we were all Hung Bang Kongsi. Our fathers had come from southern China. We built Kahala Road by hand, with just picks and shovels. It was hot, dirty work, but we wanted to show the military that we were patriotic Americans, willing to help in the war effort. At that time, we still felt like we were not true citizens of the United States. Our parents told us that the Hawaii government had burned down Chinatown in 1900 on purpose, because the Chinese were getting too strong. Too organized. We felt it could happen to us again."

He drew a line in the dirt with his shoe.

"We had built Kahala Road to about here the day that Chin Chen Yu came to visit us," he said. "We all knew who Chin Chen Yu was. He was Hung Bang Kongsi, but he also was a gangster. A member of the Jade Dragon Society, a triad based in Hong Kong. He controlled Chinatown in Honolulu. He was a dangerous man."

"Did you know he was working for the military?" I asked.

"He told us that day," he said. "He said we had to come back that night and work on the road. There would be something to be buried under the road. It was part of the war, he said. We were not to ask questions. Just bury what was brought to us. That night, he drove up in a jeep with a heavy object inside a canvas bag. We all knew what it was. We knew it was a dead body. We buried it deep. By morning, Kahala Road was just a little longer."

He stopped and looked up at me with watery eyes. "We felt we were working for our country, you see? But in the next month, Chin Chen Yu brought more bodies. The last time he came, he brought four. Two were small. Too small to be adults. He had come to trust us, so he just left the canvas bags and drove away. The seven of us for the first time opened one of the bags. It contained the body of a dead child. A dead Japanese child. Another contained the body of a Japanese woman. And the fourth was a man."

"It was a family," I said.

"Yes," he said. "Three days later it came out in a haole newspaper that a Japanese family had disappeared. The Kurosawas. The father ran a Japanese school in Kaimuki. The newspaper said he was a spy for Japan and had fled before he could be arrested, but we knew where they were. And they are still here."

He looked down at our feet and I felt goose bumps rising on my arms, what in Hawaii we call "chicken skin." Buried below me was the secret of Kahala Road. Japanese American citizens, possibly dozens, suspected of being spies for Japan, had been killed by military interrogators after the attack on Pearl Harbor.

"During the war, the military government ran legal brothels on Hotel Street and in Chinatown," So Young Hee said. "Since Chin Chen Yu was already in the prostitution business, the military let him run the brothels for them. Hundreds of soldiers a day went through those places. Chin Chen Yu also was helping the military stay in contact with the triads in Hong Kong and Singapore, gathering information on the Japanese occupation of China. The military trusted him, and he was eager to show that the Chinese in Hawaii were patriots. So when suspected Japanese spies died during interrogations, they trusted him to put the bodies in the place where they would never be found. We were young, all in our twenties, some of us just married. We wanted to show the United States we could be trusted. We didn't want to be swept up with the Japanese and sent to concentration camps on the Mainland. A lot of haoles at that time thought all Asians were the enemy. So when Chin Chen Yu brought the bodies, we buried them under Kahala Road."

Blue came back down the path.

"We should go," he said.

I agreed. We got back in the limo and headed toward Portlock. Along the way, So Young Hee finished his story.

"At the end of the war, Chin Chen Yu's controller, a Colonel Johnson, who later became a general, convinced the territorial government to make a gift of the Kahala

Marsh to us, out of appreciation for our work on Kahala Road," he said. "It wasn't such a grand gesture since this land at that time was considered nearly worthless. We created the Lodge of the Inner Eight, and the property was deeded over to the eight of us. Colonel Johnson held a small ceremony over by where the shack is today, handing us the deed, thanking us for our patriotism, and telling us that what lay below Kahala Road was a matter of national security and that as part of our agreement we must never divulge it."

So Young Hee said some members of the Lodge of the Inner Eight were not convinced that the burials, particularly of the children, were a matter of national security. But as the years went by the lodge members decided to make the best of the situation and use the land they owned to help their families, the Hung Bang Kongsi, and the Chinese community at large in Hawaii. He said they set up Four Gates Enterprises, its name derived from the cardinal directions of the compass, which the Chinese endowed with mythical significance: the North Gate associated with the color black, water, and the Tortoise; the East Gate representing the color green, wood, and the Dragon; the South Gate related to the color red, fire, and the Red Bird; and the West Gate having to do with the color white, metal, and the White Tiger.

"Under Four Gates we developed Kahala for homes and businesses," he said. "Filling in the marsh was a long, exhausting process. At first, we did not have the heavy machinery, and our employees worked with wheelbarrows and horses but the Kahala of today rose from the muck like a blue lotus plant. Over the years Four Gates has generated millions and millions of dollars. With the money we were able to help the Chinese in Hawaii work and own their own homes and businesses. Through the Blue Lotus Society, we were able to help many community projects and charities. Not just Chinese but across the island. We were able to teach the haoles and other cultures about the Chinese. Our pageants and parades have become a traditional part of life in Hawaii."

As the members of the Lodge of the Inner Eight aged, some of them, particularly Wai Lo Fat, became more concerned about what they had done on Kahala Road.

"When he became an old man it burdened his soul. Every day he looked out the window from his house and saw Kahala Road," So Young Hee said. "I asked him to move, to live somewhere else, but it's as if he felt he needed to suffer for what we had done. He needed to be reminded every day. It gave him some solace that the taro patches were here. They were not just to honor his wife, but his own memorial to the people buried there."

"Over the years, someone outside the Lodge of the Inner Eight must have known that something bad had happened on Kahala Road," I said. "I've heard that Kahala Road has become a myth in the Chinese community, that when people die, it's said they walk Kahala Road."

"I don't know how that started," he said. "Chin Chen Yu warned members of the lodge that something bad would happen to us and our families should we ever talk. He suggested that we could end up under Kahala Road ourselves. Somehow it leaked out that there was something called Kahala Road and it was a bad place where people go when they die. Only the eight of us and General Johnson knew the truth. I have eight children, Mr. McBride, and fourteen grandchildren and twenty-eight great-grandchildren and several great-great-grandchildren. You have to understand that Chin Chen Yu was a powerful and dangerous man in Hawaii. I warned Wai Lo Fat that we could say nothing of Kahala Road as long as Chin Chen Yu was alive."

"So when Chin Chen Yu died, Wai Lo Fat was ready to tell the secret of Kahala Road to the world," I said.

"Yes. He told me as much at Chin Chen Yu's funeral, and that was heard by the army colonel," he said. "The officer reminded us of our vow and said that Kahala Road was still a matter of national security. He said disclosure would amount to treason. The last thing any Chinese Americans or Japanese Americans who had been through World War II would want to be accused of is treason, Mr. McBride. I assured him Wai Lo Fat would remain silent. Then, two weeks later, Wai Lo Fat was found dead in the taro patch just feet from Kahala Road."

Chapter Thirty-six

Auntie Kealoha was gracious in accepting her new houseguest. She put a maile lei over So Young Hee's shoulders and kissed him on the cheek. Looking at the open-ended strand of green leaves hanging down to his waist, So Young Hee seemed a little overwhelmed and slightly embarrassed. Apparently he wasn't used to people being happy to see him, either.

Auntie Kealoha told him how bad she felt when she learned of Wai Lo Fat's passing and praised him for his concern for the Hawaiian people. Before she escorted So Young Hee out to the pagoda for tea, she took Tiny Maunakea aside and they chatted for about three minutes. Or rather, Tiny listened for about three minutes. Then she and So Young Hee disappeared down the gauntlet of orchid plants toward the backyard.

About twenty minutes later Tiny, Blue, and I were back in So Young Hee's palatial suite at the Moana Hotel. Blue's buddy, the night front desk clerk, had breakfast sent up, a huge spread of eggs, pancakes, bacon, toast, papaya, mango, fresh-squeezed orange juice, and, thankfully, beer. Blue and

I had been up all night and had already eaten breakfast at Zippy's a few hours earlier, so a beer sounded good. We stood drinking Heinekens on the lanai looking at four-foot waves breaking all along Waikiki Beach. The trades were holding up the faces nicely, but there were so many tourists and kooks in the water that there was no chance of anyone getting a wave to themselves. I looked at Tiny Maunakea digging into the breakfast cart while watching CNN on TV and then turned to Blue.

"You and Tiny get along pretty well," I said. He correctly understood that as a question about how a crime fighter like himself could be buddies with a well-known organized crime figure.

"I've known Tiny Maunakea since high school days," he said. "We worked on the interisland barges together during the summers. After high school, I guess you could say we went in separate directions, careerwise. When I was a cop, he was helpful to me at times."

He took a sip of beer and turned back to the waves.

I correctly understood that was all the background information I was going to get about the relationship between Blue Ho'okane and Tiny Maunakea. I also understood that there was some really interesting shit they'd been involved in that I'd never hear about.

The valet had parked Tiny's limo in the garage and moved my pickup truck right out in front of the hotel where cabs usually waited. Before getting off his shift, Blue's clerk buddy directed the coming on duty hotel staff to feel free to confirm that a Mr. So Young Hee was indeed a guest of the hotel and provide whoever asked the suite number.

That was part of the new strategy that we discussed on

the ride back to the hotel. Blue told Tiny Maunakea of our run-in with Danny Chang and his associate earlier that night. We didn't know if Chang was in direct communication with Colonel Beauregard, most likely not. Blue said an intelligence officer like Beauregard wouldn't be using landlines or cell phones for fear of someone listening in or leaving a data trail that could later be traced. He probably gave Danny Chang his marching orders days before Wai Lo Fat's funeral, which were to stay close to So Young Hee and if he did anything weird to pick him up and hold him somewhere until Colonel Beauregard could get there and deal with the problem. Knowing how well Chin Chen Yu had prospered over the years because of his relationship with the U.S. intelligence community, Danny Chang was likely eager to do whatever Colonel Beauregard told him without question.

In the Wai Lo Fat funeral photo it looked like Danny Chang and his red armbands intended to cling to So Young Hee like Chinese remora. But So Young Hee told us he became alarmed by his new constant companions and slipped away from Danny Chang and his boys by walking into the front doors of Four Gates Plaza and then out a side door, catching a cab, and disappearing into Honolulu. He went to Tantalus, to the bungalow next to the large ranch-style house, a property Four Gates owned and rented out but that was currently empty. He felt secure there until he received a call from a friend in Chinatown who said Danny Chang had spread the story among Hung Bang Kongsi members that So Young Hee was in danger and had to be found as soon as possible. Hung Bang Kongsi were fanning out through Chinatown and Honolulu last night. So Young Hee trusted that the man who had called him would not tell Danny Chang about the Tantalus house, but he decided it might not be the safest place to lie low after all. He made a quick reservation at the Moana Hotel and bolted from the bungalow, leaving behind his cell phone and Dunhills.

I thought about the strange call I had gotten from Burl Morse at midnight and could understand his paranoia. Chinatown apparently was crawling with Hung Bang Kongsi members, and not just the red armbands. Burl had gotten the Tantalus house address from one of his sources and passed it on to me from a phone booth. The line had gone dead after he told me that someone was approaching him. The last thing he said was it looked like "Danny's guys." I didn't think Danny Chang would kill Burl but he probably would have given him a taste of Krav Maga to find out what he was doing asking questions about So Young Hee in Chinatown. I was hoping that when I eventually got back to the *Travis McGee* there'd be a call on the answering machine from Burl saying how he miraculously escaped an ass-kicking. We'd have a good laugh, and I'd tell him how the information he'd dug up helped solve the mystery of Kahala Road. I was hoping that—but I wasn't expecting it.

As we killed time in So Young Hee's Moana suite, our thinking was that Danny Chang was still looking for So Young Hee. After our run-in with him last night, he knew I was looking for So Young Hee, too, with the help of some other hard-ass local guy who owned a gun. Chang had to be under a lot of pressure to find Hee, and he had to think that I might be a good place to start since I had gotten to the Tantalus bungalow before he had.

So we parked my truck outside the Moana Hotel with

the hopes that the Hung Bang Kongsi search effort had flowed into Waikiki and that Danny Chang might just show up at our door looking to get Hee and me in one fell swoop.

Blue and I were brainstorming other ways to get the information out to Danny while we stood on the lanai drinking beer and watching the kook surfers run over each other when it suddenly occurred to me that the answer was sitting in front of the TV finishing off the last of the hash browns and pancakes. Tiny Maunakea had told me during my abduction that he kept in contact with some Hung Bang Kongsi members even though he wasn't one himself. After a short discussion Tiny decided that there was one person he trusted who might be able to get our location to one of the red armbands without fear of repercussions. He made a call.

In the end, we didn't know if Danny Chang got the tip from Tiny's guy or from someone who saw my truck outside, but at about 11:00 A.M., there was a knock on the hotel room door. I looked out through the peephole; one of the organ-grinder-monkey-suited bellhops looked nervously in from the other side. Danny thought he was being clever.

I opened the door and a hand pushed the bellhop aside and two of Danny Chang's boys rushed in and grabbed me by the arms. Then Danny Chang walked in nonchalantly in his black slacks, black shirt, and gold chain, looking smug and menacing. He casually shut the door, proud of himself and considering, no doubt, what kind of retribution to inflict upon me for me breaking the potted plant over his head. He turned to me with an oily smile.

"You not going like what going happen now so much, I think," he said.

"You aren't either," I said.

Then Tiny Maunakea stepped in the room from the lanai with a 9 mm machine pistol with a silencer on it, and Blue Ho'okane walked out of a bedroom with his handgun leveled in the direction of the three men.

It was the second time Danny Chang had only brought martial arts expertise to a gunfight, first at Tantalus when Blue got the drop on him and now, here, looking at Tiny Maunakea's gun. But he decided to try to bluff his way out of the situation anyway.

"These guys my fastest kickers," he said, cocky. "They kick gun out of your hand before you even see them." The fast kickers had let go of me and were assuming a casual stance in preparation for this demonstration of kung fu prowess when Tiny Maunakea put a bullet into the right leg of each of them. The little machine gun, apparently in semiautomatic mode, just went *pfft, pfft*, and Danny's boys were on the rug grabbing their legs and moaning.

"I daresay they won't be kicking any guns today," Tiny said, his face impassive. "And you, sir, I understand you are a fast kicker, also?"

Danny Chang got the message quickly.

"No, no, no!" he said, waving his hands in front of him. "I no kicker. I no kicker."

"Pray, sit on the floor, cross your legs, and link your hands behind your head," Tiny said.

Danny sat down and assumed the desired position.

Blue walked over to him and patted him down with the revolver stuck on Danny's right temple. Then he patted down the two squirming men on the floor.

"They're clean," he said.

Tiny held the gun casually in front of him with both

hands. I wondered if it was the same gun he had used on Three Man Stone. Maybe it was his favorite gun. Maybe he had a pet name for it, like Poopsie, or something Victorian, like Algernon Charles Swinburne. In any case, I was just glad he knew how to use it, because he had to shoot the first guy in the leg, then wave the gun barrel past me to shoot the other guy in the leg. Pretty amazing accuracy when you consider the whole thing took less than a second.

"Do they speak English?" Blue asked Danny Chang.

"Only little, not so much," he said.

"Tell them to look at me, and then you repeat what I tell them," he said.

Danny said something in Chinese to his associates, and they turned to Blue.

Blue pulled out a police badge that I suspect he kept as a souvenir from his days on the force.

"Honolulu police," he said, pointing to himself and Tiny.

Danny translated.

"Do you want to go to jail?"

Danny translated, and they shook their heads. No.

"Get the fuck out of here," Blue said. "This one's under arrest." He pointed to Danny Chang.

Danny translated as Blue opened the door. The two men scrambled up on their good legs and hobbled as fast as they could out of the room. Blue shut the door.

Chapter Thirty-seven

Danny Chang's zest for life had left him. The swaggering Dragon Boy lay on the floor of Tiny Maunakea's limo cuffed hand and foot, his mouth sealed with a strip of duct tape. I sat on one couch, and Blue Ho'okane sat on another. Danny looked around the inside of the limo, his eyes going back and forth like a caged animal.

After a short strategy session in the bedroom of the Moana Hotel suite, Blue Ho'okane and Tiny had decided I should become Danny's best friend in the world, my only goal to save him from being killed by the savage local man with the police badge and the human mountain with the machine gun.

After Blue had sent his wounded associates away, Danny had defiantly refused our first invitation for him to tell us how to get hold of Colonel Beauregard. At that time, there were still a few sparks of the Dragon Boy flickering inside him. He needed time to wrap his brain around his new reality, that he was not going to become the next Chin Chen Yu, feared triad leader of Honolulu with a "never go to jail" card from the United States government. He was not going to be Tranquility, the most dangerous mixed martial arts fighter at the next Rock the Island Superbrawl at the Aloha Stadium. His Coiling Dragon Wushu Academy was history. He needed time to come to the realization, on his own, that he had only one choice: tell us how to get hold of Colonel Beauregard and then leave Hawaii never to return, or die.

I was pretty sure the option of killing him was just hypothetical. But then again, I didn't think Tiny was going to shoot anyone with a machine gun in the hotel room that morning. Maybe one of the things Auntie Kealoha had whispered to Tiny before we left her estate after dropping off So Young Hee was that she wanted Danny Chang sent back to Hong Kong horizontally in a box. Danny was the kind of random factor bouncing around Honolulu Auntie Kealoha didn't want. It disrupted the natural order, and it could lead to the perception in the law enforcement and criminal worlds that maybe Auntie Kealoha didn't have as much power as people assumed. When you're in the Godmother of Organized Crime business, that kind of thinking is not helpful.

So, to help Danny in this self-realization exercise, we decided on a long ride in a black limousine, trussed up like a pig ready to be tossed in a luau pit. While the handcuffs were needed because his hands and feet definitely were weapons, the duct tape was just an affectation. You know you're truly in the shit when someone puts duct tape over your mouth.

We were driving out to the south side of Makapuu Point where, Tiny announced in front of Danny Chang, there was a strong ocean current called the Molokai Express that was handy for getting rid of problems.

The possibility that the death option wasn't hypothetical would give me the motivation to sell it when we got him out of the car at Makapuu Point and gave him one last chance to tell us how to get hold of Colonel Beauregard.

Tiny Maunakea slowed the car as we passed Sandy Beach on Kalanianaole Highway. Blue suddenly jerked Danny Chang from the floor and pushed his head against the window, pointing out the exact spot where Chang had cornered me.

"Hey, bruddah, isn't that where you kicked my friend here in the head?" he asked. "How things change, huh?"

He let go of him, and Danny fell back onto the floor of the passenger compartment. Blue grabbed a Budweiser out of the refrigerated compartment, tossed it to me, and then cracked one open for himself. He pointed out the window with his beer.

"Check it out, Stryker, the waves are pumping at Sandy's today!" he said. "Maybe we should go bodysurfing after we send this guy off to Molokai."

I didn't know if Tiny and Blue had planned this bit of theater beforehand, but from the look in Danny's eyes, it was having an effect.

Tiny drove down a rough, sandy trail through five-foot-tall bunches of beach grass. We bounced along until we came to a small, deserted crescent-shaped sandy beach bordered on one side by the sheer lava cliffs of Makapuu Point and by a rocky outcropping the size of a house on the other. It reminded me of that little beach in the movie *From Here to Eternity* where Burt Lancaster and Deborah Kerr did the horizontal hula in the surf. I had lived on Oahu longer than anywhere else in my life, and I never knew this hidden cove existed.

Tiny turned the limo off and climbed out. I opened the big passenger compartment door, and Blue and I pushed and pulled Danny Chang until he was standing in the sand, his feet and hands still handcuffed. Tiny leaned against the right front end of the car holding his little friend Algernon Charles Swinburne, and Blue frog-walked Danny to the edge of the water. Waves were breaking along the rocks on each side of the tiny cove, and foam swirled in the middle like suds in a washing machine.

"That's the Molokai Express right there," Blue said, directing Danny's attention to the churning water. "Anything tossed in there gets dragged out through the channel out there and across the Molokai Channel. It's called the Molokai Express, but Tiny tells me few people ever actually reach Molokai."

Blue looked at me and said, "He's all yours." Then he walked over to join Tiny by the limo.

I sat Danny down on a rock sticking up out of the sand. Then I sat down next to him.

"Here's what's going to happen," I said. "If you tell us how to contact Colonel Beauregard, we're going to put you on a plane to Hong Kong. If you don't tell us, those two guys are going to throw you in the water and you're going to be dragged out to sea and drown. Those are your only choices, Danny. Nod if you understand me."

He slowly nodded at me.

"Now, I have nothing against you," I said. "You kicked me in the head and I broke a potted plant over your head. We're even. But those two gentlemen are hard-core cases. That guy Blue? He once broke a German shepherd over his knee during a drug raid. And Tiny Maunakea, well, you've seen Tiny in action. He's sort of a shoot first, apologize later kind of guy. Before he tosses you in the Molokai Express, I expect he'll at least shoot you in the legs like he did your buddies. Now, we must get hold of Colonel Beauregard for reasons you don't need to know. You're in something way over your head, and you don't even know what it is, but it's nothing you need to die over. Here's what we are going to do. I'm going to bring my friends over here. Then I'm going to take the duct tape off your mouth. You are going to have one chance and one chance only to tell us how to contact Colonel Beauregard. If anything else but that comes out of your mouth, it will be the deep blue good-bye, my friend. Nod if you understand."

He nodded. He didn't look scared anymore. He looked drained.

I signaled to Tiny Maunakea and Blue Ho'okane, and they walked over. They stood looking down at him, solemn as a couple of undertakers. I ripped the duct tape from his mouth hard and fast, because that's the way they always do it in the movies.

Danny Chang looked up at us, moved his jaw back and forth, swallowed, and said, "Mailbox place in Pearl City. I leave message there. Or he leave message. We check every two days. He check tomorrow."

Blue pressed him for more details, writing everything down. Then he made a call to the Mailboxes and More! in Pearl City, just above Pearl Harbor, and confirmed that there was a box there for a Mr. John Maynard Keynes, Beauregard's apparent nom de guerre. Once satisfied, he nodded to Tiny, who picked Danny Chang up under one arm, carried him screaming to the water's edge, and chucked him into the swirling waves. As he was dragged quickly along the left side of the cove, I looked at Tiny Maunakea, who was smiling.

"Worry yourself not, Stryker," he said. "This is merely a tidal whirlpool."

Danny was dragged across the mouth of the cove and then back toward the beach and then began the circular trip again.

"The true Molokai Express current is farther out," he said.

As Danny began his third trip around the cove, screaming and gasping for air, Blue said, "Are you going to fuck around all day, Tiny, or are we going to get some lunch? I want to try that little Mexican place in Waimanalo since we're in the neighborhood."

Chapter Thirty-eight

When it came to naval battle strategy, Admiral Horatio Nelson always said, "Never mind the maneuvers, go straight at them." I like that strategy. It's like sending a fullback straight through the line in football. Never mind the screens and bootlegs and double-reverses, just give hoss the ball and let him slam into the line all afternoon. I think Admiral Nelson would have made a great NFL coach.

So when it came to arranging a face-to-face with Colonel Beauregard, I thought it would be best to let him come straight at me. I wanted to make it easy for him to find me and feel comfortable that the meeting would be private. My plan depended on my new belief that he was working alone and was desperately trying to keep the secret of Kahala Road contained. I had become convinced that he was some kind of rogue agent.

This realization came to me after I thought about what So Young Hee had told me when we stood on what was left of Kahala Road. I believed that Japanese Americans suspected of being spies for Japan were tortured and killed after Pearl Harbor was bombed. I had no doubt that So Young Hee and his fellow members of the Lodge of the Inner Eight had buried their bodies under Kahala Road. What I didn't believe was that their deaths were part of an officially sanctioned program of interrogation by the U.S. military. It just didn't make sense.

After Pearl Harbor, Hawaii was under military martial law. The loyalty of the Islands' Japanese residents was in question. About two thousand ethnic Japanese from Hawaii were sent to internment camps in California, even though many of them were Americans. One-third of the state's population, about 150,000 people, was Japanese. You couldn't lock them all up while you were trying to rebuild your fleet and fight a war in the Pacific.

So thousands of Japanese Americans lived in Hawaii during the war, and their lives were hard. They were looked upon with suspicion and scorn by their neighbors. To insult and intimidate the local Japanese, people would throw rice in their yards. They were taunted even though thousands of Hawaii Japanese volunteered for the military, forming the 442nd Regimental Combat Team, which became one of the most highly decorated units in the history of the U.S. military. The Asian members of the 442nd and the 100th Infantry suffered so many casualties fighting in Europe that they were known as the Purple Heart Battalion.

Some Japanese in Hawaii were suspected of being spies but other than one Japanese American on the island of Niihau, near Kauai, who helped a downed Japanese Zero pilot, no spies were ever found.

But it's easy to believe that in the chaos after Pearl Harbor was bombed an overzealous military haole intelligence officer or two—who probably couldn't tell the difference between Japanese and Chinese in Hawaii—took it upon themselves to root out spies. I could imagine that Colonel Johnson, who befriended Chin Chen Yu and convinced him to secretly bury the bodies of dead Japanese under Kahala Road, was one of these rogue officers. If the deaths had been the result of officially sanctioned interrogations, the bodies would not have had to be hidden. Besides, there's no way that an entire Japanese family, including two children, could have died during a spy investigation. What happened on Kahala Road was the act of a war criminal.

I didn't know how, but it looked like Colonel Beauregard had inherited the duty to keep what happened on Kahala Road secret. It wasn't a big task. Over the past fifty years, only ten people knew about Kahala Road, and most of them steadily died off. I could imagine Colonel Beauregard's anger when, after the death of Chin Chen Yu, one of the two remaining members of the Lodge of the Inner Eight—this fucking Wai Lo Fat—says he wants to reveal the secret of Kahala Road. I could imagine Beauregard thinking the death of Wai Lo Fat would make his life a lot easier. It would have, too. Until I came along and started poking my nose into Wai Lo Fat's death and asking questions about the taro patch.

He thought Danny Chang could handle a simple assignment to scare me away and to keep an eye on So Young Hee. It turned out Danny was a loose cannon, and now everything was fucked up. These crazy Chinese guys running all over town looking for So Young Hee. So Young Hee nowhere to be found. Then Danny Chang disappears. And now he gets a note in his private mailbox from Stryker

McBride saying they should meet. The note says McBride wants to talk about Kahala Road; that the discussion could be "mutually beneficial." If McBride knew the truth about Kahala Road, he could easily have gone to the press, but he didn't. Maybe this thing still could be contained. Maybe he better have a little talk with Stryker McBride and find out just how much he knows and what he wants. Maybe it's just a shakedown. Maybe McBride just wants some money.

Assuming that was the way Colonel Beauregard was thinking—and there were a lot of assumptions piled up there—then I figured at some point he would be paying me a visit. I'd made it easy for him to never mind the maneuvers and come straight at me. And if it was going to happen, it was going to happen soon.

Chapter Thirty-nine

The day after Blue Ho'okane and I left the note for Colonel Beauregard at Mailboxes and More! I made a big show of dropping off the gods at the vet. I figured the colonel had enough experience in intelligence gathering to be able to track my movements and scope out my home turf before he approached me. I wanted him to come to me, and there's no way he would be able to get to me on the *Travis McGee* with Kane and Lono on the grounds. At least, not while they were alive. So I put them in the back of the pickup truck and tied their leashes to a ring bolt near the cab window so they couldn't jump out if they suddenly saw something worth chasing. Kane and Lono were always excited to go for a ride, even though usually it meant a trip to the vet, where they were given shots and held in small cages until I got around to picking them up. I took them to the Kaneohe Vet Center and played with them in the back of the truck for several minutes before taking them inside. I wanted to give anyone following me plenty of time to see what was going on. Although the gods were only going to be boarded for a night or two, I arranged with the girl handling their check-in to have them be pampered and paid extra so they'd have their nails trimmed, get nice baths, have their coats combed, and be walked twice a day. Then I took my time walking back to the truck so that it was clear the dogs had been left behind.

Back on the boat, I moved the recliner out of the middle of the room and put it against a bulkhead. I wanted the den to be as open as possible just in case a physical altercation ensued. One of my advantages would be that I know where everything is on the boat and a visitor wouldn't.

Then I did something I hadn't done in two years. I dug my .38 caliber handgun out of a box in the back of my bedroom closet. I bought the gun after I got the boat on the off-chance that Jake Stane was carrying a grudge and would come after me if he managed to escape from prison. Or maybe he'd make friends with a short-timer and send him to bother me when he was released. As time went on, that seemed less likely to happen, and eventually I put the gun away and forgot about it.

Now I felt the heft of the gun in my hand. It was one of those old-fashioned revolver-type guns, like Sam Spade used to carry. I pushed in six bullets and spun the cylinder to make sure it revolved. If a revolver's cylinder doesn't revolve, then the gun is not a functioning revolver. I was no Tiny Maunakea, but the few times I had shot a gun, target shooting, I was pretty good at it. I'd found that bullets generally go in the direction they are aimed. The trick was not to aim them at anything you didn't want to hit, like your foot or your refrigerator, both of which I realized I had been waving the gun in the direction of while I was loading it. If things went the way I hoped, there would be no gunplay on the *Travis McGee* that night, or whenever Beauregard decided to show up.

The last thing I did was take my wind chimes from the leeward side of the boat and hang them up under the stairs that led to the boat's stern deck. I walked up and down the stairs a few times, and the chimes made just the slightest tingling sound. Anyone coming up the stairs either wouldn't notice the chimes or would think they were ringing because of the wind, but I would know someone was boarding.

I closed and locked all the windows and doors, leaving just the door to the stern deck unlocked. Then I went to the Longhouse Bar for a few beers before turning in for the night.

I sat at the end of the bar by a wall phone, and after getting my beer, I called Dr. McCall. It was nearly six o'clock, but I hoped she still was at her office. She was.

"What's up, big fella?" she asked.

"If Wai Lo Fat had been killed by a weaponized pathogen, what kind of a delivery system would the bad guy use?"

"What are you involved in, Stryker?"

"Just sitting here having a few beers and got to wondering, is all," I said.

"Are you alone?"

"I'm alone at one end of the bar," I said. "There's a bunch of old farts at the round table telling lies to each other."

"Why don't I come out and join you. I'm just wrapping up here," she said.

"Melba, just to keep you from having to suffer the humiliation of an outright rejection, can I take a rain check?"

"Miss Congeniality doesn't take rain checks," she said. "Now, what's going on Stryker? Talk to me."

"I'm meeting a guy," I said. "I can't go into details, but just on the off-chance that he might be the kind of person that carries around weaponized pathogens, I was just wondering what the delivery system would look like."

"Jesus, Stryker," she said. "If you even suspect that someone has any of that stuff within a mile of you, run in the other direction. It's nothing to fuck around with."

"The meeting is kind of set," I said.

The other side of the line was silent. I waited.

"It's probably an aerosol delivery system," she said. "Something that would emit a narrow, directed spray. If the germs are what we suspect they are, they are probably designed to enter through the nose and mouth and live long enough to do their damage but to die fairly quickly in the open air. The delivery system could be something like a small pepper spray container. Or an aerosol spray can."

"How can it be sprayed without the sprayer inhaling some himself?"

"It would be pretty hard to spray anything in a closed space without the sprayer inhaling particles suspended in the air. The thing is, if this is a designed pathogen, then whoever designed it also could have designed a vaccination for it. In fact, I'd be surprised if they hadn't. The sprayer would already be inoculated. But Stryker, please, tell me you are just messing with me because this is serious stuff, and it would ruin my day to come in tomorrow and find you lying on one of my operating tables."

"I'll call you tomorrow," I said. "We'll talk about rain checks."

The sun was going down. I took my time walking across

the lawn back to my boat. I stopped and chatted with the commodore, returning from a trip to Heeia Kea Pier to fill his boat with gas.

"Where are the dogs?" he asked.

"On holiday," I said. "Yearly checkup. Thought I'd let them have a mani-pedi boys' night out."

"Are you okay?" he asked.

"Sure, why?"

"Because that fucking club flag has been at half mast for three days and you haven't asked me who died and if a slip was going to be available," he said.

I looked over and sure enough, the club flag was flying underneath the Stars and Stripes halfway down the pole.

"So?"

"So it was Bob," he said.

"Heart Attack Bob?"

"No, Karaoke Bob."

"I thought Karaoke Bob was Heart Attack Bob," I said.

"Heart Attack Bob, Karaoke Bob . . . whatever. The man's dead."

"What'd he die of?" I asked.

"Heart attack. Someone noticed his skiff going around in circles in the boat basin; he was dead at the controls."

"He had slip 43 on the floating pier."

"Yes he did," he said.

"Hey, my boat would fit in that slip," I said, suddenly catching on.

"That's right, Sherlock," he said. "But we have to wait until Bob is planted or his ashes spread on the water or whatever his family wants to do with him. Then his club membership goes to his wife. Christ Almighty, she's older than he is, and she never comes down here. But we have to wait and see if she wants to keep the boat there. So don't get your hopes up. I'll see what I can do. I'm tired of seeing the *Queen Elizabeth* sitting on the lawn."

"You're too good to me, Fleetwood," I said.

"You got that fuckin' right," he said, laughing. "Come on, let's get a drink."

"I'm working on something right now," I said. "Catch you later."

I ate a little dinner of leftover grilled mahimahi and wondered if I was doing the right thing. Colonel Beauregard wouldn't go anywhere near someone like Blue Ho'okane or Tiny Maunakea, but he'd already shown that he thought he could scare me by using someone like Danny Chang. I hoped he thought he could be more persuasive.

All I knew was that I was calling the shots. I wasn't going to be reacting to someone else's plans. Whatever happened that night would be on my boat this time. I would control the situation and force the action.

After dinner I took a cold shower and went back out to the dayroom to read. I realized I was on edge. I'd read an entire paragraph and then realize I had no idea what I had just read. I was listening to the night sounds. The air was still, and I could hear the squeaks and groans as the nearest boats on A Pier gently tugged at their moorings.

After an hour of trying to read I made a big production of going to bed. Anyone outside would be able to see me padding down the hallway, clicking off the lights as I went. Then I climbed into bed and turned off the light on my bedside table. I lay there still for a few minutes, and then in the dark I slipped to the floor and crawled back down the hall into the dayroom. I had moved one couch away from the corner by my office. I slipped into that corner, my back against two solid bulkheads. I felt around and found my .38 where I had left it. I thought, *This is stupid. Nobody's going to come. What was I thinking?*

Then at about 11:00 P.M. I heard the soft jingle of the wind chimes at the back of the boat, but I didn't hear the sound of anyone walking up the stairs or walking on the aft deck. I held the .38 in my right hand, straining to hear any movement. Instead I heard a knock on the stern door and a high voice say, "Hello! Mr. McBride! Are you at home? Hello!"

I walked cautiously to the door and could make out a dark figure through the opaque glass. I opened the door, and standing there was a man in slacks and long-sleeved V-necked sweater. He was short, maybe five foot one, but I recognized the face from the photo of Chin Chen Yu's memorial. He must have had to stand on a chair for that photo.

"Stryker McBride, I presume!" he said in a voice reminiscent of author Truman Capote's. "I'm Colonel Beauregard. Permission to come aboard?"

I didn't know what to think. Here I had been building up Colonel Beauregard into this villain in my mind, something akin to Orson Welles in the movie *Touch of Evil*, and instead I get Truman Capote doing Henry Stanley.

I slipped the .38 into my pants pocket and let him in. Then I turned on two lamps in the den from a switch by the door.

"Did I wake you?" he asked.

"No, actually, I was expecting you."

"Good man," he said. "I knew you were smart, Mr. McBride."

"Have a seat," I said.

He sat on the couch closest to the door. He looked more like a tennis coach than an army colonel in intelligence who, from what Blue had told me, was feared by those who knew him. I sat in a chair on the opposite side of the room. I wanted plenty of space between us.

"How's Danny Chang?" I asked.

"I haven't heard from him lately," he said. "Do you know where he is?"

"I might," I said.

"That would explain where you got my mailbox address," he said. "A shame. I had great hopes for that boy. You said in your note you wanted to talk about Kahala Road. I don't believe I know anything about a Kahala Road."

"You don't know anything about the burial of Japanese Americans killed after Pearl Harbor while being questioned as spies?" I asked.

"Sorry, nope."

"They were buried under Kahala Road," I said. "It was a road being built by So Young Hee, Wai Lo Fat, and other members of the Lodge of the Inner Eight through the marshes of Kahala after Pearl Harbor. Chin Chen Yu brought the road builders bodies to secretly bury there at the request of his contacts in military intelligence," I said.

"This the first I've heard about it."

"Among those killed and buried under Kahala Road is a Japanese American family of four, including two children," I said.

"Mr. McBride, you have me at a disadvantage," he said.

"Why were you at Chin Chen Yu's memorial service?"

"Mr. Yu was a great American," he said. "I can't go into details, but he performed many services for the government over the years. That is why I was asked to attend Chin Chen Yu's memorial service, to show that the U.S. government was appreciative of his service to his country."

"Who asked you to attend?"

"Now, now, Mr. McBride, I didn't come here to be interrogated," he said.

"Why did you come here?"

"You said you wanted to have a conversation that could be mutually beneficial," he said, his voice going higher in frustration. "So far all I am encountering is hostility about things I know nothing about. You seem to have some information you think has some value. So tell me what you want. Money?"

"Who is Colonel Johnson?" I asked.

This hit home. He looked at me, running things over in his mind. His demeanor completely changed. He no longer was a harmless munchkin.

"I knew you were smart, Mr. McBride," he said. "I do know Colonel Johnson. Actually, he's now General Jason Johnson, retired. He was promoted after World War II. He is a great man who did what he had to for his country during a time of war."

"He *is* a great man? He's still alive?"

"He's one hundred years old, and he lives over in a little convalescent center in Kalihi," he said. "It's really a sad place for such a great man to spend his final years on this earth. I see him regularly. Before his recent stroke, he was quite lucid. Now he can hardly talk. He did tell me about Kahala Road and the spies buried there. It was a classified operation and is still a matter of national security."

"It's a matter of national security that an American

family of four was killed—two children were killed—and then buried in a marsh?"

"There's collateral damage in every armed conflict," he said. "And they were Japanese."

"They were Americans," I said. "They were children."

His delivery had become flat, resigned. It occurred to me that he was telling me things that he thought would never leave my houseboat. I slowly slipped my hand into my right pocket and felt around for the gun.

"General Johnson really regretted not being able to attend Chin Chen Yu's funeral—" His sentence was interrupted by a deep, watery cough. He coughed several times, kind of wheezing in between. Then he resumed. "He really wanted to go to the funeral, but he couldn't. His stroke has left him bedridden," he said.

I gripped the revolver and put my finger gently on the trigger. I tried to remember if I had flicked the safety off.

Colonel Beauregard continued. "So I took it upon myself to represent him and to remind Wai Lo Fat and So Young Hee of their continuing commitments to this country."

He stood up and tried to take a deep breath. All he managed was a shallow gasp. "I'm sorry, Mr. McBride," he rasped. "A touch of asthma."

He felt around in his left pants pocket, searching for something. I began slowly pulling the gun from my pocket, watching his slightest move. He took a common asthma inhaler from his pocket and showed it to me.

"I don't know what I'd do without this," he said. "Sometimes I can't breathe at all. It's called a rescue inhaler because—"

As he spoke, he took a step toward me, holding the inhaler with his arm extended.

That's when I pulled out my .38 revolver and pulled the trigger three times. In the semidarkness of the dayroom, flames shot out of the barrel and the sound of the gunshots slammed off the bulkheads. Colonel Beauregard flew backward onto the couch. Dead.

Chapter Forty

Blue Ho'okane came running up the stairs and onto the stern deck of the *Travis McGee* within seconds of hearing the gunshots. We had arranged for him to position himself near the boat where he could see Colonel Beauregard approach and then make sure he had no one else with him. Then he moved below the boat by the stairs and had been listening to our entire conversation. If I felt like I needed him, I was simply to say, "Blue." But when I saw Colonel Beauregard pull out the inhaler and try to close the distance between us, I knew my only hope was to fire first. He had been so casual in bringing out the inhaler that I think he really didn't believe I would have a gun. He thought he'd just be able walk onto my boat, spritz me, and walk away, thinking that within minutes my immune system would erupt into a cytokine storm and I would end up just another mysterious unattended death.

Blue Ho'okane tried to come through the open back door, but by then I was already sprinting across the room, mouth shut and holding my nose and waving frantically at him to move back with my other hand. I had dropped the gun after firing the three rounds, knowing there was no way Colonel Beauregard would be using it. He lay slumped back on the couch, a close pattern of holes around the middle of his chest.

Once on the back deck, I pushed Blue toward the stairs.

"Go! Go! Go!" I yelled. "We gotta get outta here!"

We finally stopped over by the yacht club's front office, panting, about fifty yards from my boat.

"Why are we running?" he yelled, catching his breath.

"I think he was about to kill me," I said. "So I shot him first."

"You think? What do you mean, you think he was about to kill you?"

"Wai Lo Fat may have been killed with a weaponized pathogen, a biowarfare agent, that is distributed by aerosol," I said. "Beauregard pulled out an asthma inhaler and started coming toward me with it. I think I got him before he was able to activate it, but there's a chance some of the germs got out."

"You killed a man armed with an asthma inhaler?" he asked.

"Yeah."

"Because some other guy . . . might . . . have been killed with some kind of germ warfare bug but maybe not," he said.

"You know, the situation doesn't sound as desperate when you put it that way," I said.

"Yeah, and they said I had control problems when I was on the force," he said. "If that fucking inhaler turns out to be full of asthma medicine, we are both totally fucked."

"You are such a ray of sunshine," I said.

Chapter Forty-one

The sky was a Carl Sagan display of billions and billions of stars as I leaned my head backward onto the rim of the hot tub on the upper deck of the *Travis McGee*. God's silver eyelash was back, winking at me through occasional thin, wispy clouds drifting by on the trade winds. The boat rocked lightly on the waters of Kaneohe Bay, just between Coconut Island and the marine base, as I sipped a beer.

It was New Year's Eve, a month since I had killed Colonel Beauregard on my boat. In a few minutes, the marine base would begin its fireworks show, and if there is one thing the military knows how to do well, it's how to put on a great display of pyrotechnics. I just hoped they didn't get the play shells mixed up with the real ones. Boats full of people drinking and partying and waiting to welcome the New Year were scattered across the bay. I had been invited to join many of the parties, but I wanted to spend my time privately on the *Travis McGee*, reflecting on what a strange year it had been.

I had lived on the boat so long while it sat on shore, I had come to think of it more as a house than a watercraft.

Heart Attack Bob's widow not only did not want to keep the wet slip, she sold off his fifty-five-foot Peterson sailboat for about half of what it was worth and moved to a condo on Maui. Slip 43 was perfect for the *Travis McGee*, since it was one of the longer and wider slips on the floating pier.

After I finally put my boat into Heart Attack Bob's slip, it took a while to get used to the gentle, though constant rocking. Eventually, the rocking became soothing, and I wondered how I could have put up with sleeping on a houseboat on blocks for so long. With the serene pushing and pulling of the boat in its slip, sleeping on the *Travis McGee* was like sleeping on a three-hundred-thousand-dollar waterbed.

Beside the hot tub, the gods slept, oblivious to the coming maelstrom of booms and bursts and fire in the sky. They also seemed to like the boat in the water better than on the land. They spent more time on it now, instead of lounging around the yacht club lawn or hanging around on the docks, scrounging snacks.

The shooting of Colonel Beauregard seemed like it happened years ago. The commodore wasn't too happy about the gunplay on the property or the resulting lockdown of the entire club for more than a day while a federal hazardous materials team made sure there were no deadly bacteria lurking in or around my boat. They treated the little asthma inhaler lying on the cabin floor of the *Travis McGee* like it was a nuclear bomb about to detonate. They moved carefully around it in their bulky white hazmat suits, taking pictures of it and sniffing at it with various *Star Trek* kinds of gadgets. Then they put it in a special container that looked like a glorified ice chest and hustled it away.

Once the air was deemed safe to breathe and the boat and yacht club premises uncontaminated with any deadly bio agents, things got really interesting. Honolulu City Medical Examiner Dr. Melba McCall stood by waiting for clearance to conduct an initial investigation of the cause of death of Colonel Beauregard. HPD homicide detectives seemed a little too anxious to get on board and get enough evidence to arrest me for murder. Apparently, there still were some cops who blamed the death of Jeannie Kai on me. As it turned out, neither the detectives nor Dr. McCall got to enter the boat. A large contingent of armed U.S. Army police and crime scene investigators swarmed around and onto the boat, claiming federal jurisdiction over the scene. The detectives protested that the shooting happened on civilian property and was a local police matter, but they didn't seem ready to push their way past two army guys in camo holding automatic rifles at the base of the stairs to the boat. In any case, Dr. McCall told me later a call came from the police chief telling his men to stand down and leave the investigation to the army.

It was an interesting investigation mainly due to its brevity. I wasn't even taken to Fort Shafter for questioning. A lieutenant from the Army Criminal Investigation Command, who looked to be about eighteen years old, took me to a far corner of the yacht club parking lot away from the TV news cameras and newspaper reporters who gathered outside the club's front gate, unable to get in. The lieutenant asked me what happened. I told him that basically this crazy army colonel had broken into my boat armed with some kind of chemical or biological weapon and I had to kill him in self-defense. The kid lieutenant didn't even seem too interested in the details. I was convinced that

Colonel Beauregard had intended to kill me and that there were weaponized pathogens in that inhaler—but there was nothing to stop the military investigators from losing that one and replacing it with a regular inhaler and then charging me with murder. Although Hawaii didn't have the death penalty, the federal court system did, and the U.S. Attorney's Office could prosecute the death of Colonel Beauregard as a death penalty case. To my surprise, after only talking to me for about ten minutes, the lieutenant from the criminal investigation command just said thanks, they'd be in touch. And that was the last time I talked to anyone involved with the investigation of the death of Colonel Beauregard. A week later, an obscure assistant U.S. attorney, apparently sent to Hawaii from Washington, D.C., to review the case, issued a one-line press release saying, "After review, our office has determined that criminal prosecution in regard to the death of army Colonel R. G. Beauregard is not warranted at this time."

It wasn't exactly the warm and fuzzy kind of statement I had hoped for, one that clearly stated I had acted in self-defense and the world was better off without a murdering little psycho like Colonel Beauregard roaming the streets.

I also did not like the assistant U.S. attorney's "not warranted at this time" remark, which sort of hinted that there could come a time when prosecution would be warranted. Was it supposed to be a gentle reminder to me that it would be better if we all let the matter drop and moved on with our lives? My gut feeling was that the more army investigators looked into the life and activities of Colonel Beauregard, the more they'd rather just have everyone forget he ever existed. If keeping a possible criminal charge hanging over my head helped in that effort, so be it. My lawyer, Sue

Darling, was completely outraged that an army colonel had tried to kill me and wanted to sue the U.S. government for violating my civil rights.

"The gavyonnaya blyat should suffer for trying to hurt you, my darling," she said.

I finally convinced her it might be to our advantage to hold off on any legal action for the time being.

As to whether the aerosol inhaler had contained a deadly bio agent, the army never said. When pressed by the media, they said only that they could neither confirm nor deny that the army has developed or is developing any bioweapons and that any such program would be considered classified under the Homeland Security Act.

When I met Dr. McCall for lunch at Don Ho's Island Grill at the Aloha Tower Marketplace at Honolulu Harbor a few weeks after the case was officially closed by the U.S. attorney's office, she said that if the asthma inhaler had been a real asthma inhaler, the world would know about it.

"And you'd be living in that Supermax federal prison on the Mainland with Manuel Noriega and the Unabomber," she said.

"I'm getting déjà vu all over again," I said, picking at a wonderful piece of broiled ahi. "Reminds me of what happened in the Jake Stane affair where they tied up all the little loose ends and closed the case before I had even regained consciousness. Why do these kinds of things always come to such an ambiguous end?"

"I'd say you are doing okay," she said. "A lot of people go through life with no one trying to kill them. Now, two very bad men have tried to kill you, and one of them is dead and the other is in prison."

"What are you talking about?" I asked. "Jake Stane is

dead. He killed himself after getting a visit in prison by Tiny Maunakea."

"I don't think so," she said, sipping at her glass of red wine.

"His death was reported all over the news," I said.

"Stryker, any death in the Halawa High Security Facility is considered an unattended death," she said. "That means I have to autopsy the remains. I never conducted an autopsy on Jake Stane."

"Jeez," I said. "Can Jake Stane still be alive?"

"If this Tiny Maunakea character is as dangerous as you say he is, maybe the state thought it best for Jake Stane to be moved to another prison. It wouldn't be the first time the government staged the death of someone to put him under some special protection program. They probably named him Manuel Gonzalez and sent him off to some prison in Texas."

So now I would have the fun of wondering if Jake Stane, wherever he was, would eventually get released from prison and suddenly end up back on my doorstep. On the other hand, he said he was dying of cancer, so that was good.

There was one unambiguous element to the Kahala Road atrocities. Colonel Beauregard, thinking I'd soon be dead, told me that General Jason Johnson was still alive, living in a convalescent home in Kalihi. Since you don't often get a chance in life to observe true evil, I thought I would visit him. If only to let him know that his secret was no longer a secret.

The Worthington House Convalescent Center was a two-story, rectangular building that looked like a small hospital. I introduced myself to a nurse in a pink uniform at the front desk as Michael Johnson, one of General Johnson's great-nephews, on vacation in Hawaii from the Mainland.

"I told his daughter, my aunt, I would look in on him during our trip," I said. "How's he doing?"

She furrowed her brow and shook her head slowly. "Not good, I'm afraid, Mr. Johnson," she said. "Since his stroke he is in a lot of pain. He can say a few words but usually only asks for morphine. Of course, we can only give him so much per day."

She called for a nurse's aide to show me to his room. He shared a double room on the second floor, but his roomie apparently was out. He was in bed, cranked up into a sitting position so he could look out a window. His view was across a small plaza to a solid gray wall, another wing of the care home. I asked the aide to let me have a few minutes alone with my great-uncle.

I don't know why I always think that evil is going to look evil. In the movies, evil looks like Vincent Price playing the Abominable Dr. Phibes or Anthony Hopkins as Hannibal Lecter in *Silence of the Lambs.* But in real life, it never does. Only Danny Chang looked like he came from Central Casting—but he wasn't really evil, just dangerous.

The man sitting up in the bed looked skinny and gray. He had a mottled, pallid bald head with a few scraggily patches of white hair on the sides. Even from several feet away, he smelled the way very old people sometimes do, like the inside of an old chest of drawers. He winced every few seconds as if someone were sticking him with needles. He lifted his head as much as he could to look at me with wan, watery eyes. His right arm was attached to a plastic tube that led to a bag of clear liquid. I looked at it as I got near. It was some kind of solution used to keep him hydrated, I guess. There was a valve on the tubing through which they could inject medication without having to poke new holes in his emaciated arm.

He made a sound that I had never before heard a human make. It seemed to come from deep inside him and work its way up through his chest and escape through his nose and withered mouth in a chilling, ethereal high-pitched wail that might have come from a tortured feral animal. He squeezed his eyes closed in pain, then opened them slowly and looked up at me with a pathetic, pleading gaze. He made a tremendous effort to open his mouth and wheezed out a single, barely audible word.

"Morphine," he begged.

Like when I had tracked down Burl Morse for the first time to the Spam and Eggs Ministry with great plans to let him know what a complete piece of shit he was and maybe even smack him around a bit, I had come to the Kalihi care home with grand plans of letting General Jason Johnson know that I knew he had tortured and killed innocent American citizens and had them buried under Kahala Road. I would call him a war criminal to his face. I would curse him to hell.

But now, as I looked at him, I could see he already was in hell. A true living hell. He was like Tantalus after the gods of Olympus had cast him into Hades, burning for all eternity, unable to take a cooling sip of the lake he stood in or taste the sweet fruit that grew just out of reach. For General Jason Johnson, his respite from pain lay just out of reach, a shot of morphine into the plastic tube that ran into his bony arm.

Another person might have taken joy that this old man was spending the last years of his life in agony. They would consider his suffering small payment for his crimes. And I admit that even as I stood there with him looking up pitifully at me with his watery eyes, mouthing the word "morphine" with no sound coming out, I had the urge to lean close to him and whisper the words "Kahala Road" into his ear. But it was not my role to inflict any more misery on this man than he was already going through. Punishment, and forgiveness, for that matter, is God's business, not mine. So I left him in pain, living in Hawaii, the most beautiful place in the world, but having to stare out at the flat gray side of a building every day. I left General Jason Johnson, a truly evil man, without saying anything.

As I sat in the hot tub on my boat, waiting for the New Year's fireworks to start, my thoughts turned to Burl Morse. Danny Chang never admitted grabbing him from the Chinatown phone booth, even when Tiny Maunakea suggested we all take another trip to the beach at Makapuu Point and throw him in the real deadly current known as the Molokai Express. After Danny Chang told us how to get in contact with Colonel Beauregard, Tiny took him to the North Shore and placed him in the protective custody of the Shocka Boys. Mad Mouse Mulligan was happy to do a favor for Tiny Maunakea, mainly because he didn't want to end up like Three Man Stone.

On Auntie Kealoha's orders, Tiny apparently had sent Danny Chang back to Hong Kong, but I didn't know if it was vertically or horizontally or if any funny note was attached. I sensed a new underworld myth could be emerging, and I would certainly help it along if I could.

A week after Colonel Beauregard's death, I got a call

from Burl Morse. He hadn't been killed by Danny Chang after all. He was on the Mainland. And he was drunk.

"I'm sorry, Stryker," he said, slurring the words. "I got scared after those two Chinese guys grabbed me. They were some red armbands. They beat me up and said they were going to kill me if I didn't tell them where So Young Hee was. I didn't tell them, Stryker. I swear I didn't. They finally let me go. I went to a bar on Hotel Street and had a few drinks to calm my nerves. Then a few more. I know I let you down."

He said he took out what little money he had left in the *Honolulu Journal* Federal Credit Union and bought a ticket to Los Angeles, where he still had some family.

"I got scared, Stryker. I thought they were going to kill me," he said. "I'm not like you."

I told him he hadn't let me down. In fact, if it wasn't for him So Young Hee probably would have been killed like Wai Lo Fat.

"You broke the case, Burl," I said. "You are the one who figured out it was all about Kahala Road."

A week later I got a letter from his sister in California.

Dear Mr. McBride, my brother, Burl Morse, passed away in a local hospital due to liver failure two days ago, she wrote. *After coming home he often talked about a former newspaper reporter he knew in Hawaii, a man he admired greatly. He said this man had been good to him and helped him out when he was down on his luck. I was organizing his effects after he passed on and came across your name. If you are the man he spoke of, God bless you and I hope you have a good life.*

It was a nice thought and immediately made me feel guilty about how I had treated Burl Morse. I knew I wasn't responsible for him drinking himself to death, but I might have speeded it along by dragging him into the Hung Bang

Kongsi investigation. I guess I could live with that. I mean, I lived with the guilt of the death of Officer Jeannie Kai for a few years.

I didn't feel that guilt now. I was sorry she had died. But we literally were in the same boat when the shooting started and I had done all that I could to save her. She was an amazing woman; brave, principled, and looking toward a great future. I wish I could have gotten to know her better.

It was hard to believe that I had only seen her in person three times. First when she was walking toward me in her dark cobalt blue HPD uniform after she had pulled me over on the Pali Highway. Second when we met at the Heeia Kea Pier. And last . . . well . . . I still didn't like going through that night on a play-by-play basis. But the image most strongly in my mind was that photo of her on the "Wall of Honor" in police headquarters. Dressed in her first police uniform, looking at the camera with youthful grace and determination. A lady in blue.

Now I realized I didn't even know where she was buried. I needed to find out. Like I did with Dr. Lew Eden when I found out he was buried in Punchbowl Cemetery, I needed to go put an orchid lei on Jeannie Kai's grave. I needed to say, aloha. It's a small thing. But it's what we do in Hawaii.

"Hey, big fella, you ready for some champagne?"

The voice came from the ladder/stairway leading to the upper deck from the cabin below. Melba, wearing a bikini that made her look even more sexy than her blue surgical pajamas, walked to the hot tub with a bottle of champagne and two glasses. Since the shooting of Colonel Beauregard, we had become pretty close. And the closer she came, the better I liked it. For the past three days she had been staying with me on the *Travis McGee*. Every day we motored to a different isolated part of Kaneohe Bay and spent the day reading, swimming, and engaging in other activities that single adult individuals who like each other a lot are legally allowed to engage in.

I took the bottle from her, and she climbed into the hot tub. I popped the cork, and it flew over the deck railing into the bay. It was a rash, antienvironmentalist kind of thing to do, but I was feeling like a rebel. Earlier I even shot a beer cap at a passing sea turtle. I poured some champagne into the glasses. We clinked them together.

"To a new year," I said.

"Yes," she said. "To a new year. As we say in my business, may all your bodies be fresh and all your scalpels sharp."

"Miss Congeniality, you are a ghoul," I said.

We kissed and, as if it had been staged by a Hollywood producer, the night suddenly erupted in an explosion that left an enormous white ball of fire hanging above us. Then more fiery blossoms of color lit up the night sky, punctuated by the booms and cracks of the incendiary devices exploding above our heads.

Would the next year be a good one? I wondered, sipping my champagne. Melba cuddled up to me in the warm water, watching the fireworks. December 31 is just an arbitrary day, an artificial line between one year and the next. I kissed her neck and thought this part of the old year was pretty damn good.

The new year would be good for Blue Ho'okane. So Young Hee's lawyers had been busy while he was staying with Auntie Kealoha. As part of the legal settlement for violating the state's ban on growing genetically altered taro, So Young Hee had agreed to make Blue Ho'okane's youth outreach farming project a partner in whatever proceeds the patent from the genetic taro generated.

While some Hawaiians still were leery of genetically modified taro, Blue Ho'okane had told me he was willing to learn more about it.

"So Young Hee wants me to go to Thailand, where there has been a long drought," he said. "The government there is open to testing Frankentaro. I want to see how it does. It could end up saving thousands of lives. And the same methods used to modify the taro can be used to help other plants cope with climate change in the next twenty years. Back here, we'll be testing various legal species of plants. So Young Hee wants our little outreach farm and my kids out there to become the center of new forms of agricultural methods in Hawaii."

So Young Hee and his lawyers turned Four Gates Enterprises into a charitable trust. Michael Lee, who had run Four Gates well under the Lodge of the Inner Eight, would be kept on as CEO, but there would be no board of directors anymore, so Amber would lose out there. So Young Hee wanted to do something to repay me for my help. I tried to talk him out of it, but he insisted. So I joked that before Four Gates changed from a private company to a public trust, he appoint me acting temporary CEO for ten minutes. He could see where I was going, and both he and Michael Lee agreed. In my brief reign as head of one of the richest corporations in the country, my only official act was to fire Amber Kam from Four Gates and order her to move out of the Blue Lotus pond house on Kala Lane that the company owned. I know, it was petty, and I sometimes feel bad about it. But I got over being shot, so I think

I will be able to get over Amber Kalanianaole Kam hating my guts.

After the death of Richard Gustavus Beauregard, the big question was what to do about Kahala Road. The army would not even discuss it. There was that little matter of me "not being prosecuted at this time" that persuaded me to suggest to So Young Hee that whatever we decided to do, we should probably just leave the army out of it. General Jason Johnson was paying a painful price for what happened at Kahala Road.

Instead, we quietly approached leaders in the Japanese community. A private meeting was arranged between a blue ribbon group of Japanese businesspeople, cultural activists, religious leaders, and descendants of the Japanese Americans who were buried there. So Young Hee formally apologized for the actions of the Lodge of the Inner Eight and asked for forgiveness. He said he was willing to do anything to set things right, even though he realized they never could be completely set right. In the end, the Japanese representatives decided it was better not to make a big public issue over what happened at Kahala Road. There was no reason to set ethnic Chinese and Japanese in Hawaii against each other for something that happened so long ago. And they saw no reason to dig up the bodies buried under Kahala Road. Instead, So Young Hee donated the newly named Blue Lotus Ponds to the Japanese Chamber of Commerce. A small plaque was placed at the head of the path near the palm shack that read IN MEMORY OF THE JAPANESE AMERICANS WHO LOST THEIR LIVES FOR THEIR COUNTRY IN WORLD WAR II.

At the service, while we all stood on Kahala Road and a

Shinto priest, a kannushi in a traditional white robe and black hat, blessed the site, I thought back to that night at the Club Buy Me Drinkee when the owner, Enola Gay, the giant black transvestite in the blond wig, had Japanese nationals howling with laughter over the crude joke about his name. At that time, I had thought, *I guess the war with Japan really is over.* As I stood there listening to the kannushi recite some ancient Japanese words of blessing over Kahala Road in his nasal, singsong way, I thought, *Maybe wars are never completely over.*

Melba noticed my mind had been wandering.

"What are you thinking about?" she asked.

"Tomorrow's my birthday. New Year's Day," I said.

"Yes, I know. In three more minutes you'll be forty years old, an elderly person," she said.

"New Year's Day is the worst day in the world to be born on," I said. "Nobody remembers your birthday. Or if they do, they try to get by, by giving you a combined Christmas and birthday present."

"On the other hand, if you were born a day earlier, you'd be a year older," she said.

At that point the booming of a hundred cannon roared across the bay and the sky lit up like it was Armageddon, with the glorious finale of the fireworks show, explosions of greens and reds and yellows. Melba and I spent the first several moments of the New Year in a long kiss. The gods interrupted us, perching themselves on the side of the hot tub. Standing on their hind legs, Kane and Lono threw their heads back and howled, howled, howled into the night sky. If I didn't know better, I would say they were rejoicing.